RUN[illegible]OGY

Being a J[illegible] Futhark

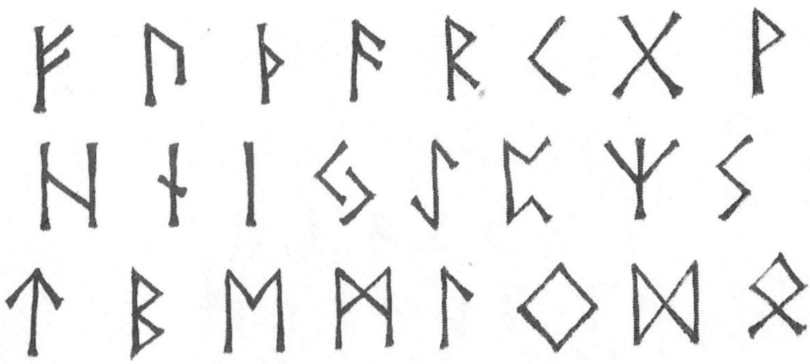

Or the Broken Chalice

By Wren

Cover art “Havamal” by Margaret Schwartz

Frames for invocations by Katlyn Breene
www.mermadearts.com

Calligraphy, glyphs and drawings by Wren

Maypole photograph compliments of Coven of the Spiral Moon 2013

Published by Moon Books Publishing
moonbooks.net

A special thanks to Margaret, midwife of theTrilogy

TABLE OF CONTENTS

Legend

All runes described in this book appear in up to four different positions (some appear in all forms, some in less). Using Fehu as an example:

Bright: 

Murk: 

Supine: 

Prone: 

Traditionally, upright runes are referred to as 'Bright', and reversed runes are termed 'Murk.' Over the years of working with the runes, I have found that the sideways runes give additional insights, and have labeled them 'Prone', face-down, and 'Supine', face-up. Prone runes generally indicate an unwillingness or avoidance, whereas supine indicate a growing awareness or reluctant acceptance.

Far and away, in the vast and icy wilderness of the Scandinavian northlands, legends tell of an ancient language; a sacred symbol system that was the voice of the Gods. It was called the Runes.

Runes were brought to the people by Odin, the wise and mysterious one. Fearlessly he hung for nine days from the branches of the great world tree, Yggdrasil. Pierced in the side by his own spear, he cried out to the Gods for enlightenment and plunged, screaming, to the earth to snatch up the Runes.

This voice speaks to us still, if only we listen.

FREYA'S

foundation
creation
mysteries to master

GRACIOUS FREYA

MISTRESS OF MYSTERIES
LEND YOUR GUIDANCE TO THOSE
WHO WOULD FOLLOW YOUR WAYS
BLESS THEM WITH INSIGHT AND
WISDOM; GUARD THEM FROM
THE WRATH OF THE IGNORANT
MAY YOUR ANCIENT TEACHINGS
BE BROUGHT BACK INTO THE LIGHT
THAT ALL MAY FEEL THE HEARTBEAT OF
THE MOTHER AND BE ONE WITH HER

In the names of the Ancient & Shining Ones

So mote it be!

Artwork by Katlyn at www.mermadearts.com

FEHU

Cattle/wealth

Mae’s Crossing ᚠ *Growth and Prosperity*

Mae’s Crossing was a small cow town, still retaining much of its early character as a crossroads trading post. Three roads led from its center, but it was no longer a stop for travelers in the fast paced world of the 21st century.

The settlement’s name came from Mae Duncan, who was widowed in 1833. She was barely 24 when her husband Derek died of a freak accident on their homestead parcel of 300 acres. Suddenly Mae was thrust into the role of managing the entire ranch as well as caring for her four children. Derek’s folks wanted her and the children to move to San Francisco, but Mae was determined to hold on to that which they had labored so hard to create. Cheerful and enterprising, Mae hung a sign on her fence defying all comers to find a better meal anywhere on this wide earth. None defied her. As her fame spread, she had a second structure built to house the trade goods she’d accumulated. Before long, Mae added a new sign for her trading post. Thus were the humble beginnings of a small town at the center of the crossroads.

Chapter 1a

Brianna ᚠ *Sending*

(Mae's Crossing; Somewhere in the Western United States, 3rd Millenium, 2nd Decade, July/August)

Brianna screeched at the sound of breaking glass, feeling like someone had just fired a gun near her head.

"Dear Goddess, forgive my clumsiness," she muttered, as she hesitantly opened her eyes to survey the damage. While she was deep in her meditative trance, she had flung out her arms in a welcoming gesture to the glowing, androgynous being who was floating towards her. The coveted crystal chalice had been swept to the floor, shattered beyond repair. Worse than that, the long awaited meeting with her Guardian, almost achieved, was abruptly ended.

"Shit!!!" Hand to mouth as quickly as she had said it. She stood up and carefully stepped back from the menacing shards of glass, and faced the Eastern portal. Sighing inwardly, Brianna performed the closing rites, and then turned on the lamp by the door.

"We will meet, my friend," she sighed as she fetched a mundane broom and dustpan.

Brianna (born Brenda Jeanne McTavish) was as energetic and vibrant at 52 as she had been at 32. There was still a natural auburn glow to her hair, and she moved with an easy grace. Brianna owned a parcel of land on the outskirts of

Mae's Crossing. Ownership, as Bri learned over the years, was a two way street. Stewardship of the land required constant attention. Planting and weeding, pruning and culling, coaxing and crooning, Bri saw to the needs of the profusion of trees, flowers, fruits and vegetables of her domain. The land repaid her efforts with a grand harvest this year, previous lean years all but forgotten. Trellised jasmine created a leafy canopy over her home's entrance, and in the evening the scent was overpowering. Birdhouses of every description hung from the trees while hummingbirds sparred at the feeder by the large windows. *Goddess, how I love this place!* Every day she recited a prayer of thanks, even and most especially so when finances were rocky and the solution unclear. Having followed the path of the Old Ones for more than 20 years, Bri had learned to trust to the Goddess.

This last ritual had been meticulously planned, from the carefully chosen tools down to the most effective lunar and planetary aspects. Firing up a bowl, Brianna kicked back and relived the days leading up to this aborted ceremony, distancing herself from the feeling of disappointment and loss.

One week earlier

Ah, he's open. Brianna entered the musty little shop with the usual objective; to find some juicy ritual tools.

Maybe I'll find it this time. What's back there in that old cupboard? Al's Antiques had been her favorite shop since her late teens; which probably had a lot to do with why she settled here. Her spinster aunt used to bring her here when she was in a scavenging mood, as Al was an intrepid collector and his array of oddments strangely alluring.

"Al, is this cupboard new? I don't remember seeing it before. What do you keep in here?" she said, as she reached for the latch.

"Wait, Bri, don't…" pleaded Al, knowing full well she would find it.

"What's this?" mused Bri as she gazed upon the most beautiful chalice she had ever seen. It was handblown, with delicate leaves and flowers worked into the entire surface of the bowl…it was obviously crafted by a genius or a magician. *Gods, was it awesome!* With honor and reverence, she lifted it down from the shelf to examine it. A shudder ran through her as she let go of the longing to own it, knowing full well it would cost a king's ransom. She oh so carefully set it well back on the shelf and closed the door, grateful for that brief moment of contact. Bri's palms tingled.

Al fidgeted, then blurt out "Lissen, Bri. I wasna gonna show dis to ya just yet, but dang it, ya found it, and now da cat's outa da bag. I know'd ya been lookin fer a chalice, and when first I saw dis, I knew twas yers. How' bout we call it a nurly birthday gift? Happy Birthday."

Stunned silence. "Oh, my Goddess, Al! How can you…and hey, my birthday's not 'til January. I can't take it…it belongs in a museum…must be worth a fortune!"

Al turned away from her and reached into the cupboard, his voice gruff with emotion "Yah, ya kin. Yull give it reason to be. Take it…please."

Brianna collapsed into the easy chair, and put her face in her hands. *How can I accept this?* An idea popped into her head. "Okay, I'll trade you. When was the last time you rang up a sale on that dusty old cash register? And what about that pitiful excuse of a garden out back? Let me do a prosperity spell for the shop and a healthy growth spell for the garden…I still can't believe you're giving this to me!"

Al reached down and grasped her hand. "Bri, ya'v been a light in my life, an be me happy to put light inna yers." He placed the chalice in her hands and dropped into his favorite chair. "Still don't believen' how I found it. Last week I was takin' my usual run through Channin' an' BigCity, lookin' fer some fresh stock. Stopped at Willum's in Channin', more fer a visit dan bi'ness. Will 'n I met fer coffee an den wenna back ta his pawn shop. Das when he brought out dis here chalice. Know'd he was just gloatin. Tol' me 'bout a youngish man, all hopped up an' bedraggled lookin' he was. Had dis chalice n' was hopin' to get a lotta money. Willum hems 'n haws den says he'll give 'em $50 on a two week pawn or $100 straight out buy. The kid says he knows it's wort more. Will says take it or leave it, so they shook on the straight buy. So's I says, Will, ya know dis smells bad. Lemme take it off'n yer hands for $200. Ya tell me, Bri, is $200 a fair price fer two spells?"

Bri chuckled at the memory, momentarily forgetting the shattered reality. But she remembered the cleansing ritual, and how the hand wrought glass seemed to come to life after the negativity had been peeled away. An ethereal light had bathed her in its comforting rays. *What a welcome gift to dedicate to the Goddess*! She had been eager to put it to practical use in her up and coming ritual to meet her Guardian.

Chapter 1b

Mae's Crossing *Arrested development*

Maybe it was its remoteness that drew and kept the folk who chose to live in Mae's Crossing, for it was situated on the lower slopes of a mountain range with a three hour drive to the nearest city. The treacherous and winding roads with deep cliffs and yawning gullies certainly discouraged the more timid motorists. Maybe it was the untouched panorama of meadows merging into the deep and leafy woods. It might have been the pure and sparkling waters filling the lake and meandering through the valley. There was a quiet beauty, and all who lived here felt the touch of Gods and magic on their doorsteps. It would come as no surprise, then, that the major portion of residents were nature worshippers, be they nudists or Buddhists, witches or shaman, or plain folk who honored the earth spirits. There was a feeling of community without a dominant tradition, for all paths were accepted and respected. Mae's Crossing, however, was no utopian wonderland. Disputes were more the norm than placid acceptance, for these folk were all 'their own people.' It was a big choice to live simply in this computer-driven age, and not an easy way out. Conflicts like Tom Bradley's goats getting into Widow Thompson's garden and feasting on her newly sprouted carrots were honest and forthright, without the fear and ignorance that fuels hatred of 'the other.'

Mae's Crossing had grown from a simple trading post to a township encompassing close to 3000. Word had spread underground throughout the country of this haven, and all who came brought their various talents. Surprisingly few of the visitors lingered, as their yearning for tech society and modern comforts drew them away.

Sometime after Jed's Folly in the 1950's, the town council wrestled with redefining their goals. Council Head Joyce Duncan, Mae's direct descendant, bullied through a ruling banning outside enterprises, most especially franchises. All businesses had to be resident owned and operated, the only exceptions being the Post Office and gas station. After much shouting and negotiating, it was agreed that the owner or a family member could get by with making an appearance once a week. Because of this, Mae's Crossing was spared the ordeal of endless chain markets and services.

Chapter 1b

Rosalind  *Reluctant Acceptance/ Windfall*

3rd Millenium, 2nd decade, July/August

"This can't be happening," she whimpered to herself. Her legs were so cramped from running that they felt as if a giant vice were squeezing them. The pursuers crashed through the underbrush, screaming her name and reaching out to grab her. Her heart lurched as her heel was trapped in an iron fist. Rose lashed out with every last ounce of her strength, aiming her foot at the captor's midsection when the reality of the hardwood floor connecting with her head and shoulder brought her awake. In the confusion, Rose had knocked her book to the floor, its pages opening to a description of the first rune of the Elder Futhark.

The synchronicity of the message was clear. Indeed, Rose was untiring in her search for meaning in the midst of chaos. Runes were her friendly guides, helping her to see the patterns and sequences of her life. So when Fehu jumped out at her, she grudgingly bent her head in acceptance. Funny, how an inheritance threw her into such a deep depression. *No wonder the scary dreams!* Even though Rose was next in line for Gram's holdings after her sister...it should be Jen taking over the business, not her. Ah, should be's. For Jen had passed on, shortly after helping Rose get settled and enrolled at the university, leaving loved ones bereft and Rosalind with a bakeshop on her hands. At 22, she was just beginning to know herself, exploring the world around her and trying out different approaches in an effort to find her niche. The usual jobs for her age -- waitress, store clerk, fast food server -- came and went as she declined college after the first semester in favor of real life experience. Fate had been doubly cruel to Rose, for her parents were on the ill-fated Flight 93 in 2001. She and Jenny had been taken in by

Gram. Gramma Dot was a generous, kind-hearted woman who opened her home to the orphaned girls. Together, the three of them embarked on the healing process, Dot mourning the loss of her only son and his beloved wife; the girls, their parents. Jenny left for college 3 years later, with Rosalind doing the same 8 years later.

Dot's Delights was a must stop in Mae's Crossing. Carrying on the Duncan tradition of fine foods, Gram's bread and pastries were unmatched. Not only did she personally supervise her workers (as if she needed to with Mabel in charge!), but she also bought the wheat from local farmers and took it directly to the mill to have it ground. Almost all ingredients were local; some of the eggs were even from her own chickens; milk, butter and cheese from Blanton's Farm; goat's milk from Tom Bradley. Once a week she made savory meat pies (with morels! compliments of woodsman Otter) that had folks standing in line. She was a most industrious woman. How could Rose ever hope to fill her shoes?

A meeting with Mabel was scheduled for next week after the funeral. Memories of the baker woman, dust covered apron and flour smears on her face saying "Stand back, girls, lest ye get burnt by this hot pan; don't know why Dot lets you all back here." filled her with dread and excitement as the appointment approached.

Days passed quickly and before she knew it, there she was facing the formidable Mabel. "Just stop your frettin', sweetie. Everything's fine and under control. You just need to learn the business; it pretty much takes care of itself. Dot made sure all would run smoothly when she weren't here; not that she was ever gone much. Caroline does books and writes checks; I take and fill orders and do most of the shopping. You'll have to take over her route with the other folk; dairy, farm, ranch, mill and probably some more I can't think of offhand. She loved goin' out and dealing with the growers and farmers. You got that good Duncan stock; no problem you can't handle." Rose noticed to her surprise that tears were welling up in Mabel's eyes as she quickly turned away. The hawk-eyed no nonsense persona that she remembered as a child melted away, leaving a grieving friend in her place.

Chapter 1c

Mae's Crossing  *Power out of Control*

In 1953, a certain Professor Jedediah Germaine, in an attempt to control and order demonic powers, had his operations backfire in a stupendous way. The old church, which was established in the late 1800's, was nearly blasted to the ground, leaving only a gutted out skeleton with a small portion of the steeple standing. Adjacent buildings were damaged in the conflagration, as well as the professor's home. This event was referred to by locals as Jed's Folly.

Jedediah narrowly escaped with his life, and subsequently ceased his ceremonial magic explorations, quite happily taking up the simpler ways of the Old Ones. Still, the scent of dark magicks lingered.

The town council, made up of a dozen landowners, smelled it. After five days of heated discussions, Alan Nelson Sr. made a generous donation (technically a land lease) of a lovely parcel on the other side of town. Alan was wise enough to know that erecting a temple on his special tract of land that had a vortex would preserve it from desecration. Word had gotten out about the spot, and he had been forced to clean up after the last group of beatniks left. A temple rather than a church was subsequently built. Bit by bit, various townsfolk lent their hands to the project, and it grew over the years to a grand design. A temple chaplain took up residence, conducting observations according to the season and caring to the needs of the building and grounds. As a balance, the temple was open to all faiths. Any group could use the building for their religious rites. It was a great success. Soon all major community events were held in or near the temple, as it radiated an aura of well-being.

Malachais *Loss of Possessions*

(1 week earlier than Bri's Guardian ritual) Channing: 3rd Millenium, 2nd Decade, late July

Gone! By all the Gods, it's gone! Malachais couldn't believe it. He'd combed the house from top to bottom, but still couldn't find the chalice. It couldn't just up and walk away. He fumed and wept, all in the same instant. Beside himself with grief and anger, he forced himself to pour a glass of water then stepped out to his 'designated smoking' area. After a long draft of water, Mal lit up, easing back into his lounger, watching the smoke dissipate into nothingness while mentally going over the last few hours. When had he last seen the chalice? That was easy, since he paid honor to it at least once a day, reveling in its beauty as the sun brought out its vibrant magic. He had even had a special glass case built for it and placed the piece in the living room, rather than hiding it away in his magickal cupboard. The price was staggering, but he had commissioned it in his hey-day at the height of Dot-com's glory. The Master Glassworker responsible for this glorious chalice was Jarnath, a fellow High Priest, and the two had become fast friends over time. Jarnath was recognized by the muggles as well as being sought out by those in the Craft (who could afford him) for his masterworks.

Malachais Merriwether was a striking figure. Tall and skinny, his queue showed more black than silver. Some might even call him handsome. His eyes, a deep brown, reflected an inner sadness born of too many failed relationships. Through it all, Mal had managed his finances well. A high paying position in the fast paced world of technological breakthroughs carefully invested allowed him to retire five years ago. Now, at 60, he had the freedom to pursue his spiritual goals full-time.

So who's been in here since I last saw it yesterday? Laura, the cleaning girl, who was as honest as the day is long, was here this morning. She'd been in Mal's employ for over six months now, and was thorough and scrupulous in her attention to detail. He smiled, thinking of how even the dust on all his hangings was non-existent. And never a misplaced object. It was as if the story book sprites came in the middle of the night to clean up. He was truly grateful for her efforts. *Might as well give her a call just in case she has some insights.* Mal scrolled through his contacts and pressed her number.

"Well, hello Mr. Merriwether. Is everything okay? I'm sorry I missed the doormats. I was halfway home when I realized I hadn't shaken them out. Is that why you're calling? I promise I won't overlook them again. I'll give you an extra half hour of cleaning without charge next time I..."

Mal interrupted her excited chatter. *Gods the girl did go on at times.* "No, no Laura, everything is fine. The house looks great. I was just wondering if anyone else was in my home while you were here this morning."

There was a pause at her end of the line, and Mal tensed in anticipation. He'd never told her 'no friends,' forgetting what it was like to be 17. Just as he feared, she went on.

"Well, gosh yeah, why do you ask? My boyfriend Gerry came by today and helped take out the trash. He was really good. Didn't slow me down any."

Bingo! Reactions were reviewed and discarded in an instant; any of which could tip off the suspect. He responded in a reassuring tone, "The reason I asked was that the trash cans were all lined up, and the wood scraps had been moved to the shed. I wouldn't expect you to take care of that, but if your boyfriend were willing…Gerry, did you say? I could use a little muscle around the place. Do you have his number, or better yet, I'd like to meet him. Do you know where he lives?" Mal hated being devious, but felt he must tread lightly in this case.

Early the next morning Mal drove out to the east side of Channing. Not a very choice location; crime reports listed the East end as a hotbed of criminal activity. While he was driving down the street Laura had mentioned, he realized he had no idea what Gerry looked like. *Rats! Why didn't I think of that before?* Lady Luck smiled on Mal that morning, for just at that moment, Laura walked out the door with a young man directly behind her. She turned and gave him a kiss then walked on out to her car. *Whew!* Gerry Le Fevre was a nondescript kid, average height and weight, colorless hair, with a bit of a slouch. The big smile on his face disappeared as soon as Laura drove off. Mal took a quick picture before Gerry swung around and kicked the screen door shut.

Malachais spent a few days covertly watching Gerry's movements; where he hung out, who he ran with, how he spent his time. Come Friday evening, Mal fixed himself his usual gin and tonic and went out to his porch to mull over all the bits and pieces. Drink in one hand, cigarette in the other, he absently raised each, watching the smoke curl around the glass. His mind raced through a dozen scenarios when aha! The clue he was looking for jumped out at him. The pawn shop! Gerry had stood staring in the window a couple of times this past week, as if he was looking for something. *Of course! That's where he must have taken it.* Mal polished off his drink, stubbed his cigarette and hurried into the house. Nervous energy had him pacing through the rooms as he planned his next move.

(Saturday)

A week had passed since the theft, and soon Laura was on his porch again waiting to be let in.

"Come in, Laura. Here, let me take that," said Mal as he took her bucket filled with cleaners and set it in the kitchen. "Please sit. I need to speak with you." He guided her to the easy chair and sat on the couch across from her.

Laura fidgeted and blurt out, "What's wrong, Mr. Merriwether? Are you mad at me for something? Am I messing up on the cleaning? I thought I was doing a good job, and you even said so yourself just last week. And what about Gerry? You said you'd talk with him, and he told me he hasn't heard from you. I don't get it. Should I…"

Mal held up his hand to stop the onslaught of chatter. "No, no, Laura. Please, listen to me. Do me a favor and look around the room. Do you see anything different?"

Laura did as he told her, scanning the room while nervously smoothing her skirt. "Different? Everything's the same… except for… oh, the pretty vase isn't in the case."

Mal gave her an indulgent smile. "Yes, Laura, the chalice is gone. Someone took it."

Wide-eyed, she looked across at him and said, "Oh no, Mr. Merriwether! You don't think I took it? I would never, never steal, specially not from you. You've always been so nice to me, and well, your stuff is your stuff and I respect that. I really have no idea..."

Once again he derailed her incessant speech. "I'm not accusing you, Laura. But I was wondering about your boyfriend. Do you think he might have taken it?"

The silence extended. Clearly Laura was debating the possibility. "Well, you know, I thought it was kind of funny that Gerry came by last week. He's never done that before. And he did go back in the house when I was getting ready to lock up. Told me he left his back pack with his keys in it and to wait outside for me. When he came out he was carrying his pack in front of him real careful like, not just slinging it over his shoulder like he usually does. Omigosh! Do you really think he took it? I can't believe he'd do that. But he's been acting sort of weird the last coupla months. Not like he was when we first got together. Omigosh! Is that why you didn't hire him? Do you think he's a thief?"

After Laura left, Malachais was going over a ritual Jarnath had sent him when he felt a sudden pain. (Meanwhile, in Mae's Crossing, Brianna had just shattered the chalice.) It was as if something broke; he could feel splinters flying and a high pitched scream. Startled, he walked out to his front deck. Nothing out of place there. Nothing happening in the street below. *Strange, it was so visceral that his stomach knotted up.* Satisfied that there was nothing amiss in his immediate vicinity, Mal chalked it up to nerves over the whole chalice affair and returned to his work.

Much as he wanted to go straight to the pawn shop, obligations blocked the way. It would be several days before he could follow up on his hunches. Right now there were business matters to tend to; issues with deadlines that couldn't be put off. So be it. He'd have a bit more time to sort things out in his mind.

URUZ

Wild aurochs/change

Chapter 2a

Mae's Crossing *Resistance to Change*

3rd Millenium, 2nd Decade

The townsfolk gathered at the Meeting Hall to discuss the ominous possibility of a freeway being built on their border. It was a logical route, as Mae's Crossing was on the mountain trail which cut through the pass and over into the next valley. Tom Bradley was adamant in his protest. "We can't let 'em do it! It'll change everything! We've got to stop them." while Widow Thompson whimpered, "I'm skeered, is what I am." Al was in the audience, joining in the general uproar. "They's got th' power. Durn politicos donna care 'bout us." Voices were raised in anger and fear, the din filling the tiny room. A bell rang out, deep and sonorous, all present falling into respectful silence. Head Councilman Ed Janssen rang the bell again as chairs scraped and benches creaked. "Order, order! Stop your dang yellin' and listen up. What we got here is a real, honest to goodness problem. And--All--Problems--Have--Solutions! Any ideas, and no talkin' out o' turn. Show of hands, please." Three hands shot up in the air. Ed pointed to Chester Burns, who stood up and cleared his throat. "How 'bout a petition? Last year Fallwater was able to stop a government development with this petition that got over 10,000 signatures." Murmurs of approval mixed with disdain echoed through the room. "Quiet!" said Ed. "Let's hear them out." Chester sat down and Ed motioned to Tom. Tom shot to his feet and blurted out, "Protest! That's what we gotta do. Make a bunch of signs, march in front of the City Hall, contact the radio and tv news stations, post it on Facebook and Twitter…we could get a huge backing!" Ed waved him down and pointed out Brianna, half hidden in the back of the room. Bri walked up to the podium and said one word: "Magic."

Chapter 2a

Brianna  *Sickness*

Much to her surprise, Brianna felt overwhelmed. Now that she thought about it, she had been feeling a little 'off' ever since the chalice's cleansing ritual. True, there were the orders piling up in her workroom, demanding her attention. Then there was this freeway thing which was really all she could think of. Normally she thrived on overstimulation, but right now Bri was feeling downright weary. Grabbing a comforting book on early Celtic fantasy, she headed for the couch. She hadn't read more than a few pages before she fell into a deep slumber.

Bri woke with a start, her hands instinctively pressing her chest. "Ow! What's happening? I can barely breathe." She slowly sat up and reached for the glass of water on the coffee table. After a few delicate sips, she slumped back into the couch. "Dear Goddess, what's wrong? I can't be sick. I don't have the time, there's too much I need to take care of. I have to finish those masks I started, and then there's the meeting with the council tomorrow. I'll just have to muddle through somehow…" as she tried to get up from the couch. *Wham!* It was like someone just pushed her back. "Can't move; can't get up. Oh my, oh my!" Bri leaned back and felt like a feathery quilt was wrapping itself around her. Her eyelids drooped and soon she was fast asleep.

Several miles away a stately mansion lay hidden in the woods; truly hidden from the sight of mortal man. Three women gathered around a large cauldron filled with water, and stared intently at the image that was forming. Nameless and yet with a thousand names, we'll call them Dawn, Sunny and Moonface (any name will do). Sunny, with eyes of a hawk, said "There! Do you see it? A grey shadow over her chest?" Dawn chimed in, "Yes, I see it! Is there anything we can do?" Moonface cleared her throat and the two women looked up at her. "Brianna needs this lesson. She failed to take into account that the chalice might have been stolen and wasn't properly protecting herself from the negative energies she released. We musn't stop it, but we can diminish its power. Hold my hands and we'll blanket her with a soft shield." The other two took her hands and together they chanted, humming and swaying, while sending the soothing energy into Bri's chest.

After hours of drifting off and coming to, Brianna forced herself to the bathroom and prepared for bed. Surprisingly, she woke in the morning with more than the usual verve. *Good!* Bri dove into her work and lovingly completed the remaining masks for her most recent order. "Bri-Gris" was wildly successful. Her cunning and daring birthed amazing masks that had enhanced many a ritual over the last two decades. That and her faery wings, which were all the rage with the younger set, had financed this home and allowed her to have a fairly high standard of living. As she put the finishing touches on the last mask *(just a whisper of glitter; nothing gaudy*), Bri mentally prepared for the meeting with the town council later that evening.

The final form of her plan clearly in mind, she cleared the dishes after dinner and sat down with pen in hand. First: pick a date and time which would best augment the work. Next: Assign each faith the task of creating a chant to discourage freeway construction. And lastly: all assemble at the temple and perform simultaneously with the final vocalizations orchestrated to end together, directing a cone of power toward the State Department of Transportation. "Yes! This will work" she mumbled to herself, humming as she slipped the note into her jacket and stepped outside. It was only a 15 minute walk to town, so she decided to walk rather than drive. Bri always enjoyed this route and the slow emergence from isolation to hustle bustle. The Nelson's had been sprucing up their yard, and she noticed a new sculpturc of three women holding hands. Charming, and so realistic that she had to look twice to determine it was truly granite. She'd have to find out who made it. Whistling a tune from Fiddler on the Roof, Bri strolled along, constructing a chant for the working ahead.

As she disappeared down the road, Dawn broke out into uncontrollable giggles. "It worked! She saw us as a statue! Oh, Granny, you're so clever!" Moonface squeezed her hand. "Hush, child. Let's get out of here."

Chapter 2b

Mae's Crossing ᚢ *Strength/ Endurance*

Rumors were flying throughout the region about some kind of magickal operation. All the various faiths had been contacted, asking for a representative to join in the work. The back room of the hardware store/lumber yard which served as a Meeting Hall was filled to bursting. Tables and chairs had been brought in, and each was abuzz with activity. Some folk bent over lists while others seemed to be composing drafts. Muted conversations were punctuated by occasional outbursts of laughter or scorn. The spiritual leaders of the community prepared to meet the enemy.

Chapter 2b

Rosalind ᚢ *Change*

Rose sat beside Mabel in the dusty old pickup, making note of landmarks. Soon she would be doing this solo; so different from the past when she and her sister played games and made airplanes of their hands out the car window. Nestled in the crook of the mountain's foot was a scattering of buildings, all painted white with a jolly red trim. The main house towered three stories high surrounded by carefully tended grounds. A large sign with the words "Blanton's Dairy" soared over the entrance to the driveway. Mabel turned in and drove past the house toward the big barn which housed the dairy.

" Hey Mabel! Good to see ya!" Billy Higgins, the man behind the booming voice, suddenly appeared in the wide doorway, grinning and taking off his hat in a mock salute. "And Miss Rosalind, pleasure to have ya here. C'mon inside where it's nice 'n cool. Yer in luck, 'cause Dan'l's here today." Daniel was the much sought after 'cow whisperer,' and his talents were called upon frequently. He could discern ailments, describe the animal's needs and preferences and tune in to their inner dialogue.

Rose ventured into the welcome coolness of the milking shed, her eyes adjusting to the dim light. She could barely make out a figure leaning over a stall. *Must be Daniel.* As her vision sharpened, she could see he was wearing a bright green cap which barely confined an abundance of honey gold curls, and seemed to be having a conversation with a cow. Just then she heard a sob behind her. Billy had taken Mabel in his arms and was comforting her. "It was so sudden, Billy! One minute she was giving orders, and the next she was on the floor. I started giving her CPR. I tried and tried…" she was blubbering now, sobs coming in great heaves. "There, there, Mabel. Ya did all ya could. The time comes to all of us, 'n she had a good life. Think on that, an' try 'n ferget the passin'."

Tears were now streaming down Rose's face as the reality of Dot's passing hit her like a fist in the gut. All of the previous days had been so jammed with activity and future plans that it hadn't really sunk in 'til now. *Gram was gone!*

Later that evening, Rose sat cross-legged on her bed in Gram's house, *My house now! all of Dot's holdings have been signed over to m,* hugging her bag of runes to her chest. Slowly inhaling and exhaling, she monitored her breath for a few moments. Rose felt the tension lifting like a palpable thing, freeing up her lungs and clearing her mind. Moving the bag to her forehead, she invoked Freya thus: "Frey-ya, Frey-ya, Frey-ya. Hear my plea. Come to me. Frey-ya, Frey-ya, Frey-ya. Guide my touch, and help me see. Frey-ya, Frey-ya, Frey-ya." Rocking and crooning, she kneaded the bag of runes. A pass through the incense smoke, and she was ready. Her hand dove into the bag and she grasped the first tile she felt. Uruz! The runes never failed her. *Of course the rune of change and strength would come up for me*. Rose put away her runes with one thought in mind; grab the bull by the horns and leap like a Minoan acrobat.

Chapter 2c

Mae's Crossing *Strength and Fortitude Increasing*

All was in readiness--each spiritual faction had worked their unique focus into a chant. Although the approaches differed (the Buddhists would send peace and serenity, the liberal Christians were concentrating on a blinding white light, the Native Americans zeroed in on the sacredness of the land, the Heathens would invoke Thor to blast an opening in an alternate route, etc.), it was agreed upon that only positive messages would be used; no harming the Capitol Building or disabling the proponents. Brianna, as representative of the Wiccan community, had settled on an invisibility spell. The optimum time for the sending was set for the following Friday afternoon. Emotions ran high as each group polished and perfected their parts. Areas were marked out within the temple, and folk could be seen walking the space and gesturing in the air. Excitement was barely contained; there was a new camaraderie within the community as they worked together for the good of all. Holding back was the hardest part. Wait they must.

Chapter 2c

Malachias *Future Change Anticipated*

The next Friday morning Malachais stepped out of his house with a spring in his step. Much as he hated to admit it, he was beginning to enjoy this detective stuff. The excitement of the chase had him looking forward to ferreting out both the criminal and the beloved glass. Today he would check out the Channing Exchange, hoping that it wasn't a dead end.

The front door bell tinkled, signaling Willem that someone had entered his shop. He hurried out to the front, wiping his hands on his pants to clean off the pastry crumbs.

"G'mornin', sir. How can I help you?"

Mal cleared his throat, searching for the right approach. "Yes, Mr. ?..."

"It be Douglas, sir."

All thoughts of subterfuge vanished as Mal spoke up. "Well, Mr. Douglas. I was hoping you could give me some information about a piece I've lost."

"Don't rightly know if I can. What are you missing?"

Mal pulled out his iPhone and pressed the picture icon, streaming through the pictures until he came to the chalice. Holding out his phone he said, "This chalice is gone, and I was wondering if..."

Willem's expression was one of shock, his eyebrows raised in alarm. "Can't say as I've ever seen the likes of this. Looks pretty costly. I'd surely remember this beauty. "

Mal was nobody's fool. Will's reaction didn't match his words. *He would never make a good poker player.* "Too bad. I was hoping…a friend said you might be able to help. It was made for me years ago, and I'm afraid someone stole it and might have brought it here. Please take my card, and let me know if it turns up."

The card was elegantly calligraphed with 'Malachais Merriwether' in white on a black background with a discreet email at the lower edge. "Sure, sure Mr. Merriwether. I'll keep an eye out for it. Not a piece that would escape my notice, that's for sure."

"Thank you for your time, Mr. Douglas. You will contact me if you find out anything, right?" Mal turned the doorknob and left the shop, the bell lightly tinkling a farewell.

Willem stood staring at the card for the longest time. *What to do?* He walked back to his tiny kitchen and plunked down on the stool. While he was pondering the problem, the doorbell tinkled again. Actually, it was more of a jangle, like someone had banged the door open. Will jumped to his feet and went out to the shop. Gerry Le Fevre was livid, and the intensity of his anger practically knocked Will off his feet. Immediately on the defensive, Will took on a placating tone.

"Hey Gerry. What's up lad?"

"I'll tell you what's up, old man. You cheated me on that fancy gee-gaw I brought you. I don't see it nowhere abouts, so I bet you sold it for a pretty penny! You owe me! Give me another hundred right now." Gerry was rocking back and forth on the balls of his feet, and his hands kept making and releasing fists.

Willem slowly eased back towards the counter where he kept a handgun. "Now Gerry, you know I can't do that. Don't have the money. Besides, I paid you fair and square. Remember we shook on it."

Gerry leaped at him, grabbing Willem by the throat. "You'll pay, old man!" Gerry shoved Will into the counter then stomped out the door. "I'll be back tomorrow, and you better have the money if you know what's good for you." The glass in the door shuddered as he slammed it shut behind him. Rubbing his neck, Will pushed away from the counter, knowing the aging skin housing his ribs would be a mass of bruises in a few moments along with fingermarks on his throat. Still holding the business card in his hand, Will locked the front door, turned over the 'open' sign and stumbled towards his living quarters upstairs.

THURISAZ

Thorn/force

Chapter 3a

Mae's Crossing *Force to be reckoned with*

Word got out about the scheduled ritual, and by Wednesday the temple grounds took on a festival atmosphere. Some folks had simply put up tents. Others brought in their RV's, while the more enterprising set up canopies. Mabel had grabbed the opportunity and sent out one of the girls with a hand cart filled with pastries. Kris Knudsen, High Godhi of the Asatru, had contacted Daniel telling him of their plans. Daniel, in turn, had sent out a crow, a falcon and a dove to the targeted area to alert the woodland creatures of the impending explosion. Ed Janssen ordered a truck to bring out the three port-a-potties the town had wisely invested in a few years back. Children were shrieking with delight at the puppet show set up on the back side of the gathering. The crowd was filled with excitement at the impending show of force.

Chapter 3a

Brianna *Force Building*

The meeting at the town hall went smoothly. All participants were busily working on their parts, eagerly anticipating the ritual which was scheduled for 2 PM on Friday. Along with being the most auspicious time planetary-wise, it was also chosen to coincide with the meeting of the Department of Transportation at the Capitol Building. There was nothing more to do but wait, so Bri made her farewells and set off on foot for home. As she neared the Nelson's property, she decided to stop by and ask about the sculpture. *Omigosh!* The sculpture wasn't there! Curiosity got the better of her, and she marched up to the front door and rang the bell. Betty Nelson swung the door open, an honest smile lighting up her face.

"Bri! How good to see you. Please come in. What can I do for you?"

"Thanks, but not right now. I'm in a bit of a hurry to get home, but I wanted to ask you about the new sculpture…"

"Umm, not sure what you mean…what sculpture?"

"Well, when I walked by this morning, there was this fantastic sculpture of three women in your yard, and I wanted to know more about it. It was so totally real…"

Betty interrupted her, and it was clear she was perplexed. "I'm sorry, dear. Did you say you saw a sculpture in our yard? True, we've thought of adding one, but haven't decided on the right piece just yet."

Bri was feeling gaslighted. She knew what she saw, but… "I'm terribly sorry, Mrs. Nelson. I've been so distracted what with all the doings at the town hall that I must have been having one of my visions again. You know how they come and go…" Brianna backed off the porch with an apologetic smile. "I really must be getting home. Thanks for your time."

Betty Nelson was about to wave her on, but stopped in mid-motion. "Wait here just a minute." She disappeared into the house and quickly returned with a container of cookies. "Fresh out of the oven, and some of my best. Please take them, and good luck with the ritual. Alan and I are so grateful for your work."

When Bri got home, she settled in the kitchen with icy milk and Mrs. Nelson's cookies. Munching and musing, she pondered on the mysterious disappearance of the sculpture. *Brilliant! Yes, that just might work, but it will have to wait 'til the weekend.* Right now Bri's priorities lay with the impending gathering. Holding on to that thought, she grabbed a rolled up tatami mat by the back door and walked out to the garden. Near the gazebo was a clear, clipped grass area surrounded by fragrant rose bushes. Inhaling the heavenly scents, she spread out the mat and laid down on it, carefully arranging her arms and legs into the star position. Bri sank into a semi-trance, storing up the gibbous moon's energy for Friday's release.

Chapter 3b

Mae's Crossing *Confusion/ Chaos*

Thursday

Late Thursday afternoon, Ed Janssen stepped up on a picnic table with a bull horn in his hands. "Thank you all for coming. As you know, many people from our local traditions will gather here," he gestured towards the temple, "at two o'clock tomorrow to blend their energies for a single purpose: to halt state government plans for a freeway through Mae's Crossing." Some people in the crowd shouted in outrage, but Ed stilled them with his raised hand. "Any folks who're interested in helping out, meet with me at 12 noon here tomorrow. After the rites are completed, please pack up and go home, and leave the grounds as you found them."

Chapter 3b

Rosalind *Trouble Brewing*

Grabbing the bull by the horns wasn't quite as straightforward as Rose had anticipated. Her first objective had been to return to BigCity, pack up and move to Mae's Crossing. Facing Shelly, her roommate, and saying adios wasn't going to be easy. The two had met during her short stint at the City College and hit it off immediately. As the friendship grew, they decided to share an apartment. That was two years ago, and the digs had become a real haven and refuge for her. She had broken away from Gram four years ago, partly to attend college, and partly to flee from reminders of her sister's absence. Succumbing to injuries inflicted by her boyfriend in a fit of violence, Jen's passing devastated Rose. She had idolized her big sister, and her loss left a deep hole. When she met Shelly, Rose could almost feel her heart mending. Over time, the friendship became a safe port in a stormy world. The two shared everything; clothes, food, transportation, deep secrets, wild fantasies…there was a closeness she had never experienced before.

"Our friendship is strong enough to survive this change." Rosalind clung to that thought and decided to go to BigCity on Saturday, opting to stay in Mae's Crossing for the big doings tomorrow. She might even 'help out' as Ed Janssen put it. On a sudden impulse, Rose called Shelly.

It only rang twice when Shelly answered. "Ro! It's so good to hear from you, sweets! How are you doing? How was the funeral? When are you coming home? What…"

"Whoa, Shelly! Slow down, girl. Had to talk with you. It's all so crazy here. Gram's gone, I'm a shopkeeper, I've got to move here."

There was a long pause before Shelly responded. "You what? No, you can't leave. Oh, shit, you've got to, don't you?"

"Shel, I'm so sorry. I didn't ask for it. I love our space in BigCity, and living together has been so much fun. I'm moving in to Gram's house, and I've got to get all my stuff from the apartment. This makes me so sad, but would you believe it, I'm excited about it too. I'm a shop owner. Me, a shop owner!"

"Why didn't I see this coming? Of course you have to move there. Oh Ro, will you be okay?" A moment's silence descended as both girls thought about Rose's fragility, and how she was plagued with abandonment issues. *How can I live alone?* She'd come so far in the two years they'd been together. Reality dawned in that instant to both Rose and Shelly, looking more like the mushroom cloud of the atom bomb than a sweet sunrise.

"Hey, I can help you with the packing and hefting and carrying and all that. I mean, like, there's a part of me that's really happy for you, and there's a part that's really pissed off that you're moving. That's okay, I can deal."

"Shel, you're the best friend ever. I love you so. Thanks for being there for me. I really, really need that. Listen, there's some big doings in town tomorrow that I don't want to miss, but I was thinking of driving down Saturday with boxes and stuff. We'll order Chinese take-out and make a day of it. Maybe drive back Sunday. How's that sound to you?"

"Yeah, that works. I'll have the coffee ready to go…we're going to need it. Give me a call when you're on the road, okay? And do you want sticky buns or lemon bars?"

Rose smiled at that. *Gods, I'm going to miss her.* "I'll go for sticky buns. Yay! What could be bad? Packing with Seattle's Best, sticky buns and the best friend in the world. What did I do to deserve this? Love you, bird's nest." Shelly's hair was always such a wild tangle; short, wiry red hair that seemed to sprout in all directions, looking for all the world like an elaborate bird's nest.

By the time Rose rang off, she was worn out emotionally. When uruz came up in her life, it was no small thing. No, she musn't ever underestimate the power of the runes.

Shelly Le Fevre sat looking at the silent cell phone, tears forming in her eyes. She couldn't imagine the place without Ro in it. *Life gets in the way, right? No, it's death gets in the way.* Poor Rosalind. She'd experienced enough death in her short life. Shelly knew she had no right to complain in comparison. But complain she did.

Chapter 3c

Mae’s Crossing *Force at Zenith*

Friday

At precisely 12 noon, Ed Janssen stepped up on the picnic table, and raised the bullhorn. “Good folk of Mae’s Crossing – thanks again for coming here today. As you know, in a couple of hours the leaders in the temple will begin their rites. You’ve all indicated that you’d like to join in, so listen up to my instructions. My son Jerrod is standing over there with the white flag. Please line up and follow him as he walks around the temple. Hold your positions once he makes the circuit. Remember where you were standing and by 2:00 be at your designated spot. At the precise culmination of the temple rites, a missile will be shot up from the temple garden. When you see the flare in the air, I want everyone to extend their arms to the center of the temple and shout out the words ‘Hear me now!’ Got it?” Ayes and yeses filled the air. “Working together we can let the State representatives know how we feel!” Murmurs of approval and bursts of excited chatter filled the air: Mae’s Crossing would not be violated.

Chapter 3c

Malachais ᚦ *Trouble/Protection/Breaking Barriers*

Willem sat hunched over his dinosaur iMac, waiting for his hands to stop shaking. He considered himself pretty fit for 73, but he was no match for an 18 year old punk who was probably high on drugs. As the shaking receded, he went through the motions to bring up his gmail account. Hitting compose, Will entered Malachais's email address and in the subject line wrote 'important'. "Dear Mr. Merriwether, I'd like to meet with you. Very important." Sincerely, Willem Douglas.

Malachais couldn't believe his eyes. He scanned the email again feeling his heart almost banging against his chest. *Yes! Breakthrough!* He inwardly cursed himself for not picking up Willem's card. Frantically typing a reply, Mal hoped Will was still seated at his computer.

He got up from his chair and walked out to the deck, lighting a cigarette and trying to calm himself. No point in jumping to conclusions; the mystery would clear itself shortly. Stubbing his cigarette, Mal returned to his computer and was rewarded with a reply in his inbox. "Please call me at 764-3058. Willem"

Mal fumbled with his phone, re-dialing after a first thwarted attempt. Willem answered; "Hello Mr. Merriwether. Could you come by the shop now? I'd rather talk with you in person."

"Certainly, Mr. Douglas, certainly. And you can call me Mal."

“Thanks Mr. Merri—Mal. Just knock, ‘cause the ‘closed’ sign is up.”

“Okay. I’ll be right over.”

The Channing Exchange was dark, but as Mal peered inside, he could see a faint light coming from the back. He gently tapped on the door, hoping it was loud enough without being insistent. He could just make out Will’s figure as he slowly hobbled to the door. *Strange, I don’t remember him as being feeble.*

Willem shaded his eyes through the window, trying to make out who was knocking. Mal spoke up “It’s me, Mr. Douglas. Malachais Merriwether.”

Will unlocked the door, “Thanks for coming so quickly Mr…uh, Mal” and beckoned for him to come to the back room. Mal saw Will holding his side as if it pained him, and his motions were jerky and abrupt.

“Please sit here, Mr. Mal. Would you like a cup of coffee, or some water? I’m going to have a brandy, ‘cause my nerves are shot.”

Mr. Mal? Funny, but it has a nice ring to it.. Mal looked at Willem closely, noticing he was fussing with a scarf around his neck. Something was wrong, and he had a feeling he was about to find out why. “Pour me a brandy too, Mr. Douglas, if you please.”

The two sat sipping in silence for a few moments. Will finally cleared his throat and began talking. “I’ll tell ya right off the bat, Mr. Mal, that I lied about not seeing yer pretty glass. I don’t usually give out that sort of information, but after what happened today…”

He broke off his speech as a coughing fit took hold of him. Will tore the scarf off his neck and Mal was shocked to see finger shaped bruises circling his throat. Instinctively, he reached out and gently touched Will's shoulder.

"Tell me what happened…"

The whole story came tumbling out; how Gerry brought him the chalice, how they bargained over it, how they shook on a deal. Mal went rigid with anger picturing the boy bringing his coveted chalice here. But when Will told him about his encounter today, Mal's composure evaporated and he jumped to his feet. "That louse! That low-life! That poor excuse for humanity attacked you? I don't believe it!" He spun around, looking for something to punch…there—a pillow…and beat the stuffing out of it. With some of his rage siphoned off, Mal returned to his chair, grabbed the brandy glass and downed it all in one gulp. Taking a few deep breaths, he placed his hand over Willem's.

"Willem, are you okay? Should you see a doctor? Can I see your side, please."

Just as Will had feared, his whole right side was a mass of bruises, and the skin was puffy over his ribs. Mal winced at the sight, then carefully pulled the shirt back into place.

"I need to think on this a bit. Do you have a spot where I can smoke? And could I please have a refill on the brandy? This may be a long night, Willem Douglas, but I'd like to be your friend and I'd like to help you. I just don't know how right now."

Will led him to the back porch, which was actually quite inviting with a wicker chair and a thoughtfully placed ashtray. Mal waved him off and eased into the chair. The anger he was experiencing had to be reined in; to be channeled into a more productive mode. His first reaction was to give the kid a thrashing, but his training forbade such an approach. Sipping on the brandy, Mal mulled over the problem. By the time he finished his cigarette, the beginnings of a plan were forming.

Back in the kitchen, Mal sat across the little table from Willem and held out a hundred dollar bill. “Please take this and give it to that little rat when he comes by tomorrow. Have my number ready to ring on your cell, and when Gerry shows up, press call. I’ll know it’s you and you won’t have to say anything. I’ll come as soon as I hear from you and keep an eye from outside. If he makes any funny moves, I’ll be in here in a flash. Are you okay with this?”

Willem fumbled with his neck scarf, and his face took on a ruddy hue. “Uh, Mr. Mal, I don’t think I should take this. It don’t seem right.”

“Nonsense, Willem. I insist. Do as I say and you’ll be fine. Are you sure you don’t want to contact the police about this?”

“Oh no, Mr. Mal. Can’t be talkin’ with no law officers. They’d be on my back for receivin’ stolen goods. Have to work it out on my own. Really thankful for yer help.”

Malachais stood up and nervously straightened his jacket. *What am I getting myself into? And by the Gods, I forgot about the chalice!* Oh well, the course was set. Nothing left but to steer the vessel to safe harbor. “I really must be off now, Willem. I’ll be waiting to hear from you tomorrow. You be sure and ring me now.” That said, Mal turned and walked towards the door, belatedly realizing that he had dropped the ‘Mr. Douglas’ in favor of ‘Willem’. Was this a friendship brewing?

"Wait up Mr. Mal, and I'll let ya out. I can't tell ya how grateful I am thatcha came by." Will made his way to the front door, shaking Mal's hand before letting him out. "See ya tomorrow."

ANSUZ

A God/communication

Chapter 4a

Mae's Crossing ᚨ *Communing with the Gods*

The temple was abuzz with activity. The building and grounds had been carefully planned to accommodate the needs of the various traditions performing their rites there. The main structure was a honeycomb shape surrounding a generous open-air garden. There were several rooms available for devotional use as well as a kitchen, cafeteria, office, library and restrooms. When the weather permitted, most preferred to perform their rites in the garden area. Today all were gathered there. Kris was off to the side with his daughter, Olga, instructing her on the use and timing of the flare gun. At 2 p.m., each contingent stood in their appointed space and began moving deosil on the paving stones which delineated a nine foot circle. Outside the circle, musicians lent their energies with the beating of drums, soft crooning of flutes, light tapping of tambourines, deep boom of dumbeks, etc. Each participant summoned their various guardians, and then began their individual chants. Brianna set the pace and all present coordinated their movements to match hers. Voices were raised in song, in shout, in entreaty. Bodies circled and robes swirled; the intensity grew as the pace around the altar increased. Clapping, stamping, drumming, ringing bells…the very trees trembled with the vibrations. Building to the point of bursting, Bri made the motion to release. Everyone stopped in their tracks, pointed their hands at the altar and shouted, "Hear me!" The noise was deafening. Olga shot the flare at the very height of frenzy. Just when it seemed like it couldn't get any louder, the folk circling the building added their voices.

On the outskirts of town, three women stood on an outcropping overlooking the village and temple. Moonface pointed at the flare and whispered, "Now!" In unison, the women extended their hands and the flare exploded like fireworks. Crazy, dancing rainbow streamers shot out from the flare, and like the ribbons on a Maypole entwined and sped towards the heavens. Inside the temple grounds, the various groups had collapsed to the earth, grounding and letting the excitement wash over them. And then, far off in the distance, a low rumbling could be heard. The ground beneath them shuddered as Thor blasted a rock formation 40 miles away. Some women swooned, others fell to the ground weeping. Men clapped each other's shoulders and children cheered. Mae's Crossing would be heard!

Chapter 4a

Brianna ᚨ *Communication*

Brianna raised herself up from the grass just in time to view the rainbow ribbons spiraling into the distance. Never had she experienced such a powerful, dynamic ritual. Her hands tingled and her head was throbbing. She looked around and saw the other participants slowly coming back to reality only to be confronted with the rainbow spiral; fruit of their working. All were in awe. Soon everyone was up. All joined hands and moved widdershins on the stones, thanking and releasing their guardians. At the conclusion, they embraced each other in congratulations, glowing with the after effects. One by one, they filed out of the temple to mingle with the group outside…and received a Hero's welcome from the townsfolk. The crowd was jubilant and full of praise for the magick raised that day.

Bri walked around in a stupor, receiving thanks and hugs from a constant stream of people. Still feeling a bit dizzy, she spied an empty bench under the trees and headed for it. *Whew! That's better.* She relaxed into the quiet comfort the isolated spot provided. A pretty blonde separated herself from the masses and approached Bri.

"Hi, Miss Brianna. I was wondering if I could get you anything? You look positively exhausted." Rosalind extended a hand in greeting.

Bri caught her hand in hers. "Hello. You're Rosalind Duncan aren't you? Thought I recognized you in the crowd. How kind of you to offer. Please accept my condolences for your loss."

Rose bowed her head, fighting back the tears that were still too close to the surface. "Thank you, Miss Bri. It was an awful shock, Gram going like that. I still can't believe she's gone..."

"I know, I know. We're all going to miss her. I hear you'll be taking over the bakery. You've got a good helper in Mabel. She'll steer you through the humps and hollows. And yes, since you asked, I'm famished. Could you please bring me something to eat and a good strong coffee, double cream, single sugar? I don't have my purse with me, but I can catch up with you later on that."

"Oh, don't you worry none about that, Miss Bri. I'll be right back." Rose turned and disappeared into the crowds as Bri sighed and leaned back against the picnic table, thanking the Gods for sending the girl to her at just the right moment. *No coincidences, right?*

Chapter 4b

Mae's Crossing *Absorbing News*

Late afternoon Friday

Back in the Town Hall, twelve members of the Mae's Crossing City Council sat glued to the TV screen. The local BigCity news station was covering the story of the proposed freeway construction. As different representatives of the State and freeway management officers conferred on the proposal, there was a flurry of activity at the side door and a messenger burst into the scene. "Senator Rawlins, I have an important announcement!" All heads turned toward the man as he blurted out "There's been an explosion, kind of like a lightning strike, and it's taken out the blockage on Rocky Peak!" Voices were raised in consternation as the Head Councilman beat his gavel on the podium. "Gentlemen, gentlemen. May I have the floor? We've all agreed that there were a lot of problems with the proposed route *(like a blotting out of all memory of the place, the sacredness of the ground, etc.),* and this opens up a whole new possibility. I suggest that we convene, and send out a survey party to see if this 'lightning strike' has made a significant difference." The cameras faded out to focus on the news team who began debating the issue. Inside the Town Hall, there was whooping and hollering as the council members streamed out of the building to let the crowds know that their works had achieved the desired ends. Mae's Crossing had scored a victory.

Chapter 4b

Rosalind  *Overflow of Divine Communication/A Need to Connect to Earthly Concerns*

"Here's your coffee, Miss Bri. Special treat 'cause Friday's Savory Pie day, and I grabbed a lemon bar just in case." Rose winked as she handed Bri the coffee, then sat on the bench, placing the food between them.

Rose fidgeted and spilled out the thoughts that had been building. "Miss Bri, I was wondering if you could tell me more about this town. Now that I'm a business owner I feel I need to have a better understanding of what makes it tick. I mean, I thought I knew it. I started living here with Gram when I was 10, and didn't leave 'til I was 18. So I know it's kind of a strange place, being cut off from everyone like it is. But what happened today, well, honestly, it's just got me perplexed. Never thought much about having a temple instead of a church, but now…"

Bri swallowed the last bite of savory pie, washed it down with the dregs of her coffee, carefully wiped her mouth and sat gazing at the young woman. "That's a pretty big question, Rosalind. I hardly know where to begin." She paused, watching the milling throng as they began the slow process of breaking down and packing up. "I guess the temple is as good a place as any to start. There was some deep wisdom in the people who suggested the concept; a place of worship for any and all paths seeking the light, whatever name they gave it. It started out simply enough with a grand final plan. Over the years, different folk added their touches and talents, some of it from my own hand. I don't think it will ever be completed, as each generation builds onto the original. So, Mae's Crossing has the temple. That makes it different. Then there's past history to think of too, which affected people's outlook. You must have seen the gutted church in decay. Rather than tear it down and pretty the space up, it was agreed to leave it as a reminder. I see it as a memorial to stupidity, but that's just me talking. We've got a ban on franchises. That's a big part of what makes this place unique. And bottom line is the people themselves…uh, hang on. Before I go any further, I need to get a refill on this coffee and stretch my legs. Maybe even take a bite of lemon bar." Bri felt like a wind-up doll that had just run down. The food and drink had revived her somewhat, but now she needed to move around and get the circulation back in her legs which had been pretty weak just moments ago. "Care to walk with me?"

Rosalind beat Bri to the task of clean-up, grabbing the paper plate and napkin. Bri held the empty coffee cup and the dessert, and together they started walking towards the coffee wagon.

"I'm not sure what I want to know, Miss Bri. It's just that, well, I hadn't really figured on inheriting the bakery and all. I mean, I guess I knew I'd be getting something; not just everything. It's all so mind-boggling. I've got a good life in BigCity and now…"

"I understand, Rose. Just keep me in mind if there's anything I can help you with or enlighten you about…" Bri broke off abruptly as there was quite a ruckus going on at the hardware store. She steered Rosalind in the direction of the bustle. Tom Bradley was running past and did a quick stop on a dime at her side.

"Hey Brianna! We just got news about the freeway guys, and it looks like they're going to drop the Mae's Crossing proposal! We did it!" Tom grabbed Bri around the waist and swung her up in the air. Laughing uncontrollably, Bri admonished him. "Put me down Tom! Oh yay, hooray! Oh happy day!" She did a few pirouettes out of sheer exuberance, then threw her arms up saying "Thank you Goddess!"

"You know, mum, she makes it all worth the effort, don't you think?" Sunny looked across the cauldron to Moonface. Dawn pouted and said "She should have said Goddess<u>es</u>." Granny reached out her hands to the two women, giving them an affectionate squeeze. The three of them stared into the water, grinning faces reflecting back at them.

Chapter 4c

Mae's Crossing *Hidden Inspiration*

The next day, being a Saturday, was a busy one for a town with only three streets of businesses and many of them closed. Kids lined up at the movie theatre for the Saturday matinee, while groups of women in twos and threes window shopped. The pub, 'Crossing Point', was already doing a brisk business, and the town was fairly bursting with cheer and light-heartedness. Mae's Crossing emerged from this latest conflict with a determined populace; confident in being able to preserve and protect their hard-won freedom. There was a new sense of self esteem buoying up the folk that made the sun seem brighter, the breeze more refreshing, the town itself much grander than ever. Ed Janssen and Chester Burns sat in the corner of the pub, nursing their ales while hunched over the checkerboard between them. "You know, Chester, this whole freeway thing has put new life into our town, and folks are just bustin' to have a celebration. I think we should have some kind of a festival. Whatcha think?"

Chapter 4c

Malachais (Channing) *Bad News*

Laura arrived promptly at 9:00 am to a highly agitated employer. Malachais resisted saying anything about Gerry yet, as he waited impatiently for his phone to ring. Thinking about the injuries the kid inflicted on the older man made him see red; he needed to calm down and approach this situation with a clear head. Pouring a tall glass of ice water, he let himself out onto his porch and lit up. The phone rang, and an errant memory of lighting up in a restaurant just as the waiter appeared jumped into his mind. Dropping his cigarette in the ashtray, Mal raced inside to see that it was, indeed, Willem calling. He blurted out something about staying away from Gerry, grabbed his keys and left the house, taking care to keep his foot light on the accelerator. No sooner had he pulled up to the curb when he saw Gerry leaving the shop. Dear Gods, how he wanted to grab that kid and knock him senseless! Waiting until the boy turned the corner, Mal got out of his car and entered the shop.

"Hey, Mr. Mal. No problem. The kid took the money and skeedaddled."

"I have a feeling this isn't the end of it, Willem. Is there someone you can stay with for a few days until Gerry cools off some?"

"Funny you should say that, Mr. Mal, 'cause I was thinking the same. I'll need to check with him first, but I'm sure my friend Al up in Mae's Crossing would put me up for a time. Thing is, I don't drive no more. Have to check out the bus schedule. I'm pretty sure it goes out there pretty regular."

"No need to take a bus, Willem. I'll be happy to drive you up there. I've never been to Mae's Crossing, but I've been curious about the place. I really don't think you should stay here tonight, in any case. If you'd like, you can stay at my home for a couple of nights."

"Don't know why yer going to all this trouble for me, Mr. Mal. Ya hardly know me, and…oh, it's the pretty glass, isn't it? Yer hopin' to get it back maybe?"

"I don't want to see you get hurt again, Will. But you're right, I am anxious to get my chalice back…if I can…"

"Well, Mr. Mal, fate has a funny way of puttin' stuff together now, don't it? Just so happens that Al bought it from me."

Mal's pulse quickened at the news; *one step closer to reunion!* Barely containing his excitement, he urged Willem to pack what he needed and close up the shop. Half an hour later, he welcomed Will into his home.

Later that evening as they were finishing up a meal and sharing information about their personal lives, there was a frantic pounding on the door.

"What in the world? Who…" Mal hurried to the front door and opened it to find Laura, trembling and apparently weeping. It was hard to tell through the sunglasses she was wearing. "Laura, what's wrong? Come in, come in. Here, sit down over there. Let me get you a glass of water." He rushed to the kitchen and came back with a tumbler of ice water, placing it in her shaking hands. She gratefully took a big gulp, and seemed to calm down some.

"I'm sorry to bother you, Mr. Merriwether, but I didn't know where else to go. Oh, dear, you have a guest. Maybe I should just go…" She started to get up, but Mal gently pushed her back into the couch. "Laura, this is my friend, Willem Douglas. Willem, this is Laura Black. She is responsible for the spotless order you see around you. And now, young lady, tell me what's going on."

"Well, Mr. Merriwether, I went over to Gerry's today and I was going to ask him about the vase. When he let me in I saw a glass pipe and a pile of white powder next to it. So I says, "Gerry, what's this? I thought you didn't do drugs. You told me you'd never touch 'em, but look at this. What's up?" Gerry, he gets all huffy and says it isn't his; belongs to a friend who just left. But Mr. Merriwether, he was all jittery and nervous, and like I told you before, seemed like he changed from when we first started going together. I mean, like he'd get angry at the littlest thing. Anyway, it just sort of burst out of me, I mean, asking him about the vase. That's when he blew up. He started beating on me, punched me in the face, and says he's leaving this crummy town and going up to BigCity with some of his friends. Yells at me and tells me to get out, 'cause his friends are supposed to show up any minute. So I asks him, "What about us?" and I was kind of sorry I asked 'cause I sure didn't like him anymore. Not after what he did to me. He just punches me again and shoves me out the door saying, "Get out! Get out of my life! I don't want nothin' to do with a dumb cleaning girl! Don't know what I ever saw in you in the first place. Just get the hell out!" At this, Laura broke down and started crying in earnest.

Mal sat on the couch next to her and tentatively reached out to her, only to have her come tumbling into his arms, sniffling and crying, wetting his shirt with mucus and tears. "There, there, Laura. Here's a handkerchief," as he pulled a fine linen cloth from his pocket. He patted her on the back then disentangled himself from her clutching embrace.

"Here now, Laura, let's see that eye," as he removed her sunglasses and saw the shocking evidence of Gerry's anger. Her eye was puffed shut, and blood was flowing freely from a nasty cut above her eyebrow. Laura lifted her skirt slightly to reveal bloodied knees. Inwardly seething at Gerry's mistreatment, Mal fought to keep his composure as he gestured to Willem; "Will, please get me some hydrogen peroxide from the bathroom. You'll find some gauze pads in the drawer. Bring me some of those, too."

While Mal was cleaning up her face, he asked if she had anyone she could turn to for help. At his suggestion of her parents, she stiffened and said, "Oh no, sir, I can't go to them. They're mad at me for hanging out with Gerry, and they'd just say I told you so and probably throw me out. No, no I can't go to them," and a fresh burst of tears started flowing. Then Mal suggested a battered women's home; he'd heard of one opening up downtown. Laura squirmed and said, "I don't think so. I don't want strangers asking questions; it could make trouble for Gerry, though I don't know why I care about that. No sir, I just wouldn't feel comfortable there." Through his growing frustration at the girl's rejection of his suggestions, Mal chose his next words carefully. "Surely you have friends that would take you in…" An uncharacteristic calm descended on Laura as she gave the question some thought. Finally she muttered "Maybe Shelly, Gerry's sister. We always got along pretty good, and I like her, and she'd let me stay there for a while, I'm pretty sure."

After calling her friend and making arrangements, Mal saw her to the door. He counted out fifty dollars and stuck it in her purse. "This is for next Saturday. I'll be out of town, and I want you to just rest and get better, okay?"

No sooner did Laura close the door behind her than Mal marched into his bedroom and brought out his Bozo the

Clown. After fifteen minutes of brutally punching the blow-up doll, sweat rolling down his face, Mal collapsed onto the couch. Although the anger had been somewhat dissipated, he was still left with a powerful rage; powerful enough to compel him to put a stop to any further damage Gerry Le Fevre might do.

R A I D H O

Chariot wheel/journey

Chapter 5a

Mae's Crossing *Journeys Thwarted*

The annual re-election and selection of new board members was under way in the back room of the hardware store. The original charter, drafted more than fifty years previous, still held water. Once a year there was a review, a discussion centering on the council members themselves. Firstly, there was a show of hands on how many of the present members wanted to continue in that position. This year there were two drop-outs: Widow Thompson and Caroline Spivack. Both declared pressing home issues which demanded more of their time. The remaining ten councilmen wanted to continue in their positions. That would necessitate a vote of confidence. Tallies were taken and counted, and all ten were approved for another year. That left two openings for new council members. Eligibility hinged on being a property owner in Mae's Crossing for at least 5 years, nothing more. There were actually four candidates this year, no doubt inspired by the recent doings at the temple. First was the temple Chaplain, one Samantha Sunrise (property ownership was not mandatory for her, as she had been caretaker of the temple for the past seven years). Next was Tanya Blanton, then Betty Nelson and lastly Bors Larsen. Each in turn spoke of how they would enhance the council and what talents they could bring to the table. There was a short break for necessities; bathroom, snack table, smoking section, etc. In fifteen minutes, all were present in the main room, and again a tally was taken and counted. The new council members, Samantha Sunrise and Bors Larsen were sworn in. The first order of business for the new council was a proposed 'Glory Days Gala' to give all a chance to celebrate the amazing success of the freeway conflict. It was unanimously approved and set for the next month. A sense of pride permeated the group as they relaxed later with food and drink, reveling in the town's ability to divert a freeway which would inevitably be filled with curiosity seekers and disrupters of local customs. Mae's Crossing stood strong.

Chapter 5a

Brianna *Journey Cancelled*

Brianna awoke Saturday morning with a pounding headache. She had really stretched herself to her limits yesterday, and now it seemed that she would be paying for it. Bri had tentatively planned to drive down to BigCity today to stock up on materials, but she scratched that idea. Better to just stay home and finish up some wings that were floating around her workroom. Besides, she wanted to carry through with her thoughts on the sculpture in the Nelson's yard; it was still in the back of her mind, eating at her with visions of self-delusion and possible hallucinations.

By the time she finished lunch, Bri's headache had abated. Clear-headed at last, she started gathering together the things she needed for solving the statue mystery: An incense burner, her special scrying blend of herbs, a purple candle and her coveted sheen obsidian scrying orb. *Oh, and don't forget the matches*. Because the original vision had happened outdoors, Bri decided to do her rites in the garden. Putting everything in a basket with her favorite altar cloth covering it, she went out to the gazebo. The timing was perfect. The sun was just beginning to set, and the lavender twilight filtered through the latticework. Laying out the altar cloth and arranging her tools upon it, Bri could feel the rightness of her procedure. *Yes, this will do nicely.* She lit the incense and walked around the center table, humming 'we all come from the Goddess'. Satisfied that the tone was set, she sat before the orb, positioning it so the 'eye' faced her. Bri placed her hands on the stone, raised it above the incense smoke so that it curled and coiled around it, then called upon the Goddess. "Gracious Goddess, Mighty Mother of Magicks, bless me with inner sight that I might see into this mystery. So mote it be!" Time passed and soon her vision blurred. As it cleared, she saw the statue again. While she watched, the figures came to life and were clearly identifiable to her: Maiden, Mother and Crone! *Oh my Goddess! They're here among us!* Oh, but now it all made perfect sense; the success of the temple ritual, the spiraling rainbow ribbons, the blast by Thor, the hesitation of the planning department of the Transportation Board...*Oh My Goddess!* The vision faded and she put away her things. The Fates were with her, and she was humbled by their presence.

Chapter 5b

Mae's Crossing ᚱ *Plans Put in Motion*

The myriad of details in putting on a festival were placed squarely in the laps of Samantha and Ed. Rising to the task in record time, within days of receiving the assignment, they issued an announcement heralding "Glory Days Gala" (to be held in thirty day's time). It was posted online and distributed to local businesses as a small poster. The wheels were turning. The gathering was to be located in the pasture directly adjacent to the temple. This space had been used for large get-togethers many times in the past with great success. Already Sam and Ed were receiving requests for booth space as vendors and food booths vied for the choicer spots. The parking lot on the west side of the temple was designated as the entertainment area where musicians could 'plug-in' and dancers could dance. It would commence on a Friday afternoon (giving all participants ample time to set up their various venues) and wind down Sunday afternoon. A detailed map of the area was drawn up, and Sam laboriously laid out the booth plans, numbering the spaces as she went. Power lines were brought in, with branching lines ending in multiple plug-ins. One of the perks of being an earth-oriented community was an independent attitude regarding electricity. There were a few lines coming up the mountain from BigCity, but their main source of power was self-generated. The methods varied, but the results were the same; virtual power autonomy.

Deep in the woods, three women were hard at work in the potting shed. Dawn, being bright and industrious, had sniffed out some fine red virgin clay. Sunny was in the process of working it into forms which she would then decorate. Moonface stood over her, instructing her. "Make it a little thinner, Sunny. There, that's good. Now make two circles…" Having created the shapes to her satisfaction, she handed Sunny a paper with signs and names. "Put these signs on one side with the futhark circling the rim. On the opposite side, do the names like this," as she indicated with her long, bony finger. Sunny followed her commands, eventually handing her the completed circles for inspection. "Good, good. Perfect! Now glaze and fire them." Much later in the evening as they sat in the atrium, Sunny presented Moonface with the fired pieces. "Excellent! Dawn, hand me that kerchief and the candlestick, please." The old woman carefully wrapped the cloth around one of the pieces, set it on the table, and gave it a firm whack with the candlestick. Opening the cloth, two perfect halves lay, not a single speck amiss. She repeated the process with the other circle, then slid each piece into a pouch with a name stitched on the outside. Handing the one that said "Rosalind" to Sunny, she said, "See that Rosalind gets this."

Chapter 5b

Rosalind ᚱ *Journey*

When Rosalind woke up Saturday, she sleepily groped for the rune bag on her nightstand and drew her daily rune. Raidho! *Wouldn't you know it?* Here she was, on the verge of driving down to BigCity, and she gets Raidho. *Thank goodness it's upright*. She reflected on the seemingly chance meeting with Brianna. Rose had been surprised at the easy familiarity Brianna exhibited towards her. Feeling at ease with the older woman, she looked forward to spending more time with her. Wasn't much of a chance on 'Frenzied Friday,' but sometime soon she'd ask for a lunch date or some such thing. Reflect was all she could do, for the days following that Friday were busy and demanding. She jumped out of bed, ready to face the day.

Later in BigCity

"Here, Shel, let me help you with that chair. I should just leave it, but I've got some more sitting to do in it." The two young women wrestled the chair through the doorway and out to the rental van, ever vigilant to keep the door out of the path of the constant flow of traffic. While they were trying to figure out the best way to pack it in, Laura Black drove up.

"Oh, Ro, I forgot to tell you she was coming over. It's my little brother's girlfriend, Laura. She's a real sweetheart. She's having troubles, and I said she could stay for a few days. Still don't know what's up, but it'll come out in its own time....maybe she can lend a hand with the fetching and carrying."

The two jammed the chair into the van and walked over to Laura's car. She seemed a little edgy, but Rose chalked it up to revealing her problems to a stranger. "Come on inside, Laura. Do you have a bag or some stuff you want to bring in? My name's Rose and I'm Shelly's roommate. I mean was. Damn that's hard to say." Rose looked over to Shelly, tears starting to form in her eyes. "Damn it anyway!" She hastily mopped the tears with her sleeve and took the bag Laura had pulled out of the back seat; a paper shopping bag stuffed with clothes and USB cords spilling out of the top. The three of them walked into a living room strewn with books, clothing, odds and ends, etc…in other words, pure chaos. Shelly steered her into her bedroom while Rose set her bag inside the door. Overwhelmed by their kindness and generosity, Laura broke down in tears, reaching for the edge of the bed.

Shelly and Rose shot questioning glances at each other, raising their eyebrows and mouthing "What?" Shelly sat next to her on the bed, putting her arm around the girl who promptly responded by throwing both arms around her shoulders. Laura was shaking uncontrollably, but Shelly managed to soothe and calm her. Soon enough, she'd straightened up and wiped her face (with a fine linen handkerchief), clearing her throat and getting up the courage to tell her story.

When she was through talking, maybe half an hour later, the two older girls looked at each other with shock on their faces. Shelly exploded. "Gerry did that to you? That little shit! Wait 'til I get hold of him!"

Seeing the damage Gerry had inflicted on Laura, Rose felt a clenching in her stomach as the vision of her sister's last hours flashed through her mind. Heavily bandaged and on life support, Jen had been unaware of Rosalind and Dot kneeling by her bed. Rosalind stayed by her side and held her hand for hours before it finally turned cold. She looked pleadingly at Shelly, mouthing "Can't do this!" Making her apologies to Laura, who was smiling now like a lost puppy that's found a home, Rose backed out the door and returned to packing and schlepping. Mostly she packed and sorted. What a mountain of stuff she'd accumulated in two years! By the time the other two emerged from the bedroom, Rose had methodically created three groups of 'stuff'.

"You guys ready to help me pack this pile in the van?" she pointed to the closest grouping. "That pile in the middle is total trash. The last bunch of stuff is still pretty good, but I'm leaving it for whoever wants it. Or Goodwill it."

Happy for the diversion, both girls grabbed armfuls and headed for the van. Within a short time, everything was packed and they were on the long road to Mae's Crossing.

Chapter 5c

Daniel *Immobilized*

Out at Blanton's Dairy, fear and apprehension tainted the air. Bessie, their prize cow, had fallen ill. Billy Higgins was at his wit's end. He'd tried every remedy he could think of to no avail. Bessie lay on her side in the sweet smelling straw strewn manger, her breathing labored. Tanya Blanton put out a call for Daniel through the grapevine. He didn't carry a phone, and was seldom found in his little cabin off Dutchman's Creek. Billy stayed at Bessie's side, crooning to her and stroking her stiff hide.

Daniel emerged from Honeycomb Hollow, his foraging for burdock and comfrey successful. When searching for herbs such as these, he would purposely wear his deep green cap. Seen in this setting, his eyes were his most startling feature. Usually hazel, they now seemed to echo the green of the forest. Most folks couldn't tell you what color they were as they kept shifting into variant shades of brown, gold and green. Hiking up the hillside to his mountain bike, woodland creatures chattered and chittered. Many were the thanks he heard that day as stories of dens, lairs and burrows being vacated in time to avert the disastrous blasting of Rocky Peak swirled around him. As he was peddling back to Dutchman's Creek, Otto waved him down. "Hey, Dan'l! Just heard yer needed out at the dairy. Sumpin 'bout Bessie. Ya better get there quick."

Daniel thanked him and turned around, taking the quickest bike route over to Blanton's. Quick still meant another forty-five minutes of peddling, but it was the best he could do.

Chapter 5c

Malachais *Preparing for Journey*

The silence stretched between Malachais and Willem until Will finally broke it. “Uh, Mr. Mal, are ya okay? Poor girl. I thought I got roughed up, but lookin’ at her just gives me the willies. Gerry’s a real creep!”

Mal extended his arms, working out the tightness in his muscles. “I hardly know what to say, Willem. We’ve got a real monster on our hands. Only good thing about it is that he’s leaving town, and you don’t have to hide out with me.”

“I was thinkin’ on that some, and was kind of lookin’ forward to a visit with Al. Do you think we could still do that, I mean, go on up to Mae’s Crossing?”

“I believe we could, Willem. Just let me take care of a few things tomorrow, and we can set out first thing Monday morning. You say it’s about a four hour drive? Do you mind if I smoke in the car? I can always make a stop if it’s uncomfortable for you.”

“Sure Mr. Mal. I’ll just roll down my window and be fine. Smoke all you want. I actually like the smell of tobacco; just that my old lungs can’t handle it no more.”

“If you don’t mind, Willem, I’d like to turn in now. I’ve got a lot to sort out and really just want to lie down on a soft pillow and let my spirit take over the task. Here’s the guest room” he said as he walked Will to the door. “The bathroom has fresh towels.” He gestured towards the bathroom. “I usually get up around seven, so I’ll try to be quiet in the kitchen. Would you prefer coffee or tea in the morning?”

And so the gentlemen settled in for the night, each with his own set of challenges to work on. The next day was spent in relative relaxation, as the departure time for the road trip was scheduled for the following morning. There was a cautious probing of each other's character throughout the day, but by evening it was a sure thing that they had become friends independent of the circumstances which had brought them together. Mal's reclusive life style was hardly that anymore; his world was getting larger.

KENAZ

Torch/enlightenment

Chapter 6a

Daniel *Fire Gone Out*

By the time Daniel showed up at the Blanton's, Bessie was on her last legs. Daniel camped out in the barn with her, knowing there was nothing he could do to cure her, and curled up at her side, cradling her head in his lap. In the morning, he went up to the main house to break the news to her grieving owners. What followed was most extraordinary.

Muttering a few hasty words to divert folks' attention from his head, Daniel removed his cap, ceremoniously bowed and announced Bessie's passing, then turned to face Tanya. "Well, Miz Blanton, you may not believe this, but Bessie wanted me to give you this message. She said she was tired of folks pulling on her tits, and that she was coming back as a horse next time. She also wanted me to tell you not to waste all her good flesh; tan her pretty hide and please have a party on her. Like I said, it's pretty weird, but those were her exact words."

The group assembled in the sitting room stared at Daniel in disbelief. Then he looked at Tanya, tipped his head and winked. When he made that familiar gesture, Mrs. Blanton gasped and fainted into her husband's arms. When she came to, Tanya exclaimed that that was the same motion Bessie had used to greet her. There was no mistaking that Daniel's words rang true.

Gordon, the butcher, was contacted and showed up shortly afterwards with his flatbed and winch. As he drove off, back wheels digging deep ruts in the road, Tanya stood watching from the comfort of her husband's arms. Tears were streaming down her face in sharp contrast to the bright smile she flashed at James Blanton, secure in the knowledge that they were following Bessie's last request.

Chapter 6a

Brianna *Creativity Sending Forth Blossoms*

Sunday morning found Brianna back to her usual high energy self. After spending some time on her craft *(her newest mask design was positively the cat's meow)* she fixed lunch and took it out to the back porch, admiring her garden in full bloom. *Full bloom! Oh my Goddess!* She had clean forgotten about the spells she had promised Al. No wonder, with all the goings on, but no more putting it off. Grabbing a pencil and tablet from the kitchen, she returned to the porch and started scribbling down thoughts and possible chants. Looking for further inspiration, she grabbed Maria Kay Simms' 'Circle of the Cosmic Muse' and the Farrar's 'Witches Way'. Thumbing through the pages, she found the rites she was searching for. Within the hour, Bri had rough sketches for both spells. Tomorrow she would go to Al's to schedule the best times for each working. She wrestled with the guilt of the broken chalice, and wondered if she should tell him about it.

Back to her workshop, Brianna laid out the pieces for three more sets of wings. She'd gotten wind of the 'Glory Days Gala', and wanted to be sure and have plenty of stock for that event. Bri put a note on her board, reminding herself to call Samantha in the morning. She'd already been accepted for an annual event in BigCity; one which always brought plenty of business. Not having any employees, Bri had to put a bit of hustle-bustle into her work routine with two shows on the horizon. Putting all thoughts aside of the myriad niggling details vying for her attention, she buckled down and spent the rest of the day making stock. Thanks to the Goddess's inspiring presence, she went to work on a trio of masks in red, white and black; a fitting tribute to the Triple Goddess. This would undoubtedly be a hot item with the Pagan shoppers. When Bri went to BigCity next month for the

'Fantasy Festival', she'd need to do some shopping for materials, as she added three more items on her 'must have' list.

Three women, their heads nearly touching as they held their nightly vigil 'round the cauldron, presented a striking picture. Immune to the aging process (Goddesses could appear in any guise that pleased them), Moonface's hair was inky black. It spread out around her like a silken cloak. Sunny's hair was a flaming red that was carefully braided and wound about her head. And Dawn—well, she was Dawn, and the sun rose when she smiled. Her hair was achingly white, and looked like thistle down, wild and fluffy. Dawn exclaimed; "Wow! Aren't those masks terrific?" The other two readily agreed.

Chapter 6b

Mae's Crossing 〉 *Unknowable*

Later that week, with the cow grieves' behind them, James and Tanya had more pressing issues to deal with. Their wild mare, which they had tamed and subsequently bred to their top stud, was giving birth. Tanya preferred to distance herself from the labor, making herself comfortable on the porch while still within hollering range from the horse barn. It wasn't a long wait. James called up to her "It's a filly! White with brown spots." Tanya promptly rose and hurried down to the barn. She stared in amazement at the newborn foal, its coloring and patterning so much like Bessie's. When the filly looked up at her with its wet brown eyes, it nodded and winked. Tanya, true to form, fainted in the arms of James who was so thoughtfully standing behind her.

Chapter 6b

Rosalind 〉 *Drained of Energy*

Sunday

By the time the girls had unloaded the van, it was close to midnight. Rosalind was exhausted, but glad she had decided to drive 'home' Saturday rather than Sunday. The four bedroom home easily accommodated the influx of bodies, who were all deep in slumber before 1:00 am rolled around.

Sunday morning, the girls gathered in the spacious kitchen. Shelly was familiar with the place, as she and Rose had visited frequently over the past couple of years. Laura was all agog at the estate, and let them know so in an unending stream of comments…"Oh my gosh, look at that old clock. And the hutch with all those pretty plates in it. Wow, this couch is so comfortable…" All three had Monday commitments; Laura back to school *How can I go to school with this black eye? Everyone's going to ask about it!*, Shelly back to her position as manager of 'Classy Chassis,' an up-scale dress shop, and Rosalind was scheduled for her final run-through of her pick-up route with Mabel. Rested and refreshed, they piled into the van and drove back to BigCity.

As soon as the vehicle was out of sight, Sunny emerged from the woods, a silk pouch dangling from her wrist. Finding the front door locked, she pointed at it and said "Open." The door swung inward, and she entered. Sunny wandered through the house, looking for the right spot to leave the talisman. She wasn't sure which room Rosalind would be sleeping in until the rune pouch caught her eye. Of course! She opened the pouch, dropped the talisman in, and carefully set it back in its original position. Humming a tune from the Wizard of Oz, she let herself out the front door and disappeared into the woods, a smile wreathing her face.

After dropping off the rental van and retrieving her car, Rosalind spent some time with the girls. Inwardly, she was glad of Laura's distraction; it made the parting so much easier. After a chummy meal of Chinese take-out she was yawning, but forced down some coffee *(with sticky buns!)* to fortify herself for the drive home. Making an unavoidably tearful farewell, Rose slipped into her car and drove away. It was dark when she finally parked in front of Her Home. She thought she was exhausted last night, but tonight was worse because of the emotional drain of leaving Shelly. Usually, Rose drew a nightly as well as a morning rune, but she was too bleary-eyed to do a reading. Maybe she'd pull two in the morning. With that, she turned out the light and was asleep before her head hit the pillow.

Chapter 6c

Daniel < *Aha!*

Daniel rummaged through his cabin, frantically throwing clothes and shoes about, searching for his red cap. To outsider's eyes, his living quarters would look messy and unkempt. In actuality, Dan'l was a scrupulous cleaner, and the floor underneath the disarray was shiny and spotless. *Why put something in a drawer or a cupboard or some other hiding place when who knows when I might need it next? Aha, there it is!* Grabbing his cap, he pulled it over his unruly curls and tugged it over his ears. Red was definitely the color for today. Daniel would be searching for amanitas muscaria, and he was a firm believer in sympathetic magic.

Chapter 6c

Malachais < *Attraction*

Monday dawned bright and clear. Malachais and Willem climbed into the vintage Mustang and settled in for a pleasant drive up to the mountains. Fortune smiled on them, as the traffic was light and the journey filled with good conversation. They only stopped twice on the road, and Mal carefully blew smoke out his window, keeping his consumption down in respect for Willem. It was 1:00 pm when they pulled up in front of Al's Antiques. Will had called ahead, and sure enough, Al was standing in the doorway with a welcoming grin on his face.

"Hey, Willum. Made good time, did ya? And ya mus be Mr. Mal?" as he reached out and grasped Mal's hand in a strong grip.

"Malachais Merriwether, at your service," said Mal with a theatrical bow. Al and Willem chuckled at his display, as Al ushered them into the air conditioned comfort of his dusty den.

While closing the door after them, he directed, "Will knows where guests sleep. Whyncha take yer stuff on up, do what ya need, and come on down in say, half hour?"

In due course the three sat around the small table in the back of the shop, drinking coffee and making serious inroads on an assortment of Dot's Delights. Speaking around a mouthful of pastry, Willem piped up, "Al, 'member that kid I tol' ya 'bout? The one that brought me the purty glass?" Al nods his head. "Well, would ya believe it, he shows up at my place this weekend wantin' a hundred more. Starts yellin' at me an' pushin' me 'round," at this he pulls up his shirt to show the bruising and swelling. Al stiffens and starts to rise at the sight of his friend's injuries, fury burning in his eyes.

"That scum! Let me get my hands on 'im!"

Willem reaches out and presses Al back into his chair. "That's not the half of it. Mr. Mal here, he gives me a hundred to give the punk. Next day kid comes back, takes money an' scoots. Me an' Mr. Mal figured he might try agin, so I go to stay at his place until the kid cools off some. Den it gets really wonky. We be sittin' in his purty living room when the door almost comes off its hinges from some'un bangin' real hard. Turns out it's the creep's girlfriend Laura, really sweet girl, and he's roughed 'er up too. Long story, but she's Mr. Mal's cleanin' girl, an 'er dumb boyfriend stole his glass when she was workin' there. Now Mr. No Good ups and says he's leavin' for BigCity. So didn't really need to hide out, but after all these shenanigans, well, ya know, just wanted to get away fer a while."

At the mention of Mal's ownership of the glass, Al's head jerked up from his coffee, spilling some on his shirt. Fussing with the stain, he mumbled "Sorry ta hear about yer stuff, Malakai."

"Well, Mr. Cooper… I know Willem sold it to you." Al threw a withering glance at Willem, who shifted uncomfortably on his chair. "I was hoping you might point me in the right direction to retrieve it. I'd be willing to pay for it." Mal looked at him expectantly.

Making a display of busily cleaning his coffee stain, Al mumbled something incomprehensible under his breath.

"I'm sorry. I didn't quite make out what you said."

“Well sure, ya got the rights of it. Can’t do more than fess up to that. ‘An I sol’ it. Client confidenchal, though, can’t say who.”

“I can respect that, Mr. Cooper. Why don’t you give your client my card and tell him I’d pay handsomely for its return,” Mal handed him his card.

Al took the card, carefully scrutinizing it and reluctantly admiring its simple elegance. “I’ll do just that, Malakai. I’ll do just that,” as he tucked it into his shirt pocket.

Mal changed the subject, trying to work his way into a more genial exchange. “I’ve never been here before. I was wondering if you could recommend some sights to see. I’d like to stay for a few days and just soak it all up. Gods know I’ve had enough excitement and could sure use a little R&R. Is there a hotel or a bed and breakfast you could steer me to? It feels good to get away from the usual routine -- as well as the BigCity noise and smell -- and Channing with its yuppifying do-gooders.”

Relaxing into more familiar territory, Al followed the lead, warming up to the question. “Well, now, I’d say ya got to take a look at the temple. Folks here in Mae’s Crossing are right proud of it. Years in the making, it was, and a sight to see fer sure. An prolly the Ruins too. Yep, both worth the lookin’ at.”

At that, Al rose and gestured that Mal should follow him to a map on the wall. He started pointing out the best routes to the two places, when he caught movement out of the corner of his eye. Brianna! She was peeking in the window, so Al motioned to her to come in. *Ain’t life strange?*

GEBO

Gift/Sacrifice

Chapter 7a

Mae's Crossing *Harmony*

Old Man Blanton sat in his wheelchair on the front porch, watching his son James direct the workers. Big doings at the dairy today, making a party out of Bessie's passing. Men were hefting large planks onto the lawn, positioning rounds under the corners to create temporary tables for the feast to come. Tanya was in the kitchen, helping out with the baking. Tomorrow the guests would be arriving to hold a wake in Bessie's honor. The elder Blanton cursed his useless leg which kept him from a more active role in the dairy. It was Bessie's dam who crippled him years ago, forcing him into a wheelchair and a background position in the managing of daily affairs. Not that the farm suffered; on the contrary, it seemed to thrive under James' supervision. Pride in his son made the old man straighten up in his chair, just as James approached.

"Hey, Pa, I was wonderin' about that old haywagon out back. Do ya think we could fix 'er up to take the children out fer a hayride tomorrow?"

The elder Blanton gave it some thought. "James, ya'v come up with a good idee. Shouldn't take much to get it movin'; the axles 'r good. Mebbe grease 'em up some, put a new plank in the side; yes indeed's a good idee," he patted James' hand, beaming up at him. The two shared a comfortable silence, watching the activity in the yard.

Chapter 7a

Brianna X *Meeting of Equals/Mutual Attraction*

It was close to two in the afternoon before Brianna could finally tear herself away. A last minute order (account called as she was walking out the door) took priority, and she went back to her studio, packed the order and left for the post office. When she finally stood at the Antique store and looked in the window, she saw that Al had some customers. Just when she was deciding to come back later, Al spied her and beckoned to her. Bri would never openly discuss plans for the spells. There had to be another reason for her to be here.

“Hi Al. Just thought I’d do some browsing on my way to the market. You can go back to your customers. No need to tend to here. Go on, Al, I’m fine.”

Al noised, somewhere between a grunt and a snort, the hint of a smile hanging from the corners of his mouth. “Yah, well tanks, as I’d be talkin’ wi’ friends.” He nodded and walked back to where the two men were standing. She recognized Willem, but who was that beautiful man? He glanced in her direction *(such an old soul looking out of those dreamy brown eyes)* and she quickly ducked her head to surreptitiously examine a silver candy dish.

She wouldn’t be in the dark for long. The three men shared a chuckle over some such thing, then Al ushered them to the front of the shop where Bri was browsing.

Brianna gave Willem a hug, though he didn’t lean in to her like he usually did; actually pulled away a little as though she had hurt him. *What’s up with that?* She backed up and gave him a big smile and a kiss on the cheek. "Good to see you, Will. What brings you up to Mae's Crossing?" Willem beamed with her attention, then indicated the handsome man. "This be my friend, Mr. Mal. He drove me up here."

Al interrupted with introductions: "Thought ya might like to meet a new friend of ourn. Malakai here lives in Channing, an' he brought Will up fer a few days' stay."

"Malachais Merriwether," he said as he held out his hand, palm up, to Brianna. As she placed her hand in his, he lifted it and brushed it lightly with his lips. *Oh my, such gallantry!* Bri actually blushed, doing a slight curtsey and said "Brianna McTavish." She was so glad she had decided on the green dress today. Although her eyes were usually a deep blue, there was a hint of green to them, which was accentuated by this dress.

Al cleared his throat and put forth an idea. "Just struck me, Bri, dat mebbe ya could help out some. Malakai here's lookin' to see the sights. Now me 'n Will, we got some catchin' up to do, an' I was thinkin'…mebbe ya could show 'im around some."

Bri's heart fluttered. *Oh my Goddess!* Not wanting to seem too eager, she hemmed and hawed, saying "Gosh, Al. I'm up to my ears in orders. I'd like to help out, but…"

Malachais cut in. "If it's okay with you, I could watch you work. Al was just telling me about your fabulous masks. I'd really like to see some."

Now she was beginning to feel cornered. This was all happening so fast. Bri thought about the haphazard appearance of her workshop, and how it might make a bad impression; like she was a sloppy worker or something.

Before she could give it more thought, she blurted out, "Well, sure, Malachais. Why don't you come by tomorrow morning?" Bri scribbled hastily on a scrap of paper. "Here's my number. Let me know when to expect you." *Oh Gods! Did I just say that? What am I getting myself into?*

Brianna excused herself from their company, stating her need to shop before the market closed. Indeed, it was close to closing time when she emerged from Hillside Market, carrying much more than she had originally intended before making a 'date' with Malachais. After unpacking her bags, Bri grabbed her pipe and settled into her favorite chair in the living room. The sun was sending its last rays through her windows, illuminating the chalice fragments she had strategically placed to catch the light. She hadn't the heart to just toss them in the trash; even bits and pieces of the remarkable glass seemed to emanate a powerful glow beyond the capacity of a merely decorative goblet. Sighing with contentment and just a dash of excitement about tomorrow's meeting, she lit up and took a deep drag.

Chapter 7b

Mae's Crossing *Gift/Sacrifice*

There were about 30 people invited to the Blanton's bash. Ed Janssen and his wife Hester attended along with their five children as well as the crew from Dot's Delights and some close friends and family. All present knew Bessie and how she was doted upon, especially by Tanya Blanton.

James Blanton stood on the porch, and motioned for everyone to gather in close to hear his words.

"Now, we all know why's the party today. Bessie died last week." Murmurs of sympathy and a couple of 'sorry for your loss' sentiments came from the group. "You may have heard some gossip, so let me make it straight with you. Dan'l here," he paused and waved his hand at Daniel in his bright yellow cap, "sat with Bessie at the end, and she told him some things." A scornful laugh was heard, though quickly hushed. "Yah, I know it sounds screwy, but there ain't no doubt 'bout what she told him. She said to tan 'her pretty hide' and have a party with all that good meat. I'm askin' you to keep this in mind while you're enjoying the fine steaks and barbecue we'll be servin' up. Bessie was a willin' sacrifice, and I bet she'd be plain p-o-ed if we didn't honor her. Folks in BigCity are so distanced from the animals that fill their bellies that they don't honor the spirit that feeds them, and here we are, presented with a fine gift." Ed Janssen shouted out "Thanks, Bessie!" and others chimed in. James raised a hand and said, "And that ain't all. Bessie said she'd come back as a horse." At that, he beckoned Billy to come forward, a filly in his arms. "This here is Tessie, and I believe she is Bessie reincarnated. Just take a look at her coloring." Hoots and hollers erupted from the group, but there was no denying that the new filly had the exact same colors and patterns as Bessie. "So let's all give thanks and enjoy the feast!"

Responding to James' request like cows following the sound of a bell, everyone headed for the heavily laden tables, while the younger ones gathered around Billy to admire the new foal. One of the parents called out to his children "You can't go on a hayride until you eat your dinner." No more enticement was needed; the children raced to the tables to join their elders.

Chapter 7b

Rosalind *Gift of the Goddesses*

Rose yawned and looked at the clock. Omigosh! 8:30! She was supposed to meet with Mabel at 9:00. Once more, she neglected her runes as she jumped out of bed and headed for the shower. Rose arrived at the bakery, hair still wet and clinging to her head, to find Mabel waiting impatiently by the truck.

"Oh Mabel, I'm so sorry I'm late. This has been such a busy weekend, what with my driving back and forth to BigCity, getting all my stuff. I promise to be on time in the future. I've just been so…"

Mabel cut her off, waving her hand towards the truck. "So we'll be a little behind today. Folks can adjust. Now missy, let's get moving."

This time Mabel sat in the passenger seat, handing the keys to Rosalind. Such a small gesture, such big consequences.

The first stop this morning was Tom Bradley's goat farm. The pickup was fitted with a large cooler which Mabel had filled with ice. Tom came out of his cottage, hefting a canister of goat's milk. "Mornin' ladies. Fine weather we're having now, aint it?" He juggled the container into position in the cooler, piling up ice around it. Mabel glanced at the invoice and handed him a check. "Yep, sure is fine. Hopin' we have a nice long Indian summer 'round the bend. Thanks for the goods. Rose here will be comin' out next week by herself. You be sure and treat her right now, ya hear?"

"Yah, and I treat all you ladies right, doncha know?" Tom winked and tipped his hat to the women as they waved goodbye.

The next stop on their list was to Farmer Johnsons to pick up some wheat. Mabel showed Rosalind how to inspect the wheat and what to look for, so that it was truly hand chosen. From there they went on to the mill. By now it was lunchtime and Miller Burns invited them to stay for some eats.

Back on the road again, Mabel glanced at her list and said "Hmmph! Right that be!" Rose responded "What's that you're saying, Mabel? What's right?" "I says right that be close by Dutchman's Creek. Why not swing by and see if the lad's at home. Like to pick up some fresh herbs if'n I can." It took Rose a moment to realize the 'lad' must be Daniel. She never had a chance to really talk with him as the only time she saw him was at Blanton's when Mabel broke down. That had certainly put a stop to any possible conversation. As Rose recalled, he was kind of cute. They pulled up in front of a rustic cabin nearly hidden by all the vines growing over it as well as a roof garden spilling over the eaves. The lack of human presence was apparent. Quiet, so very quiet. "I'll just try the door, Rose. He might be sleepin'." After a few soft raps on the door, Mabel returned and said "Keep this location in mind, girl. He's hard to track down, but Dan'l brings in the best herbs in the county."

Rosalind was like a sponge, soaking up all the necessary bits and pieces of her grandmother's steps so that she could duplicate them *(I hope Gram, Goddess bless her, approves).* By the time she got home, had a light dinner, caught up on her email and showered, she was worn out and ready to hit the sack. While lying in bed, Rose reached out for her rune bag. She sat up, waited a moment to calm and center, then opened the bag to grab a rune and jumped back at the alien feel of silk where it shouldn't be...Cautiously, she put her hand in the bag again and pulled out a beautiful red silk pouch. *Wow!* There was her name, 'Rosalind', stitched in gold thread! *What in the world? How'd this get here?* Curiosity overcame fear and she opened the little pouch to find a broken piece of pottery. There it was again; her name was pressed into the clay before it was fired. Turning it over, there was half of the elder futhark going around the rim with a symbol in the center flanked by the break. *Oh my Goddess! Is this good or bad?*

In a stately mansion hidden deep in the woods, three women leaned over the water-filled cauldron. Dawn was fidgeting and clearly agitated. "We can't just leave it like that! She might be afraid and block the whole thing. I'm going!" Granny reached out, just a shade too late, as Dawn vanished into thin air. Whoosh! Dawn popped into Rose's bedroom. "aiee!" Rosalind reflexively drew her knees up to her chest and clutched the covers, wondering if she was hallucinating. Standing before her was the most startling creature she had ever seen. Clearly a girl, might even be her age, but that was where the similarities ended. This 'girl' had white hair that looked like a huge powder puff on her head. She was strikingly beautiful, thin and delicate, and <u>she had appeared out of nowhere</u>! And she speaks…"Rosalind, it's okay honey. I just wanted you to know that this talisman is very, very good, and it's going to make you really, really happy." With that the apparition disappeared as mysteriously as it had materialized in the first place, leaving Rose in a state of utter shock, the talisman held tightly in her hand.

Rosalind

Chapter 7c

Mae's Crossing ╳ *Partnership*

Ed Janssen, Chester Burns, Kris Knudsen and Alan Nelson sat together at the Crossing Point. The idea Ed came up with had found fertile ground in this company. All four were deeply involved in working out plans for a community playground. Not just a wimpy little kid park but a place where adults could enjoy the swings and slides and such as well. Kris, being a smith and familiar with welding and forging, volunteered to supply the metal and labor. Ed, owning the lumber yard and hardware store, could supply materials from there. Chester, though his livelihood was through the mill, was a master woodworker, and his talents would come into play as well. Since the property proposed for this venture was adjacent to the temple, ownership technically fell to Alan Nelson Jr., the final cog in the wheel of progress. They were hoping to have it completed by the time of 'Glory Days Gala'. As the event drew closer, more people joined in the effort, adding their various skills. It was an ambitious undertaking, and each new addition fleshed out what would eventually be an incredible playground.

Mae's Crossing was blessed in its populace. Many were the improvements and contributions made over the years in a gesture of good will. No bills were issued. What was created was given freely for the good of all.

Chapter 7c

Malachais ✕ *Partnership/Attraction/Friendship*

Malachais was truly enjoying the men's company; when was the last time he had felt so totally relaxed and at ease? Not to say that his life was stressful in any way. It was just so predictable. The missing chalice was becoming a blessing for him in ways he would never have imagined. Because of it, he'd made two new friends, driven to a location he kept putting off going to because of distance and lack of motivation, and most interestingly, had encountered an intriguing female. Feeling buoyed up by the sheer novelty of it all, Mal decided to let the two old friends visit in private while he took a stroll around the village.

First Street ran about six blocks, the main attractions being in the center three. Nelson's Department store was flanked by Widow Thompson's 'The Sewing Basket' and Dot's Delights. Malachais ventured into the bakery, drawn by the delicious smells wafting on the air. Looking over their cases, he decided on rugelach and cannolis. The cannoli was for him now, as he knew it wouldn't keep that well 'til tomorrow. The rugelach was for Brianna; he hoped she liked it. He continued down the street, taking occasional bites of his superb cannoli *(Dot's Delights gets high marks on this confection)* and peered through the store windows. The corner store was a coffee shop/restaurant, Cup 'o Life, where customers could overflow to the outside tables under spreading umbrellas. Malachais found himself slowly and surely moving towards total captivation. *What a sweet town this is!* He continued around the block to 2nd St. just in time to see Brianna pulling out of Hillside Market. She was driving an old, buttercup yellow Karman Ghia in mint condition. *Sharp car!*

Malachais' phone vibrated in his pocket. Pulling it out, he saw it was Jarnath calling.

"Greetings, Jarny. What's up?"

"Mal…oh Mal," sobs broke his speech. "Could you come quick? Something terrible's happened." Jarnath's breath caught, "Nellie just died, terrible car accident. I don't know what to do. Please...I'm having kind of a hard time," again his voice trembled.

"Oh my Gods, Jarny!" Mal looked around frantically for a place to sit; his legs had gone all rubbery. "Oh no...Oh no...I was just talking to her a couple of days ago -- some landscape ideas I had -- and, oh my Gods! Oh Jarny. Of course I'll come, but I'm in Mae's Crossing right now, and it'll take me four hours to get there. Don't you worry. I'm coming as soon as I can. You just hang in there, buddy, maybe watch some TV to keep your mind off of things. I'll be right there."

Malachais hurried back to Al's shop, mentally organizing everything he'd brought in from the car so he could pack up and get on the road as quickly as possible. He burst into the shop, startling the older men who were playing chess at the back table.

"Gentlemen, I'm so sorry to say that personal business demands that I return to Channing immediately. I've really been enjoying myself; you've been quite hospitable and –and oh my Gods! Brianna. Look, I bought these rugelach for her. You can either keep them or give them to her. I've got to call her. Excuse me." Mal stepped back out the door, pulling the slip of paper with her number out of his pocket. He was acutely aware of how abrupt his manners were, but his mind was in a jumble. Brianna answered after the first ring. "Hello, who's calling?" "It's me, Malachais. Listen,

Brianna, I'm afraid I'm going to have to cancel our meeting tomorrow. My best friend's wife just died in a car wreck", at this, Mal faltered, stifling a sob, "and I'm driving back to Channing to be with him."

Brianna could feel his distress, and wanted so to comfort him. "Oh, my Goddess. I am so sorry. My condolences and of course, go. Drive safe."

WUNJO

Joy/celebration

Chapter 8a

Mae's Crossing *Unhappiness*

Tom Bradley was rudely awakened from his nap by a loud banging on his door. "What the *#! Hold on, I'm coming!" He stumbled out to the front door to be confronted by his neighbor John Simpson. "Oh, it's you. What the dang fooey do ya be making such a ruckus about?"

John was red-faced and his fists were clenched tightly. "I should just punch you and get it over with. When are you going to pen in those dang goats of yours? They've just cleaned out my sheep's foraging range like a dang lawnmower!"

"Yah, well why doncha just go ahead and hit me…see where it gets ya, ya little wuss!"

John knew his slight 5'7" frame was no match for Tom's hulking 6'2". Fuming and sputtering, he backed off the porch. "This aint the end of it, Tom. I'm takin' this to the council!"

"You just do that, Mr. Wussy." Tom hocked one just short of John's feet, then turned and slammed the door.

After John Simpson informed the town council of his grievance, the council had summoned the two of them to a hearing later that week. Each speaker was given the floor to state his case. There was a short recess for the antagonists as the council put their heads together. The men were called back and Ed Janssen stood up, giving them a disgusted glance before announcing the verdict.

"It is the considered opinion of this committee that you are both stubborn headed as mules. It is also our opinion that you need to separate your animals with a proper fence. By order of the Town Council of Mae's Crossing, I do charge the two of you with the task of erecting a fence on your adjoining property lines, and to have it in place within thirty days of today. You are to do this without outside help, and to share the cost between you. I'll supply the materials on credit, but you will be billed. So be it. The Council has spoken. You are dismissed."

Chapter 8a

Brianna ᚹ *Bright Prospects*

As Brianna ended the call, a wave of sadness swept over her. Sadness for Malachais' friend and selfishly, sadness for herself that he wouldn't be visiting tomorrow. She didn't realize until now just how much she wanted to get to know Malachais Merriwether. Pulling a Coppola Chardonnay *(intended, of course, to share with the beautiful man)* out of the fridge, Bri poured herself a glass and fell to musing on possible futures.

The following days saw Brianna hard at work, bulking out her stock. Soon there was a profusion of wings hanging from the ceiling and a crazy collage of masks covering the walls of her workshop. By weeks' end, she was dog tired and totally pleased with her production. There was more than enough stock to entice and hopefully captivate the crowds at 'Fantasy Festival' and 'Glory Days Gala'. When Friday evening rolled around, Bri headed back to town to schedule the spells with Al.

Brianna walked into Al's Antiques with determination. Finally, she could get the spells in motion. Al looked up from his novel and gave her a welcoming smile. "Ho, Bri, good to see ya." She settled into the chair across from him and got directly to the point. "Al, it's high time we completed our bargain. I was going to talk to you about the spells on Monday, but with a stranger in the shop I couldn't." She fairly tingled when she said 'stranger'. *My Goddess, what's going on with me?*

"Right cha are, Bri. Could sure use a boost in bi'ness."

"Well, I brought all my stuff with me, just in case. If it's okay with you, I'll do it now. You will have to close the shop, though."

Al rose and went to the front door, then hesitated. "How long ya be wit' it?"

"Oh, it shouldn't take more than half an hour. I just need some undisturbed quiet."

He turned the 'Open' sign over, locked the door, and headed for the stairs. "I'll just go on up 'n intrude on Will. He's really gettin' too comfy here; gonna have to send 'im home soon." Al's grin belied his words. Bri stopped him before he left the room. "Al, I was wondering about Willem. Is he okay? He seemed a little edgy to me, though I can't put my finger on it."

Al hesitated, wondering how much to share with her. "Well, 'member I tol ya 'bout the kid what brought the chalice to him?" She nods. "He came back and roughed 'im up a bit, wantin' more money." Bri stiffened at the mention of the chalice and the unfortunate run of circumstances surrounding it. "So I tells 'im he kin stay wit me for a time; get away from that dang kid."

"He did what? How dare anyone lay a hand on sweet Willem! What a jerk! And to think it's all over the chalice. Wow. Funny thing, after I did a cleansing ritual on it, I got sick. Lot of bad ju-ju there. As a matter of fact, I've been meaning to tell you about the chalice." Bri stumbled over her words..."Oh, Al, I broke it! It was an accident. I didn't mean to. I'm so sorry." She hung her head in shame as a realization hit her. "Now I'm thinking maybe it was a good thing, all things considered." Al, stunned, recovered from the shock of her confession. He knew no good could come from revealing its owner; he wasn't oblivious to the spark of attraction he saw between Mal and Bri. "Ya know, maybe it's fer the best. Dang glass just brought nothin' but trouble."

Bri felt the guilt melt away. "You're too good to me, Al. I'm truly blessed with your friendship. Now, please tell Willem I hope he gets better real soon. I'll light a candle of protection and another for healing when I get home...It's time I finished what I came here for, if it's okay with you." Al nodded in agreement and went upstairs.

As soon as he was gone, Bri lifted the cloth off of her basket. Placing the incense burner on the table, she lit a brick and sprinkled a little prosperity blend on it. Nine pennies were arranged in a circle around the burner, with a tenth one tucked under it. Athame in hand, she faced the East and described a large circle with the intent to include the entire shop, upstairs and downstairs. The quarter portals were opened, and she called in the 'money Gods'...Hermes for commerce, Jupiter for expansiveness, Lakshmi and Ganesh. With each name, Bri sprinkled more incense on the brick. Pointing her blade at the cash register, she intoned "Fill this till with good will. May prosperity flow as wallets grow. So mote it be!" As a final gesture, she walked the perimeter, sprinkling ground cinnamon. Returning to the East, she kissed her blade and released the quarters with heartfelt thanks for their presence, wishing them a happy journey to their pleasant and lovely realms.

Brianna sat in the peaceful silence for a few minutes before calling Al back, breathing in the incense and catching just a whiff of cinnamon. Already,she could feel a lightness and an attraction emanating from the little shop, or is it just pure relief from releasing the guilt she'd been carrying? Her spell was short, sweet and to the point; often the best approach for an effective working.

Chapter 8b

Mae’s Crossing ᚹ *Celebration*

Work progressed on the playground at breakneck speed. Everyone seemed to take a hand in it: even children were enlisted to run errands and fetch tools. They were by far the most enthusiastic participants. After all, it was a playground! The last of the wood chips had been scattered. There were ribbons and bows on the shiny new monkey bars, jungle gyms, rings, (two sets of each of these in adult and child sizes) swings, slide, whirling disk, etc., an astounding two weeks before ‘Glory Days Gala’! An impromptu party was held on the site, with young and old eagerly trying out the new equipment. Even Widow Thompson went down the slide, screaming the whole way. Rosalind dared Mabel to a ride on the whirling disk, and before long they were both whooping and hollering while the children pushed them faster and faster. Jerrod Janssen proved to be a master at the rings, and was soon doing amazing moves on them to the cheers and applause of the observers.

Standing back from the celebration, four men stood together fairly bursting with pride.

Chapter 8b

Rosalind *Underlying Optimism*

Rosalind awoke in high spirits. Not willing to lose or break her magical talisman by carrying it around with her, she decided to keep it on her newly erected altar. Rose hoped it was properly constructed. The books she read about altars seemed to be contradictory; God (statue) on the left, Goddess on the right. Or was it the other way? Trusting her instincts, she kept it simple with a bowl of water filled with blossoms flanked by a red and green candle. The new talisman looked right at home in front of the bowl, the red silk glistening in the morning sun. *Good!* Giving the piece one last caress, she hurried out to the kitchen for breakfast.

Rose's new life was unfolding in a series of strange and fascinating encounters. This was the last week Mabel would accompany her on Dot's ambitious route. She found herself looking forward to meeting all the suppliers and seeing their various trades in progress.

Mabel handed her a printout of the weekly run, pointing to the day's stops. "This here's where we're going today. Just take the left fork out of town; we'll be driving up to the Bee Man's place." Rose dropped the truck into first gear and chattered the clutch. "Yull get used to it, Rose. Easy as fallin' off a log. Just have to do it over 'n over 'til ya don't think about it no more. There's the turnoff up ahead. Take it on up to the end; there'll be a sign."

The sign, black letters on a yellow background, said "Honey Hill." Rose drove past it and pulled into a driveway flanked by a meadow resplendent in wildflowers. Bordering the meadow was a meandering row of white beehives. A little yellow cottage appeared at the end of the road, looking like something out of the Wizard of Oz. Bee Man stepped out on the porch carrying a carton of honey jars. He surely had a name, but folks had been calling him Bee Man for so long that he even forgot sometimes that his name was Oliver.

"Howdy, Miss Mabel. Here's your order. Really good batch this year. And this must be Miss Rosalind, right?" Oliver tipped his head in her direction as he secured the box in the bed of the pickup.

"Sorry I cain't visit a bit, but I'm showin' Miss Rose here the route, and we's got a few more folks to see today. She'll be comin' out by herself next time. Mebbe ya could show her around then." Mabel cheerfully traded a check for his bill.

As they continued on their prescribed route, Rose could see someone waving at them in the distance. It was Daniel looking highly upset. She stopped the truck and called out the window, "Hey Daniel, what's up?" He ran over to her side of the pickup, a limp fox in his arms. "Howdy Miss Rosalind. I was hoping I could get a lift from you fine ladies over to my place. I can't ride my bike and carry Mr. Crafty here at the same time, and he needs some serious doctoring. I think he got in a tussle with Old Man Blanton's hound, least that's what it sounded like he said. He's pretty badly chewed up." Rose took one look at the torn ear and quickly turned away, choking down the rising bile in her throat. "You got it, Daniel. Climb in and I'll get your bike." Mabel grumbled something under her breath, then chimed in. "Suppose it's the right thing to do. Customers can wait." Her tone certainly didn't match her words.

Chapter 8c

Daniel △ *Latent Joy*

Back at Dutchman's Creek, Daniel cut the thread on the last stitches on Mr. Crafty's ear. The animal lay in his arms, twitching and whimpering, while Daniel spoke soft words to him. He gently laid him on his bed, and brought over the broth he'd been cooling after simmering on his stove. "You're not going to like this, but you've got to drink some. It'll help you sleep and heal." With half of the broth soaking into his blankets, Dan'l was satisfied that Mr. Crafty had ingested enough to do him some good.

As he was watching Mr. Crafty drift off to sleep, a memory of Rosalind flashed in his mind. Something about the way she didn't hesitate to lend a hand, even hefting the bike into the pickup bed without help…Something about the yellow dress she was wearing… Something about her eyes, looking like cornflowers peeping out between the golden wheatstalks of her hair…Something about…*omigosh!* Daniel looked infatuation square in the eyes and dove into its seductive arms.

Chapter 8c

Malachais *Sadness*

Nellie's funeral was depressing; what funeral wasn't? Malachais stayed by Jarnath's side and helped him through the trying time as friends and relatives extended their condolences. After the last well-wisher was gone, the two men moved off to the kitchen and pulled some stools up to the breakfast bar.

Mal reached over and placed his hand on Jarnath's. "Jarny, I was thinking. I'd like to do a proper ritual for Nellie while her spirit is still hanging around, if it's okay with you."

Jarnath looked at Mal, tears welling up in his eyes. "Yes, yes! That's just what's missing. This whole funeral, eulogy, sad folk stuff just doesn't cut it. Nellie'd be wondering about all the fuss, knowing she was in a good place if only they could see it. Sure, and she'd be sorry to leave me, I know." Sobs burst from him, the memory of her passing still too painful to deal with. "Let's do it soon."

Malachais rose from his chair and put his arms around Jarnath, giving him the comfort of a loving embrace as his friend broke down and truly cried.

The next day the two men brought all their ritual implements out to the garden that Nellie had created. Surrounded by flowering bushes and climbing vines, the gazebo had been planned as the focal point for ritual work. Indeed, many fine celebrations had been held in it. A more somber tone ruled today as they laid out the different items and prepared for 'A Rite for a Departed Soul.' All went well. The final gesture of walking about the garden and scattering her ashes on the plants that thrived under her hand sealed the moment. Releasing the circle, Mal caught a glimpse of a stronger soul emerging from Jarnath's grief. *Well done! And fare thee well, Nellie.*

Hagall's

movements of nature
bridge to a new reality
the Hero's journey

Hagalaz

Hagalaz, Hagalaz!
Your slumber ended,
You stretch awake
The trembling earth
Doth heave and shake
Hagall, Hagall, Hagall!
Alert and wise
Now hear my call
Hella's mercy on us all

Artwork by Katlyn at www.mermadearts.com

HAGALAZ

Hail/outside forces

Part II: Chapters Nine through Twelve: *Objective: Outside Obstacles to Overcome*

Chapter 9a

Mae's Crossing *Storm Coming*

Chester Burns checked his barometer again. No doubt about it; storm coming. Rare that such a thing would happen in late August. As he recalled, it was back in August of '96 that a mighty storm had ripped through Mae's Crossing, destroying crops and wreaking havoc upon the town. Pray that this was not as violent. Grabbing his phone, Chester called a warning to Ed Janssen. Ed would see to it that all were alerted to the approaching storm.

Responding to Ed's warning, homesteads throughout the Mae's Crossing region prepared for the worst and hoped for the best. The day's crops were hastily brought in; haystacks were sheeted, animals out to pasture were herded into their barns and lean-tos. At exactly 9:00 pm on Sunday night, the howling winds descended, bringing torrential rains into the peaceful valleys. There were even scattered reports of hail. It was a long and frightening night as folks huddled in their homes, shutters banging and loose furnishings outdoors getting tossed about. In the morning, all was calm. The storm was over. Although there was quite a bit of damage (Widow Thompson's greenhouse glass was shattered by a falling tree), the only fatality was one of John Simpson's sheep; the one who eluded his search the previous night. Death was swift with a flying branch through its neck. Butcher Gordon dressed it out, and soon John's freezer was filled. Woodsman Otter was gifted with the hide. Old Man Blanton's hounds got the big bones.

Chapter 9a

Brianna  *Minor Delay /Latent Feelings Working to the Surface*

The storm had battered Bri's garden. Monday morning found her in the midst of the worst of it, piling plants and other debris in her wheelbarrow. She looked on the harrowing as a necessary culling. *Mother Nature just shaking her shoulders and flicking off specks.* Still, it was with some sadness that she discovered her prize fern tree had been uprooted. After examination, Bri was sure she could save it, and carefully wrapped the exposed roots in wet burlap. By lunchtime, she was a muddy mess. Her garden looked orderly in comparison. Famished, Bri opted for lunch first and shower later. As circumstance would have it, it wasn't until two in the afternoon that she finally checked her phone for voicemail and discovered a message from Malachais…he'd called at 10:00 am! *Damn!* She'd been up to her elbows in dirt then. Berating herself for her schoolgirl reactions, it was nonetheless with shaking fingers that she pressed voicemail.

"Hello Brianna, Malachais Merriwether here. Sorry I missed you. I wanted to apologize for cancelling our meeting last week. I was hoping to reschedule, if you're still willing to let me see your workplace. Please call back and let me know. Be well."

'Be still my heart'…It was with great determination that she would not allow herself to swoon…although a delicious thrill ran through her at the thought. His voice had a melodious tone to it, almost as if he were singing to her. Bri couldn't trust herself to call him back right this minute. She needed some time to calm down and cultivate a less eager approach.

Pouring herself a glass of wine, she grabbed her pipe and settled into her favorite lounge on the porch. After a sip and a hit, Brianna slowly melted into the cushions. While she was sorting through her feelings, Bri heard a rustling, well actually more of a wet slapping, of leaves behind her. She turned to see an old woman wrestling with the branches and mumbling something like “Let go! Let go of me right now!” The really amazing thing is that all of the leaves and branches and vines that had been clinging to her immediately stopped and fell limp. Moonface emerged from the foliage, pulling leaves out of her tangled, inky hair.

Muttering to herself, “Got to work on that entrance,” she walked straight up to a gawking Brianna, grabbed her by the shoulders (she had a pretty fierce grip) and kissed her on each cheek. Looking around, she spotted a chair and pulled it up alongside of Bri, plunking herself down on it with an audible ahhh.

Brianna steeled herself to normalcy and blurted out, “I know who you are! I saw you and the other two in my scrying ball. You’re the Crone, aren’t you?”

“Well, dearie, that’s one of my names, yes. For now I’m Moonface, but you can call me Granny. I just wanted to give you this,” Granny searched her pockets, showing Brianna an embarrassed smile. “I know I’ve got it. Now what did I do with it…green silk, gold letters…should be easy to see or feel but I can’t seem to...”

Bri reached out and tugged on a pouch of that description hanging from Granny’s wrist. “Is this what you’re looking for, Granny?”

“Oh ha ha, gotcha didn’t I? Knew it was there all the time, I did. Say, do you have another glass of that Coppola stuff? ”

Brianna jumped up and came back with a glass for Moonface. She took a long sip and smiled. "Fine vintage here. Thank you for your kind hospitality." Granny took another long draught, then waved Bri back to her lounge.

"Now you're probably wondering why I'm here. I wonder myself sometimes. Never mind. We've been watching you, and your story is running faster than anticipated. I wasn't going to give this to you yet, but here, take it." Granny untied the pouch from her wrist and handed it to Brianna.

Brinna

"You made this for me? How lovely. Thank you so much." The pouch was a beautiful deep forest green silk with 'Brianna' stitched in gold. She removed a broken piece of pottery from it, carefully examining it and turning it over. "I'm sorry. I don't understand. This is broken. What use is a broken talisman?"

Moonface emptied her glass and stood up. "It's not broken. It's separated. Find the other half. Oh, and thanks for the wine. Hail and farewell." Poof! She disappeared in a flash of light.

Giving up on any hope of rational thought, Bri picked up her phone and pressed call. Malachais answered on the first ring. "Hello Brianna. Glad you called back. So what do you think about a get-together?"

Brianna winced at 'get-together' but blustered her way through. "Uh, yah, Malachais, why not? When were you thinking of?" *Boy, that was a dumb answer. Surely I could have come up with a better reply.*

"Let me talk with Al first. I might be able to give Willem a lift back to Channing. I'm so glad you'll let me see your work. Give me a couple of days to get back on this, but I'm aiming at Saturday---the morning traffic isn't that heavy."

"I'll be home. So, good, you let me know what works for you. And thanks for being interested in my work. It's my life, you know." *Well, that was a little better. Sounds like I might have a brain under all this gorgeous auburn hair.*

After the call ended, Malachais and Brianna each wondered what they were getting into.

Chapter 9b

Mae's Crossing ᚺ *Acts of God/Goddess*

Woodsman Otter came upon the crumpled car early Monday morning. Moans issued from the front seat as he rushed to the driver's door. It was young Jason from the Miller homestead, and he was pinned by the tree which had caved in the hood of his car. Frantically trying to open the door, Otter found he couldn't budge it. "Hey, Otter, am I glad to see you!" Although there was blood oozing from a cut to his scalp, Jason looked to be okay; just stuck. "Hang on there, buddy. I'm calling for help." Otter pulled out his old Nokia pay-as-you-go cell phone, *no fancy iPhones with their fancy monthly fees for me,* praying that he could get a signal. The fates smiled on him as Ed Janssen's voice came on. "Ed, it's Otter. I've got an emergency here. Young Jason Miller's car got hit by a tree, and I can't get him out. He seems okay, but I need help gettin' him out. We're up on the Old Pine Ridge Road just above Coyote Cut-off. D'ya think ya could send someone up with crowbars and such?" Ed Janssen answered in the affirmative, signing off and calling for help. Otter went back to the car and gave Jason some water from his canteen, reaching through the broken windshield. "Thanks Otter. My throat's so dry." He fumbled with the canteen, guzzling the water down in big gulps. "Folks are out of town, so I was comin' down to sit out the storm at the Blanton's when wham! This tree just fell on me. Can't move my legs, but it's prolly 'cause I'm pinned down so hard.

Can't reach my cell…it's there in my backpack…but it's prolly dead…can't charge it 'cause the car won't start…" Jason made a hiccupping sound, holding back the tears that were threatening to fall.

Otter patted his arm, trying to soothe the youngster. "We'll get ya out o' there as quick as we can, Jason. Yer gonna be fine. Just ya relax and don't go upsettin' yerself none."

It was an hour later before rescue workers arrived with toolbars and a stretcher. "Grab my backpack!" Jason groaned as they pulled him out of the driver's seat, his legs bloodied through the thick denim covering them. As they drove down the road to the emergency clinic, Otter staggered to a tree stump and dropped onto it, holding his head in his hands. He didn't like the look of the kid's legs; no he didn't like it at all.

Chapter 9b

Rosalind ᚺ *External Influences Affecting Future*

Rosalind sat in her bed and reached for her rune bag. Making the customary intonations, she felt for a rune and pulled out Hagalaz. "I know this rune. It's like the Tower in tarot. My gosh! Haven't I had enough disruptions and emergencies? I'm going to study up." She pulled out her favorite rune author, and started reading the passage for Hagall in 'Leaves of Yggdrasil.' Rose noted the connection to the Norns. This was certainly illustrated most graphically by Dawn's appearance. Obviously, something of importance was playing out, and according to Aswynn, it indicated a part of her past demanding her attention. Laying aside the book and turning off her lamp, Rose snuggled into her feather pillow and willed herself to explore the deeper meanings of Hagall in her dreams.

Rose awoke with visions of planes crashing and a woman screaming in terror. *Enough!* She knew she'd requested this sending, but it didn't make it any easier to relive those horrifying times. *My Goddess!* She'd received three inheritances in her short 22 years. *Send it back! Turn back the hands of time!* All she wanted was her happy family alive and well. Rubbing the sleep out of her eyes, Rose dragged herself out of bed and went to sit cross-legged before her altar. "Dear Goddess, have mercy on me. Deliver me from this pain. Let me know love again." When her trembling subsided, Rose reached for her talisman and held it to her chest. Somehow, it seemed to calm her.

Resuming the routine of picking up supplies from the various individuals that helped make Dot's Delights a success, Rose drove with Mabel at her side. Today they would be picking up the ground flour from Miller Burns. A short run, and then a welcome respite from the ongoing demands of shop ownership left Rose with a free afternoon. On the spur of the moment, she decided to check in on Mr. Crafty.

Pulling up to Daniel's whimsical cabin, she saw him sitting on the porch, cradling Mr. Crafty in his arms.

"Howdy, Miss Rosalind. I'd get up, but Mr. Crafty here..." He signed for her to take a seat next to him as he shifted the fox in his arms. "He's going to make it. It was a tough go, but he's coming around." Rose tentatively reached out while Daniel turned in her direction. Wow! His fur was so much softer than she expected. Mr. Crafty made a low sound in his throat, and she drew back.

"It's okay, Miss Rose. He's only sayin' that feels good. Go ahead and touch him some more."

After petting him a bit, Rose looked up at Daniel's eyes. They seemed to be glowing a deep golden brown. *Awesome!* She quickly looked away and searched for words.

"So, Daniel, how come the orange cap?"

"Well, Miss Rosalind, I choose the color according to the work I'll be doing. Since I'm in the 'healing mode' I'm wearing orange. If I'm searching for herbs, I'll wear green. For mushrooms, it's brown, unless of course, I'm searching for the magic mushrooms. Then I wear red. Wish it had polka dots."

Rose sat back and studied him carefully. *He really is cute, even in the ridiculous caps he always wears.. Pretty hair, good build, and amazing eyes.* If she didn't know better, she'd say she was falling for him. *But that's ridiculous!* A few thwarted attempts at 'partnering' made it clear that close relationships were anathema to her. She'd seen where they led, and wanted no part of it. Shelly was the closest thing to a 'love' in her life, and that suited her just fine. *No, there was no chance of anything serious happening here.*

"You did a great job on his ear. I can hardly tell it's sewn. You have quite a talent with animals."

Daniel blushed and pulled his cap down tighter around his ears. "Yeah, well you might say it's in my blood. Runs in the family. We're all healers, of animals and the land."

"So where's your family, Daniel?"

"Oh, they're around and about." He shifted uneasily, then rose and took Mr. Crafty into the cabin. Settling him onto his bed, Daniel returned to the porch.

"I was wonderin', Miss Rose, if you'd like to go herb hunting with me sometime? It's real fun, and I could show you some fine patches."

Rose was taken aback by the offer. *Herb hunting?* He really was an odd one. *Well, what the heck. Might be interesting.* "Maybe, Daniel, maybe. I've got a pretty busy schedule. Only time I've got free is on the weekends."

Daniel lit up. "That's great, Miss Rose! Come by Sunday in the afternoon. Best time for gatherin' is twilight or dawn."

How did I get roped into this? "Okay, Daniel. I'll try to be here by 5:00 pm this Sunday." As she got up to leave, Daniel bounced up and said. "Be sure and wear soft shoes and old clothes. Don't want the plants to hear us comin'...they can hide if'n they don't want to be seen."

Shaking her head in wonder, she waved goodbye and drove off.

As soon as she was out of sight, Daniel leaped for joy and threw his cap in the air.

Chapter 9c

Mae's Crossing N *Act of the Goddess*

Later that week, young Jason Miller tossed about in a drugged stupor in his bed at BigCity Memorial Hospital. He kept moaning "My legs, my legs." Off to the side, Dr. Victoria Cellini conferred with his parents. "I'm so sorry to tell you this, Mr. and Mrs. Miller, but Jason is going to lose his left leg." Gasps from the couple escalated to uncontrolled sobbing by his mother, as Mr. Miller held her tightly and bowed his head, saying, "The boy's only 17. It just don't seem right." The doctor continued. "The bones are too fractured to mend, but I have hopes for the right leg. We'll give him a couple of days to regain his strength."

Huddled together in the grand living room of their palatial estate, three women embraced. Sunny spoke: "Oh mum, isn't there anything we can do? " Moonface replied, "I think I remember reading something about just this kind of situation. It's been eons, but let me see." She reached into the air above them, grabbing a heavy tome with the title 'Elder Goddess Handbook,' and started flipping through the pages to the section under the heading 'Healing.' "Ah, here it is." Granny read from the book: "Whereas, if the injury sustained is the result of an act of God/Goddess/All That Is and whereas if the injured party is under the age of 18, it is judged permissible to perform a complete healing."

The next day, Dr. Cellini met with Jason's parents. She was clearly dumbfounded as
she announced that not only would Jason keep his left leg, but that both legs were miraculously healing at a tremendous rate! It was her opinion that Jason could walk out of the hospital in a matter of days.

Chapter 9c

Malachais ᚺ *Shake-up/Change Brewing*

Malachais' mind was in a whirl. These last few weeks appeared to be life-changing.
He found himself loosening up and going with the flow in a state of complete trust.
As a devoted Priest of the Goddess, Mal had no fears of the future. For the present, though, there were tasks he had set for himself that needed tending.

Al answered after three or four rings. "Ho Malakai. What up?"

"Hi Al. Say, I was wondering...I was thinking of driving up there on Saturday, maybe spending the night with you if that's okay, and bringing Willem back on Sunday."

"Ho an' aint I glad ta hear that! Dang old codger's gettin' on my nerves. Not ta say I don' luv 'im, just that, oh dang…Hell ya, Malakai. Come on up. Could ya bring some of that BigCity sourdough? An' not a word to Miss Mabel at 'Dot's' 'bout it, ya hear?"

"You got it. And thanks so much, Al. I really appreciate it. I'm going to be visiting with Brianna at her workshop and I'll be able to see how she makes those incredible masks."

"Yeah, well ya be spendin' time wi' my Brianna, ya just mind yer manners, hear?"

Mal chuckled. "Yes sir, Mr. Al. I'll be on my gentlemen's best...well, great. I'll let you know when I get into town; probably around noon."

The next call was to Brianna. One ring and she answered. "Greetings, Malachais. How's it going?"

"Hi Brianna. I'm just calling to let you to know I've arranged with Al to spend Saturday night with him. I'll be driving Willem back on Sunday. So it's settled. I'll get there around lunchtime, and I was wondering, how about meeting me at that corner café, think it was called 'Cup 'o Life' near Nelson's Department Store for a bite to eat? Unless you have another place you'd prefer..."

Brianna's favorite lunch spot was right around the corner on 2nd Street; Tito's Diner. They made heavenly tortilla shells mounded with goodies; her mouth watered just thinking of them. "How about Tito's Diner? It's on Second Street; you can't miss it. And yes, that's a great idea. Looking forward to it."

"Great! I'll give you a call when I'm close, and we can meet there." Mal rang off, plans set in motion.

His final call was to Laura Black.

"Hello, Mr. Merriwether. Glad you're back. Will you be wantin' me to come do some cleaning?"

"Yes, Laura. I was hoping you could work here sometime during the week. I'll be out of town on the weekend. And say, how are you doing? Are you feeling better?"

"Oh gosh, yes. The swelling's down, and my eye's just a little yellow around the edges. And Shelly was so good to me. She took me to my parents. I was so scared. Shelly told them all about how Gerry had hurt me, and omigosh, I thought they would be so mad, but my mom hugged me and told me how much she loved me and what a jerk Gerry was. My dad was spitting fire, wantin' to report him and all, but I talked him out of it. So yeah, I'm back home and am I glad. And sure, I could come by maybe Thursday at 5." At this point, she seemed to have run out of breath, and Malachais jumped in with "I'm so glad to hear you're back home. It's really the best place for you. Thursday is fine. I'll see you then. Bye."

NAUTHIZ

Need/desire

Chapter 10a

Kyle Porter *Harm Restricted/Needs Tended*

On rare occasions, the township of Mae's Crossing took advantage of the government aid to which they were entitled. "Hag's Wail" demanded it (Brianna had referred to that freak storm as 'Hag's Wail,' and it soon caught on). The main road into town, RM 12 (ranch to market), had been heavily damaged. Although still passable, traffic was restricted to one car at a time through the more difficult passages, making the wait sometimes a full thirty minutes. When 'needs must,' patient drivers sat at their wheels. Some even got out of their cars and visited with other strandees. It was during such a wait that a fortuitous meeting took place.

Kyle Porter, a young billionaire, was on a quest. He'd heard of Mae's Crossing; how the people pretty much ruled themselves and took care of their needs independently of the State and Federal Government; how there were no chain stores, all business locally owned and operated; and the biggest plus of all, that the religious/spiritual views nurtured there were revolutionary and life-affirming. Having sparred in the arena of corporate business for more than 15 years, Kyle was ready to give up that fight. His spirit yearned to live in beauty, and this town just might be able to give it to him.

Kyle Porter and Ed Janssen met at the edge of the rain eroded road, both of them watching the men in the trenches with chain saws chattering away. Having just come from BigCity Memorial Hospital, Ed was trying to get the disturbing vision of young Jason out of his mind when he noticed the man next to him. "Quite a storm, quite a storm. Did a lot of damage." Kyle responded with, "Yah, well, I sure picked a fine time to go sight-seeing." There was more humor to his voice than annoyance.

Ed, always ready to sing the praises of Mae's Crossing, countered with "Funny thing; after a storm our little town looks brighter, what with the wind and rain takin' away the dust. I'm sure this is a fine time for sight-seeing." Friendly nods came from both men. Ed held out his hand and said, "Ed Janssen, Head Councilman to Mae's Crossing." Kyle grabbed his hand. "Kyle Porter. Seeker."

"So, Mr. Porter, are you looking to see anything in particular? Reason I ask is I've got a little spare time, and since we're both going there, maybe I could point out some stuff and answer questions. For me, my first stop is going to be at Cup o' Life where I can get some of the best dang coffee in the world and goodies from Dot's Delights. Always makes getting' home the best thing."

"Well Mr. Janssen, that's a most generous offer, and one that I would be a fool to turn down. By all means, let me follow you to a 'Cup o' Life.' Under his breath, Kyle whispered "I could use some of that," a warm smile lighting up his face.

Chapter 10a

Brianna ᚾ *Desire/Need*

Brianna studied the 'separated' talisman in her hand. A clean break created a kenaz facing the 'separation,' with just a faint line making a wall in front of it. A wealth of meanings jumped out at her: Creativity, sudden inspiration, controlled fire, sexual force, and on and on. Which one? She chose sudden inspiration. Focusing on the implications of inspiration, Bri entered familiar territory. She smiled as she curled her fingers around the fragment, memorizing the contours and sharp edges, then returned it to its pouch.

Bri's first inspired act was to feverishly clean her workshop, top to bottom. It was a daunting task, one she had always put off until 'later.' Well, later had arrived with a vengeance. Expecting a guest to survey her inner sanctum, Bri wanted the 'guest' to focus on her work, not the chaos it created. It took all of two days to finally get her work space presentable, and she was thrilled with the results. Now she couldn't wait to mess it up again. While doing the cleaning and organizing, Bri started a list of supplies she'd need to pick up in BigCity next month. 'Glory Days Gala' was the first weekend in September, and the Fantasy Festival in BigCity was set for the third weekend. September was shaping up to be a very busy month for 'Bri-Gris.'

Her next inspired act was to stop by "Cut 'n Curl" to get her hair done. It had been ages, and her hair was a wild tangle of wayward curls and split ends. When Bri stepped out of the salon, she felt younger, lighter and ready for excitement to enter her life. The prospect of courtship had not been a priority in her life for a long time; not since she and George split up six years ago. Bri had been content in her solitude. With Malachais entering her life, she found herself flushed with anticipation. *Where will this lead? Do I really want this?* Time would tell.

Chapter 10b

Kyle ⸻ *Needs Surfacing*

Ed and Kyle sat at a table under a green umbrella at Cup 'o Life, downing their coffee and sweets. Kyle steered the conversation toward rentals; he'd pretty much decided to try living in Mae's Crossing to see if it suited him. Ed was the right person to ask, for he was a veritable font of information, making suggestions and forwarding his own personal inclinations. By the time they finished their coffee, Kyle had an impressive list of contacts. What a lucky meeting this was for him! They rose, shook hands, and left on their own journeys.

Kyle Porter had set out on this trip already predisposed to like Mae's Crossing. Having seen the busy town center with folks waving and yelling greetings to each other, he was impressed by their outgoing friendliness. The surrounding mountain vistas were rugged and uncluttered by overbuilding. It was like the land itself was beckoning him to stay awhile. He drove around the outskirts of town, admiring the homes and the way they seemed to blend with the land rather than dominate it. It came as no surprise, then, as he followed Ed's explicit directions, to find himself drawn to an attractive older Victorian style home that might as well have had a 'Welcome' sign on it. Widow Thompson answered the door, and after exchanging a few words, directed him to the path at the side of the house. The approach was bordered by flowering bushes, the walk itself a carefully laid pattern of herringbone in bricks. The cottage in back was charming, painted a soft ivory with dark green trim. The porch extended around the small building, and as he walked around to the back he was greeted with a paved area complete with barbecue pit and benches. Kyle was sold before he walked in the door. The little house was cheerful and inviting, with built in bookshelves and a river stone fireplace. Returning to the main house, he negotiated with the widow and signed the necessary papers, handing her a check to secure a year's lease. He wanted to jump for joy, but held to a proper demeanor for propriety's sake. *Hooray! I've done it! I made the leap.* Now for the monumental task of packing, sorting, storing and schlepping. Kyle looked forward to the whole process, a new vitality animating him.

Chapter 10b

Rosalind ⸻ *Desires Suppressed*

Rosalind got off the phone with Shelly, snickering to herself about a juicy piece of gossip they'd just shared. Their friendship was as strong as ever, in spite of Rose's fears that they would drift apart. *My Goddess!* It wasn't as if they were separated by a continent or an ocean! Each of them was in a position of importance in their respective jobs, and they both thrived on the headiness that comes with exerting authority. In Rose's instance, she was learning the intricacies now, but she knew that in the future she would be able to take over the reins. One of the intricacies was in place today. Rose worked in the bakery, taking orders from customers. There was a fairly steady stream of folks that frequented 'her' shop *(still sounded strange),* and she was getting to know some of them by name. Farmer Johnson had just walked out the door with a dozen fresh donuts when He entered. Rose was a big fan of old movies, and if she didn't know better, she'd have sworn it was Russ Tamblyn from "Westside Story" walking in.

He approached the counter and caught her gaze. "Hi. I just had some of your goodies over at Cup 'o Life. Fantastic! I'm on my way back to BigCity, and thought I'd get some for the road. Those lemon bars look great. Why don't you give me two of those, and two of the macaroons, please." Kyle flashed her a big smile.

Rosalind flushed. *What's going on with me?* First she was drawn to Daniel, and now a perfect stranger had her pulse racing. "Yes, sir, right away." As she handed the baked goods to Kyle, she said "That'll be $5 even, and by the way, could I have your autograph?"

Kyle, taken aback by her strange request, handed her five dollars. "I'm sure I don't know why you'd want my autograph…"

"Oh, ha ha. Just a joke. You look so much like Russ Tamblyn. I couldn't resist. Sorry, didn't mean to offend you."

"No offense taken, Miss…?"

"Rosalind. These sweets should get you back home with a happy tummy." She smiled and ducked her head, feigning interest in straightening the cases.

"Kyle Porter here. I'm going home to pack up, Miss Rosalind, because I'm moving here. Just rented the cottage from Widow Thompson, and I'm looking forward to being one of your best customers. 'Til then, adios." Kyle made a slight bow and walked out the door, leaving Rose fantasizing about his remarks.

Chapter 10c

Daniel ᚾ *Need-fire/Desire*

Daniel couldn't get Rosalind out of his mind. He puttered around his cabin, not exactly straightening up, but making pathways through the clothing, baskets, boxes, cages, books, and various paraphernalia of his workings. Herbs were strung from the ceiling, giving the tiny room a pleasant aroma. As he hurried outside on some inconsequential errand, Dawn crept up to the cabin door. She entered Daniel's space with some hesitation; somehow she felt like an intruder. *Oh well, best to get the job over and done with.* She scanned the room, wondering where in the world she could leave the talisman so it wouldn't be overlooked in all this mayhem. Mr. Crafty spied her from the comfort of Daniel's bed and made a low sound that almost sounded like purring. Dawn patted him on the head, admiring the artistry of the stitches in his ear. "Mr. Crafty. Would you please see that Daniel gets this? It's very important." Mr. Crafty blinked and nodded. As Dawn was tucking the pouch under Mr. Crafty's belly, Daniel came flying through the door. "Oh!...Oh my, it's you, Dawn. What are you doing here?" She never spared him a glance; merely disappeared in a cloud of mist.

Daniel rushed over to Mr. Crafty and crouched on the floor, looking him in the eye. “I know Dawn. She wouldn’t just stop by for a friendly visit, and besides, she didn’t even say hi. Something big’s brewing, Mr. Crafty.” The fox blinked his eyes at him and rolled sideways, exposing the yellow silk pouch. Daniel grabbed it up and saw his name stitched in gold. He recognized Sunny’s handiwork. Pulling the talisman out, he puzzled over it. There was his name again, and yet, on the other side there was only half of the runes with a large symbol that he didn’t recognize in the center. It had apparently been broken with intent; the break was so clean that only a Goddess could have done it with such precision. “Oh, this is big, Mr. Crafty. This is real big.”

Chapter 10c

Malachais ✝ *Needs Must*

Malachais pushed thoughts of Brianna aside, puzzling over the dilemma with Gerry. Even though the kid was supposedly out of town, Mal was concerned not only about Laura's well-being, but Willem's also. What if he suddenly reappeared and caused more havoc in their lives? Something had to be done about the boy, and as a High Priest, there was one sure avenue available to him: A proper restraining ritual. It would have to be constructed carefully, as his oath demanded 'no harm.' Mal turned to his reference books and BOS's, searching for the right approach. After considerable research as well as soul-searching to make sure he wasn't being vindictive, he settled on a well-crafted working. Although he had created a temple room in his home, it didn't have the right 'feeling' for his ritual. No, what he really needed was something spooky; something with an edge of darkness to it. Malachais resolved to be alert to likely ritual space, but it would have to be soon. As he was settling in for Friday night's rest, he appealed to the Goddess to show him the way.

Mal awoke in the middle of the night, trying to hold on to the vision. Fast fading, the only impression he managed to remember was a burned out building near the ruins of a church. He knew there was more...a lingering feeling of being lovingly held teased his memory. Try as he might, it was all he could retrieve. Mal busily wrote in his bedside journal, committing to words what recall might elude. He punched his flattened pillow and returned to the warmth and comfort that beckoned to him in his dreams.

ISA

Ice/freeze frame

Chapter 11a

Mae's Crossing | *Restriction*

Tom Bradley was rudely awakened by a loud banging on his door. "What the dang phooey!!! Hold up a second; I'm coming." Tom opened his door to see a very irate Mikos Stauros, his neighbor to the south. Mikos shouted at Tom; "I've had it with your dang goats, Tom! I should take this to the Town Council."

Tom steadied himself on the edge of the table. He was dizzy with the realization of experiencing déjà-vu, *or are the Goddesses just laughing at me?*

"Mikos, Mikos. Hey man, calm down. Ya know I'm dang sorry about my wanderin' goats, and I'm gonna fix it an make everything right between us." He was taken aback by his very words. *Did I just say that?*

Mikos edged closer, clearly mystified by Tom's attitude. "Did I just hear you say you were going to 'fix it'? And just how do you plan on doing that, goat ass?"

Tom bristled, but held his ground. *I may be slow, but I'm dang well not stupid.* "I'm gonna let that be, Mikos…If'n ya like, ya kin call it 'divine intervention,' but I'm gonna put in that fence that I said I'd do two years ago. 'Bout time I followed through, an I guess I owe ya an apology fer takin' so long."

And so it was that Tom Bradley made peace with his neighbors. Such is the strength of community in Mae's Crossing that eventually all bow to it.

Chapter 11a

Brianna | *Hold on to this Moment/Caution*

Saturday dawned bright and clear that August morning. Brianna knew in her gut that she awoke to a turning point in her life, and took mental photographs of the trees, flowers, house; everything her eyes lit upon. *Hold on to this moment!* There was a sharpness and a clarity she hadn't noticed before, and the day sparkled with promise. Bri filled her morning with 'busy work,' trying not to will the clock to speed up. She was fiercely proud of her accomplishments *Would Malachais be proud?* as she looked upon the life she had built totally on her own; a life she thought was a complete picture. Now she felt there was a 'missing piece.' *Could it be him?*

By 11:30 am Bri was ready, dressed in a layered green and brown skirt with a lovely green silk blouse (almost the same color as her magickal pouch). She set it off with her favorite Tree of Life pendant, a blatant understatement of her path. Bri was chomping at the bit for the phone to ring. Sure enough, Malachais called fifteen minutes later to let her know he was driving into town, and would be waiting for her at Tito's Diner. Bri picked up the poplar branch by the door and went out to her car. There was a space right behind a cherried out '79 Mustang. Bri admired the car, remembering how she was torn between one like it and the Ghia that she settled on years ago. She looked in the window to see Malachais looking back at her. Nervously patting her hair, she walked into the diner, poplar branch firmly in hand.

"Hello, Malachais. It's so good of you to come all this way just to see my work. I hope it will be worth your time."

Mal pulled a chair out for her and gently pushed it in as she sat down. *Always the gentleman. What an anomaly in this jet age.*

Brianna tightly gripped the poplar branch in her lap, focusing on its power to combat fear. *What am I afraid of? That he's not a good person; that I'm vulnerable and may be threatened; that he may be the answer to my unspoken prayers...*

She realized he was talking to her. "What was that? The 'Bonanza Tostada'? My all-time favorite. You'll love it."

Malachais commented on her pendant affiliations, rising to the bait she had intentionally chosen. Bri loved his directness.

"Since you ask, yes, I am Wiccan. And you...?"

With an affirmative reply, *a 'Blessed Be,' no less,* Bri loosened her stranglehold on the poplar and relaxed. The meal progressed, light chatter sprinkled with occasional laughter. Hunger assuaged and feeling a mild buzz from the margarita, she led the way to Al's Antiques. Malachais gave Al a package with a firm "See ya later, Al." The very Mustang she'd admired earlier pulled up behind her *Wouldn't you know it?* and followed her to her home. She parked and stood at the door to the studio, poplar branch in hand. Watching him emerge from his car, Bri was struck by his air of self assurance. It showed in how he carried himself, filling out his height with confidence. So many tall people tend to stoop in efforts to seem less intimidating; not so with Malachais. There was a certain pride in his carriage that made her catch her breath. *Careful now.*

As he approached, she stepped forward, holding out the branch in both hands towards him. "Are you familiar with

Ellen Evert Hopman's works? She calls poplar a messenger of the Gods. When held by two people, spirit speaks through them. Will you hold it?"

Malachais placed both his hands between hers, curling his fingers round the branch, then looked her in the eye. Getting her courage up, Brianna continued. "Before you enter my home, I must know that you mean me no harm." His gaze never left hers as he intoned "an' it harm none."

"Then, welcome, and enter." She said with a flourish as she opened the door to her studio.

Brianna watched him as he wandered through her studio, making appropriate remarks and zeroing in on some of her special touches. She was pleased with his reactions, seeing an astute and sensitive side of him. When he chose the Raven mask, though, she was taken aback. It was a bit dark; she wouldn't have thought he'd be drawn to that. Business concluded, Bri wanted to invite him into her home proper. Once again, she lifted the poplar branch to him and surprised herself by voicing her concerns. "By the Goddess, do you swear that you are not involved with another?" Relief flooded through her as he swore he was unattached.

Brianna felt some trepidation as he entered her inner sanctum. *Will he fit in my world?* Seeing Malachais stagger and fall into a chair, dropping his head into his hands, set off alarm bells in Brianna's mind. *Is he having a seizure?* "Oh my Goddess, Malachais, are you okay? Do you need some water? Is there anything I can do?"

Malachais merely pointed at the window, moaning, "My chalice, my beautiful chalice!"

Chapter 11b

Mae's Crossing | *Plans Solidified*

For the up and coming 'Glory Days Gala,' it was agreed between Samantha Sunrise and Ed Janssen that vendor co-ordination fall in her lap with final approval by Ed. Sam was beginning to feel the enormity of her task. She had more applicants than the space allowed. Should she expand the space and set stiffer requirements? A lesser soul would develop a migraine, but Sam doggedly worked through the details. Jerrod and his buddy, Bjorn Knudsen, would show up at 6:00 am Friday morning, ready to chalk mark out the spaces for the vendors who would start arriving at 7:00 am. The spaces needing electricity had been carefully mapped out; the boys would help her lay out the electric feeds.

Ed was busy on his end. He'd arranged for port-a-potti transport at 7:00 am, with the cleanup crew scheduled for 7:00 am on Saturday and Sunday. The entertainment area would be getting the heavy duty electrical set-up; it was laid out in his garage right now, ready to lift and put into place by noon on Friday. An odd assortment of outdoor furniture was beginning to pile up, all destined to be placed around the dance area, with an audience area of fold up chairs also in readiness. Signs were placed for vendor and public parking. One of the boys would be directing traffic to the appropriate areas, making sure that they parked in an orderly manner. The greens would take a beating, but they'd spring back eventually. Trash cans had been strategically placed near the food booths and at various intersections. Parade instructions were handed out to the various groups and individuals wishing to be included. Ed had recruited several council members to assist, as it was way more than he could handle on his own. Not a detail was overlooked.

The Township of Mae's Crossing's booth would be at the entrance, with a discreet 'donations' jar on the table. Ed had learned over the years that it was best to leave the amount up to the donor; they had lean fairs and fat ones. One of his sons painted a banner for the booth: "Off the Grid!" with a big smiley face, to be hung at the back.

Chapter 11b

Rosalind | *Chilling Out/Introspection*

Rosalind was totally confused. She was meeting with Daniel tomorrow, herb hunting of all things. But her mind was filled with fantasies of Kyle. He was moving to Mae's Crossing! *Oh my Goddess!* When she consulted the runes and drew Raidho, she felt that they advised a ritual. That made sense. Perhaps it would clear her perceptions.

I thought I knew what I was doing...Rose had done a lot of research and had long talks with some self-avowed witches in BigCity. Accordingly, she had spent an hour in meditative practices and fasted all morning.

And yet...here I am at the very heart of the ritual, and all feeling of connection has deserted me. She stared blankly at the altar, knowing full well this was the moment when she was supposed to state her case and weave a cone of power. What she saw was herself as ridiculous and wretched: a self-centered fool in a carefully arranged 'play,' 'dressing up' to vie for magickal powers. Rose felt like crying and burst into laughter. She had the presence of mind to properly release the energies she had summoned, then promptly walked out to the porch to clear her mind. She made a promise to herself to follow up on her intentions to spend some time with Brianna. Rose was pretty sure she was a witch. Maybe Bri would be willing to train her.

Chapter 11c

Kyle — *Blockage/Progress Restricted*

Moving to Mae's Crossing presented a major challenge to Kyle. He'd lived in a large house in Big City for the last seven years, and had managed to accumulate an inordinate amount of 'things'. Diving into the thick of it, he sorted as he packed, often getting sidetracked by going down memory lane. *What a relief it will be to free myself from all the excess baggage in my life.* Some few things he couldn't part with; those would go into storage. The bulk of his hoard would be going to charity. Contracting movers to take away storageables and charitables, Kyle pared down to the bare necessities. He felt like he'd graduated from Gold's Gym; not only had he lost excess weight but he'd also beefed up. He aimed for the first week of September as his move-in date, partly due to a big festival in town that weekend and partly due to unavoidable hang-ups. Whistling and doing an improvised two-step between boxes, Kyle prepared for a new life.

Chapter 11c

Malachais — *Caution/Self-preservation*

Malachais was on the road by 7:00 am. He'd checked the traffic patterns, and knew that there would be a delay through the storm damaged areas, hoping that he'd calculated the extra time into his journey. Sure enough, by 10:00 am he encountered the first of three reconstruction sites. It wasn't until quarter to 12 that he passed the township sign of Mae's Crossing. A quick call to Brianna to let her know he was on schedule, then a drive down First Street to Cup o' Life. A left and a left brought him directly to the door of Tito's Diner. Parking right in front, he walked into the south of the border ambience of chiles and onions.

Ten minutes later, a perky yellow Karmann Ghia pulled up behind his car. Smiling inwardly, Mal thought the cars made a good pairing. *There she is. Wow, she looks even better than I remembered.*

While helping her get seated, he admonished himself for the quickening heartbeat. *Just a meeting between an artist and a prospective client...wonder what the stick's for?*

"I've been looking over the menu, and I think I'll go for the 'Bonanza Tostada.' Is it any good?" Receiving a positive reponse, he said, "Then it's settled, good." He signaled for the waiter and put in their order. Turning back to Brianna, he hesitated then bluntly asked, "I see you're wearing a Tree of Life. Are you Wiccan?" With an affirmative reply and a 'back atcha' attached, Mal straightened in his seat. *Touche! A fellow traveller. Careful now, Mal.*

Malachais raised his hands in surrender and uttered "Blessed Be." She broke into the most joyful grin he'd ever seen.

Enchanting The meal lived up to its reputation. *Delicious! This would be a regular spot for me if I lived here...where did that come from?* Brianna was charming, and the conversation flowed comfortably between bites. After the meal, Malachais and Brianna walked over to Al's Antiques to drop off the bread. They exchanged pleasantries, and then went back to their cars. Mal trailed her yellow Ghia to her place in the country, inhaling deeply on his after-meal cigarette. Driving up to her house made him feel as if he had left the real world behind and entered a magickal realm. The house exuded such a strong spirit that he could almost see it. *And oh yes, there really was a golden aura! Am I the only one who notices this? Are you speaking to me, Goddess?* Brianna was standing in front of the door of what must have been her studio, and there was a lovely calligraphed sign over it that said 'Bri-Gris.' *Great name for her work.*

Mal steadied himself as he received a challenge from her. *Gutsy girl! So that's what the stick was for.* Having passed muster, he entered her workspace and was overwhelmed by the sheer magnitude of her creativity. Masks and wings everywhere! He walked about, examining each mask, noting the details and the power that radiated from each one. All different; all special. A particular one caught his eye, and he knew immediately that this was meant to be worn in his ritual. "I'll take this fine mask. Is a check okay?"

When Brianna asked about his 'involvements' he was taken aback. *Suspicions confirmed! She is interested in me!.* "I swear by the Goddess that I am truly single," and saw the relief sparkle in her *(lovely)* green eyes. *Or are they blue?*

Walking into the living room, Malachais was hit with a sudden blow to the gut. His knees went weak, and as he searched for a place to sit, he saw why. There in her windows with the sun streaming through them were fragments of his chalice!

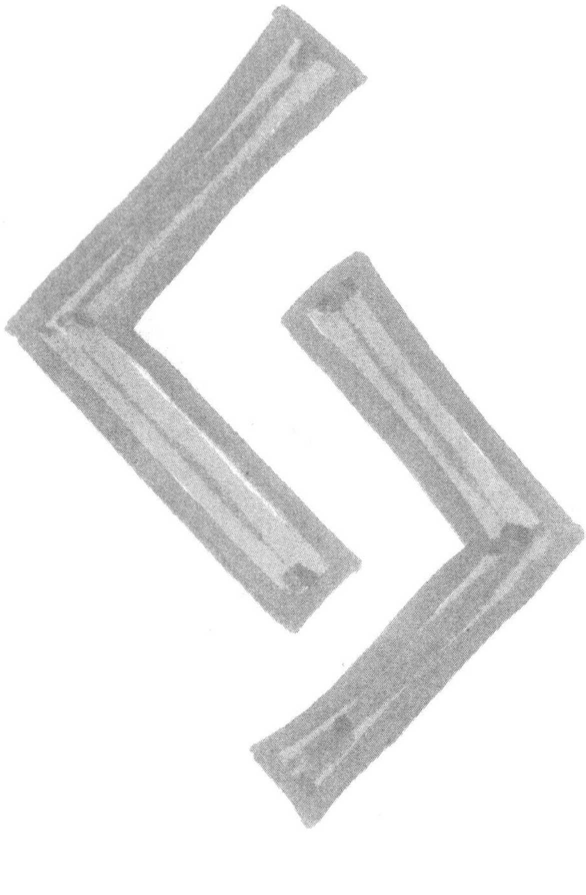

J E R A

Harvest/reward

Chapter 12a

Kyle *Fruits of Labor Unfold*

Moving day! Kyle directed the movers, keeping a watchful eye as they hefted his grandmother's treasured hutch…his only family heirloom. The workers handled it with care, and soon the moving van was packed and ready. He led the way in his old XKE.

I really need to get something more suitable for the mountains. Kyle had called ahead to Widow Thompson to alert her to their eta. Keeping a slow pace and an eye on his rear view mirror, he guided the van up the winding mountain roads to the heart of Mae's Crossing.

Chapter 12a

Brianna & Malachais *Reward in Sight*

Brianna dropped to the floor at Malachais's feet, boldly placing her hand over his. "Oh my Goddess, Malachais! It was your chalice! I am so, so sorry I broke it! It never registered with me when Al gave it to me that it was stolen." Malachais raised his head, looked at her stricken face, and took her hand in his. *If she can break my chalice and I still feel this way...well...* "Bri, Bri. It's okay." He brushed her hair away from her eyes and found himself drowning in the watery blue-greens. He stood and walked over to the windows, reaching out and caressing the broken glass. "It's over and done. All the puzzle pieces from the moment it disappeared have come together. Ah, Brianna," Malachais turned to face her..."My blessed chalice brought me into your life and now you've captured my heart. I am so humbled by the Gods' manipulations."

Sunny peeked in the window and saw the two of them talking in the living room. Perfect! With them being so deeply engrossed in each other, it would be a snap to deposit the final pouch. Granny was right; Brianna's story was unfolding much quicker than expected. Sunny walked over to the Mustang, opened the driver's door and placed a blue silk pouch on the driver's seat. She carefully closed the door, took one last look at the couple in the window, then melted into the woods.

They sat in silence for a while, then Brianna told Mal the whole story; how she had coveted and then received the chalice from Al, the cleansing and the sickness, the Guardian ritual...When she finished, he stroked her hand, then lifted it to his lips and kissed it. In his turn he told her his story; how Gerry took the chalice, sold it to Willem then roughed up Willem and Laura. He told how things developed between

Will and him, bringing him eventually to Al's. They both marveled at how the two stories intertwined. When Mal mentioned the ritual he'd devised and how perfect the mask would be…if only he could find the right spot…

"I've got it, Mal! I know the perfect place to perform a restraining ritual. It's still light; let's drive over to the Ruins."

They walked out to their cars. Mal offered to drive, and as he opened his door, he saw the pouch. "What the..? How did this get here?"

Brianna peered around him and saw him holding a blue silk pouch, almost identical to hers. "Wait here just a minute, Mal. I'll be right back." She raced into the house, grabbed her pouch and ran up to him, swinging it in the air. "Talk about puzzle pieces fitting together! I just bet this is the other half!" Malachais had taken the token out of the bag, and was carefully scrutinizing it when she came rushing up to him, thrusting her talisman at him. He took the two pieces and fit them together. *Oh My Goddess!* They looked at each other in amazement. Brianna blurted out, "I know that symbol! It's an old Belgian bindrune for Union." Before she could stop herself, she said "Isn't this where he takes her in his arms and kisses her?"…"Damn right!"…He barely got the words out of his mouth before their lips met.

Malachais

Chapter 12b

Rosalind *Bountiful Harvest*

Rosalind attempted a 'lazy' Sunday; she didn't succeed. She was working on a painting, and couldn't walk away from it. Time and again, the colors on her palette changed as the picture emerged. She was trying to combine her vision of Dawn with a misty forest background. It was coming along famously. So much so that she lost track of time until she looked at the clock and it was 4:15 pm. *Oh my Gods! Daniel! ... What was it he said about clothes? Old clothes and soft shoes?* Rosalind cleaned her brushes and rushed upstairs to change. On a whim, she grabbed her talisman for luck and protection. By 4:30 she was on the road and arrived at Daniel's at 4:55. *Whew!*

When she drove up to the cabin, the door was open. Rose could hear a flute playing a light and airy tune. She crept up to the door, hoping that the music would continue. It stopped.

"Miss Rosalind! You're here. Oh good, come in, come in please."

Rose poked her head in the door. "I know. You're wearing a green cap because you're going herb hunting, right?"

"Yes m'am. So, ya ready? Let's get out there and find us some lovelies."

Rosalind followed Daniel into the woods, being careful to step where he stepped and to keep her movements as silent as she could. Daniel's progress was awesome; not a whisper of a sound, and the bushes hardly stirred as he passed them. He turned to her and held his finger to his lips…shhh…and pointed to a bush that was so hidden she wouldn't have noticed it if he hadn't indicated it. He crept up to it, humming, as he reached out and broke off a couple of leaves, putting them in his herb basket. Daniel pulled a dime out of his pocket, and stuck it near the roots. They continued in this manner for about an hour, filling his basket to overflowing.

Back at the cabin, Daniel had dumped the contents of the basket on his table and was busily sorting and bundling. While he was occupied, Rose looked around his cramped space, marveling at how much he had managed to jam into it. Some jars on the top shelf caught her eye.

"Dan'l, what are those up there?"

Daniel looked up from his sorting. "Oh, those are magic mushrooms in honey. Really yummy."

"So what's so magic about them?"

"Well, they kind of take the veil off your eyes, sort of. You see the world in its essence."

Rose mulled that over. "Can I try some?"

"Well, sure. I'll take some with you. You'll really like them."

Half an hour later, Rose was doubled over with laughter, tears streaming from her eyes.

Daniel grabbed her hand and joined in the laughter. Soon they were rolling around on the floor, holding their sides. Rosalind had never experienced such pure joy. It was intoxicating. Somehow, their rolling turned into rocking as their bodies joined in ecstasy.

Pulling her disheveled clothing about her, Rose sat up, not really self-consciously but certainly bewilderedly. Her eyes lit on a pouch peeking out from under Mr. Crafty. "Oh my, is that a silk pouch? Does it have your name on it?" She turned to look at Daniel, and couldn't believe her eyes. His cap had come off during their tussle, and *Oh my Goddess!* he had pointed ears!

He hastily straightened his clothes, tugging the cap over his ears, and crawled over to where Rose was sitting, grabbing her hands. "Miss Rose, please promise you'll never tell. Please, please! My folks aren't happy that I'm here, but I like the people in Mae's Crossing. They're real special. And I'm sorry 'bout what just happened. I didn't mean for it..."

"Oh, Dan'l, it's okay. Really. I like you, and well, it just happened, right? No blame. This is all so nutty. So you're an Elf! Oh my Goddess! And that pouch. Could I see it?"

Daniel pulled the pouch out from under Mr. Crafty and handed it to her. Rose ran over to her packsack and retrieved her pouch. Daniel's eyes widened with wonder as she took the two talismans out and showed that they fit together perfectly! She puzzled over the bindrune for a few moments, then looked up in shock. "It's a fertility rune!"

Chapter 12c

Mae's Crossing *Harvest*

The day had finally arrived. It was Friday and vans, pickups, SUV's, food wagons, etc. were lined up at the entrance to the vendors' parking lot. Some had gotten in line as early as 6:00 am. By 10:00 am, a small village emerged in the broad expanse of quiet countryside adjacent to the temple. Canopies of every color vied for attention, a few with banners, balloons, pennants, flags…It was glorious. So apropos for a true 'Glory Days Gala.'

Brianna drove up around 10:00 am, ready to set up for the afternoon opening. Harp music lingered in the air, and she wondered if that was Jim with 'Just Rewards.' As luck would have it, *or maybe Samantha's insight,* her neighbor turned out to be Wren with Myth and Magic. *Oh, this is going to be a good fair!* They belonged to a 'mutual admiration society,' each one sincerely impressed and inspired by the other's works.
Getting approval by a fellow artist was as good as it gets. There she was now, probably coming back from a cigarette break. "Hey Bri! I was so pleased to see they put us together! How you doin' girl?" Wren smothered her in a big hug, then held her out at arm's length, carefully scrutinizing her. "Something's different." "I just got my hair done." "No, that's not it, it's…wow! You got a man in your life, don't you?"

With a piercing whistle from the conductor, the parade started at noon at the far end of First Street, making its way towards the festival grounds. Mae's Crossing High School's marching band took the lead. They were followed by the Spiral Scouts; boys and girls proud and shining in their uniforms and badges. Next were the grade schoolers with their instruments, not always delightful to listen to, but delightful to watch. Blanton's Dairy had the first float. Old Man Blanton was secured in his wheelchair with Tessie the pinto foal next to him, while the rest of the hay wagon was jammed full of younger children. They responded to the crowds' cheers and whistles by tossing candy out to them. Ten more floats followed along with the Volunteer Fire Department truck. After that, it was the classic car group; Brianna was sorry she couldn't leave her booth to show off her flashy Ghia. Overhead, Outback Jack buzzed the air in his helicopter pulling a banner that said 'Glory Days Gala.' The group entered the festival grounds, made the rounds before all the booths, then exited amidst whoops and hollers from the onlookers. The gates were opened and the crowds streamed in.

What a turnout! If today was any indication, this just might be the best fair Brianna had ever done. *Where did they all come from?* Right around closing time, she caught a glimpse of a man melting into the throng, and could have sworn it was Russ Tamblyn. But a Russ as he looked fifty years ago. *Ain't life strange?*

There were two motels (privately owned) and five bed and breakfasts in Mae's Crossing; all were filled to capacity. The township was a popular vacation spot, and what with the recent victory over the Transportation Department, it had become downright famous. Curiosity seekers sorely tested the wards so carefully placed by Samantha Sunrise. *I will need to strengthen them soon.* The town prospered; all restaurants were busy, and Dot's Delights had its best weekend on record.

Rosalind was in line Saturday morning with a large crowd awaiting admittance. She had taken to carrying her pouch with her, and had tied it to her wrist.

Three women leaned over a water-filled cauldron watching the scene unfold. As usual, it was Sunny with her sharp vision who spotted Rosalind in line. "There she is! And how convenient," she looked at the others with a mischievous grin "she just happens to be wearing her pouch on her wrist!" Moonface forced herself to a standing position, *(old bodies!)* and said, "I'll take it from here, girls. You go get the clay ready." Poof and poof! Granny was in line behind Rosalind. She bumped into her, quickly removing the pouch as Rose rounded on her. Rose spoke: "Oh, gosh, I'm so sorry. Are you okay, ma'am?" Moonface raised her right hand to her head and tousled her hair as she quickly deposited the pouch she held in her left hand into her pocket. "Sorry me, dearie. My eyes aren't as good as they once was. Didn't mean to jostle you so."

It wasn't until an hour later that Rose noticed her pouch was missing. She searched the grounds for another hour, and finally gave up, desolation setting in. *Where has it gone to? I suppose someone could have picked it up. Damn!*

EIHWAZ

Protection/shaman's ladder

Part II: Chapters Thirteen through Sixteen : *Subjective: Path to Self Discovery*

Chapter 13a

Mae’s Crossing ᛇ *Blessed by the Gods*

Glory Days Gala was a grand success. It was a major effort, but Ed Janssen had a good team. By Tuesday, all was back to normal with the exception of flattened grass and deep ruts in the field. Time would heal that. Ed was in high spirits as he counted out the take from the fair; donations and booth fees put $23,034 into the town treasury! *What a blessing!*

Chapter 13a

Brianna and Malachais ᛇ *Divine Guidance*

When he finally got to see the building, Mal had to admit that it was tailor made for his workings. So much was falling into place at such a dizzying pace that a light-headedness overtook him. Feeling giddy, he laughed and twirled; catching Brianna by the hands, they twirled. The Gods were certainly smiling on him.

Brianna tracked down the owner, Samuel Germaine, and Malachais arranged for a one week rental. With her first festival over and another one two weeks later, they had settled on the week between the two shows for the ritual. That was providing, of course, that the portents were correct.

Mal instructed Brianna: "Once we settle on the right day for the ritual, and it must be at midnight, I'll come back for a few days. I'll send you the write-up; let me know if you think it needs more. Could I take another look at your masks before I go?" Malachais followed Bri into her studio. "I noticed this piece, and thought you might wear it for our rites. *Did I just say 'our' rites?* What do you think?"

Bri had unknowingly shrunk into herself, already lamenting his departure. Her response was slow and soft spoken. Mal put his arms around her. "Ah, Brianna. What a blessing you are. You make my heart sing. I must go, but please know, that to paraphrase a great poet, I carry your heart in my heart." As he spoke, Mal stroked her hair and kissed the top of her head. Tears formed in her eyes as she hugged him even tighter.

Holding to his promise, Malachais left Sunday after lunch to drive Willem back to Channing.

Chapter 13b

Mae's Crossing *Sacrifice/Yearning for Divine Connection*

Kris Knudsen and Bors Larson met at the temple, copies of the Asatru Fallfest ritual in their hands.

Kris paced the garden circle. "I was thinking Odin could approach from the South, meeting up with Uller, coming from the North. We'll place the altar to the North to keep the center open for their meeting. They'll tussle, Odin falls then retreats, Uller takes up the staff. What do you think?"

Bors walked the path Kris indicated. "Yes, I like it! Even the Wiccans will be able to relate to the story."

Chapter 13b

Rosalind *Twists and Turns*

Rosalind was heartbroken over the loss of her talisman. She shouldn't have worn it on her wrist; too late now to think of that. The glyph for fertility blazed across her inner eye. *Oh my Goddess! Of course, that was the intention. Did that mean...?* She would have to keep close track of her courses. Rose was fond of Daniel. There was no denying that. But the possibility of them becoming a couple was nil…after all, he was an Elf!

Worry and apprehension ate at her. She was a nervous wreck. Trying to divert the direction her thoughts were taking her, Rose took up her brushes and was soon lost
in the process of bringing Dawn to life in her painting. Reaching deeply into her subconscious, Dawn's image was transforming from a flighty, ineffectual creature into a powerful Goddess. She stood back in awe at what her brushes had revealed. *What was it Dawn had said? 'And it will make you very, very happy.'*

The image of Kyle Porter kept popping into her head. *And he's moving to Mae's Crossing!* Rosalind felt overwhelmed. Up until now she had been resolutely single, and suddenly there were two men in her life! *That's it! I need to call Brianna.*

Brianna answered after the third ring. "Yes, who's calling?" Rosalind piped up, "It's me, Rosalind. I was wondering if we could get together for lunch sometime soon. I'd like to speak with you in private." Brianna liked what little she had seen of the young woman, and was happy to hear from her. "Of course, Rose. How about Thursday noon at Tito's?" Rosalind warmed to her tone. "Terrific! It's a date. I'll see you then, and thank you so much for your time."

Chapter 13c

Malachais ᛇ *Shaman's Ladder*

Malachais paced the tiny room, a mere five lengths back and forth, his brow furrowed in deep concentration. His thoughts were racing as he mumbled to himself, "not yet… Wait!" Every ounce of determination sped him towards his goal, and still he held back. Not until the moon had passed into Scorpio at midnight would all be in readiness. Weeks of planning had brought him to this moment and for Mal the waiting was excruciating. Now with Brianna joining him in the effort, he had no doubts concerning the successful outcome he was aiming for.

The autumn winds rattled the windowpanes, howling like wolves and threatening entry into the attic room. If only it hadn't had such a superb view, he would have passed up this drafty place. Mal knew the moment his foot touched the stairs that this was the spot he was looking for. His mind went back to that moment of discovery when he forced the shutters open to the breathtaking vista: there, laid out before him, past the broken down buildings were the remains of the old steeple towering over a neglected cemetery. All of it exactly as he had seen in his dreams. Even now, his pulse quickened with the memory. Dealing with the dark forces holding Gerry would be best dealt with if the starting point, physically, was equally dark. Hence the rites here, rather than in the comfort of his private temple room.

Although Mae's Crossing was over a four hour drive from his home in Channing, the old house was well worth the journey. *Not to mention the chance to be with Brianna.* Situated in the abandoned section of town, without nosy neighbors, made it a perfect setting for his magickal operations. Even the owner, on handing the keys over, had shown no curiosity as to his choice. Better to have a few coins in his hand for this derelict building.

At precisely midnight, Malachais and Brianna walked the perimeter of the chalked out circle. Mal conjured the circle and Bri followed up with calling the quarters. Tyr was invoked for justice, with Nauthiz, Isa and Thurisaz for containment. The first glyph, drawn in chalk on the floor with a picture of Gerry's head in the center, was activated. This symbol would hold Gerry for the next phase. Both of them concentrated their efforts on a positive change of heart in the second glyph holding the fragmented photo of Gerry's torso. Mal and Bri walked the circle and lit the 12 candles on the perimeter, pouring divine light into his heart. The last symbol was a transformation of the first symbol with 'justice served' and a new outlook resulting in a changed man. The lower section of the photo of Gerry's body lay in the center, as they empowered the legs to stand tall and walk in the light. To make manifest the bright new outlook, the large candle in the center of the final glyph was set aflame. By the time they released the circle, sweat was running down Mal's face, so fierce had his intentions been. Brianna and Malachais grinned and hugged, satisfied that they had put things right.

In concert with their workings, three women stood within a paved pentacle in their garden, their hair of black, white and red glowing in the moonlight. Holding the image of Gerry in their minds, they added their energies to Bri and Mal's ritual.

Glyphs employed in 'Restraining / Transformation' ritual

All glyphs hold the focus in center crossing point (i.e., photo, item of clothing, hair, etc. or a strongly projected mental image placed in center)

Glyph of Binding

Three Thurisaz pinning object in center, directing force of surrounding runes: three Isa holding object immobile enclosed by three Nauthiz, the fettering rune.
Light candle in center.

Glyph of Enlightenment

Dagaz. *Light twelve candles encircling glyph, then light large center candle.*

Glyph of Transformative Action

Three Thurisaz pointing outwards. Isa melts to allow Tyr through.

Fetters (Nauthiz) are removed. *Light large center candle.*

PERDHRO

Mystery/opportunity

Chapter 14a

Mae's Crossing  *Death*

When James shook his dad's shoulder to wake him for morning coffee, he could feel the coldness of his skin through the sheet. Weeping, he fell to the floor beside him and held him close. "Pa, oh pa."

The sign over the Blanton's driveway was swathed in black ribbons. Whereas there was the usual sadness and sorrow surrounding a death, there was also a comfort in knowing that he was released from his infirmities. A wake was planned, and all would have a chance to speak of him.

Old Man Blanton had acquired a lot in his lifetime, and the bulk of it rightly went to James and Tanya. There were a couple of surprises in the will. He gave a small cottage on the northern edge of his land to Billy Higgins, the dairy foreman. Jason Miller got the old '82 Chevy pickup. To the township of Mae's Crossing he willed $10,000. The old man was a sweet-tempered soul, well-known for his generous manner. He had a fierce pride in his town, helping to maintain its independence while contributing to myriad improvements. He would be missed by many (for various reasons) but none as much as his son James, who never made a secret of his deep love and respect for the man.

Out at the Green Cemetery, Samantha Sunrise had completed the eulogy when James took over. “Thanks, folks, fer comin’ here today. Pa would be surprised at how many of you there are. I’m not. I wrote out a few words to say, but I just can’t…” at this, James gulped and fought back the tears that were threatening to overcome him. He cleared his throat, gripping the paper in his hands, and continued: “My Pa was a good man. He took care of his own, and a few more to boot.” Ripples of affirmation sounded from the crowd. “Now that his time is done,” a few more gulps and sobs escaped his lips, “now that he’s gone, we gotta know just how much we’re gonna miss him. Pa wouldn’t like to see us all mopin’ about feeling sad. I know that fer sure. So I propose that we all fill our glasses with his favorite whiskey and pour it on his box so’s he kin go out in style!”

Chapter 14a

Brianna  *Mystery/Opportunity on Horizon*

Brianna sat in her favorite lounge on the back deck, toking and musing. She felt like her world had been turned upside down, but not in a bad way. The beautiful man seemed similarly perplexed at the turn of events in their lives. Each of them had carved out a comfortable space in their respective worlds, and neither had felt a lack. And yet, and yet… they were inexplicably drawn to each other. Bri had her suspicions regarding the Goddess' hand in it, but there was no denying the passion that burned between them. At one time, she would be counting her blessings at the excellent fair she had just done, hoping the next one would be as profitable. Work and recognition had taken second chair to the wonder of Malachais. Bri was looking forward to her trip to BigCity next week, as Mal had invited her to stay over at his home in Channing.

Next on her 'to-do' list was a spell for Al's garden. As usual, more pressing needs had gotten in the way of this obligation. Not so now. Bri puzzled over the rite, adapting an older one she had successfully used on her own garden. Satisfied with the final draft, she gave Al a call.

"Ho, Bri. Good ta hear from ya. What's up, darlin'?"

"Hi, Al. I've got the spell finished for your garden. When would you like me to do it?"

"How 'bout now? Ain't got nuthin' happening, an' I'd sure like yer company."

"You got it, Al. I'll be right over." Brianna gathered up the necessary items and drove over to Al's Antiques.

Al's garden was a disaster area. The tomatoes were sickly, the lettuce thin and weak, the pole beans drooping and tiny. This was a bigger challenge than she had originally thought. Al was following behind her, keeping up a steady chatter. "That prosperity spell ya done was a good un! I had two big sales whilst folks was busy at the fair. An' a bunch a little sales, too. Ya have some powerful magic in those little hands o' yurn."

"I'm so glad, Al. That's just great. Now could I have some privacy while I do some work on this pitiful garden?"

"Yes ma'am. Just wanted ya ta know how grateful I be." Al turned and walked back into the shop.

Brianna set about doing her spell, glad she had brought plenty of dimes. By the time she was done, she'd worked up a sweat. *Good! I'll smear some on these leaves over here.* Satisfied that she'd done all she could, she collected her tools and went back inside for a visit.

Settled in his parlor, they shared a cup of coffee. Brianna fairly burst with the news about her and Malachais being 'an item.' Al sputter-spatted coffee on his knees. "Well dang, looka there. Di'na mean to do that, now, Miss Brianna." He fussed over the mess, mumbling "Tha's great, Bri. If'n yer happy."

Chapter 14b

Mae's Crossing ᛈ *Mystery*

Mae's Crossing concealed many secrets and mysteries in its wild woods, not the least of which was the magnificent estate of Dawn, Sunny and Moonface. The palatial home was only two stories, but it was topped by an open air terrace complete with a garden and fountain. It was there that the three women gathered one September evening under the star-strewn sky. The cool winds brought nothing but exhilaration to them as they worked the finishing touches on a new talisman.

Moonface looked on the other two with affection. "Dawn, this is some of the finest clay yet. Well done!" and to Sunny, "Your hand is so steady and sure. You've created a mighty talisman here." Both women beamed with the compliments. "Now go ahead and fire it, and can you give it a thin golden glaze? That would be perfect. Tomorrow we'll finish it and the two of you can deliver them."

Chapter 14b

Rosalind *Opportunity*

Rose was glad they were meeting at Tito's. It was her favorite lunch spot, with its yummy smells and cheery deco. She arrived early and grabbed a table by the window. *So much better for people-watching. There's Brianna in her cute little yellow car.*

Brianna walked in and spotted Rosalind by the window. "Hi Rosalind. Glad you suggested this meeting. I just love this restaurant, and I see you picked the best spot in the house." She smiled at Rose and pulled up a chair.

"It's my favorite lunch spot too, Miss Brianna. I'm so happy you could find the time to meet with me. I know you must be terribly busy, what with all those beautiful masks and wings you make. Are you doing the Fantasy Festival this year? I saw your booth there last year, and just love your work."

"Thank you, Rose. Yes, I'll have a booth there. And yes, I am terribly busy replacing stock from our fair which was just fabulous. But that doesn't mean that I can't take the time to visit with you."

They were interrupted by the waitress, and both of them declined menus and ordered their favorites. Rose squirmed in her seat, anxious to get to the heart of it. "Miss Bri, I was wondering if you could help me out some. I'm all mixed up and having a hard time figuring out what's going on with me. The truth of it is, I'd like to choose a path and dedicate myself to a stronger, more capable me. If I'm not being too forward, I think you might be a witch, and was hoping that you might take me on and train me." *There, she said it*!

Brianna looked at her long and hard. She liked her directness, and decided immediately to take her on as a candidate. "Well, Rose, you're right. I am a Priestess of the Goddess. What you're asking for is not a simple course in self development. It calls for a lot of reading, memorizing, paying attention to detail and ultimately a willingness to serve the Goddess. I would be willing to train you, but I'd like you to read a couple of books first, then give it some hard thinking. The training itself would take a year and a day." Bri wrote down the name of a few books and handed it to her. Just then, their food arrived. After hungrily working her way through half the food on her plate, Bri paused. "Would you like to tell me what's troubling you?"

Rose gulped down the bite she had just taken, drank some water, and replied, "Uh, well, some of it's 'man stuff.' I've been spending some time with Daniel." Brianna's eyebrows rose at that. *Does she know he's an Elf?* "And then there's Kyle. Not that anything's going on with him, it's just that I'm really attracted to him and he's moving to town and he said he'd be one of my best customers."

So that's it. Figures, pretty girl like her. "It's been my experience, Rose, that following the path of the Old Ones tends to put things in perspective. You see the world a little differently. You'll know who fits and who doesn't. Doesn't mean your heart will, but your spirit always knows. Create a strong connection with spirit and let it guide you." She smiled inwardly, thinking how spirit had brought her and Malachais together.

Chapter 14c

Daniel *Mysteries Deepen*

A tremendous crashing sound outside his window startled Daniel from his sleep. He rushed out his front door to see Moonface dusting herself off, spluttering; "These dang brooms! How do those women do it? Most uncomfortable ride I've ever had!" She picked up the broom and marched to Daniel's door.

"Granny! Are you okay? By gosh a golly, you've taken quite a fall."

"Fine, fine, Daniel. I'm fine. Just trying to get your attention. Ha! Worked, didn't it? Look, I just wanted to drop in and trade you this fine magickal broom for that worn out old talisman of yours."

Daniel quickly acquiesced to the Goddess's request, knowing full well it was a command and nothing less. A bright flash and she was gone, leaving him staring at the bedraggled excuse of a broom in his hand.

Chapter 14c

Malachais 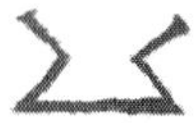 *Secretive Work Completed/Results Beginning to Show*

Back in Channing, Malachais fell into his usual routine. After his greeting of the Sun, he wandered out to the kitchen, fixed his coffee, then took it out to the deck. Sorting through his mail, Mal came upon a note from his broker. *Good news!* The stocks he had invested in were doing fabulously, and his agent recommended selling them now. *Ah, life is good.* Laura showed up for her cleaning duties, and Mal left her to it as he went out on errands.

Malachais was driving past the corner drug store when he did a double-take. *Is that Gerry standing out front?* He slowed down and pulled over, cautiously looking over his shoulder at the young man. Yes, it was Gerry, but he looked different. He was cleanly dressed and seemed to be standing taller. Mal would have to ask Laura about that. He checked his watch, and figured he could get home right as she was finishing up.

Just as he thought, Laura was closing the door behind her as he drove up. "Hold up, Laura. Could I talk with you?"

"Why yes, Mr. Merriwether. What is it?"

Mal looked down at her anxious features and put a reassuring hand on her arm. "Not to worry, Laura. You know I'm very pleased with your work. It's Gerry…I thought I just saw him downtown. I felt you should know to be on your guard."

“Oh, Gerry. Well, yeah, I know he’s back. But you know, funny thing is, he told me he was really, really sorry for being so mean to me. I’d like to believe him, but what he did was so awful, and I had such a hard time with it and now I’m pretty much putting it behind me when Pow! he shows up and apologizes. Honestly, Mr. Merriwether, I’m so confused. We was so much in love in High School; planning our lives together, wondering what our kids would look like…then he goes and changes bad, real bad. Scared me, he did. So now he’s paying attention to his looks and says he’s got a new job and wants to take up where we left off. Well, I just don’t know…”

Malachais lifted his hand to her shoulder, willing her to silence. “Thank you, Laura, for telling me this. I still recommend caution around him. I am so relieved to know that he hasn’t threatened you. I don’t want you to get hurt again. Now I really must get back to my office, but thanks again for being straightforward with me. Don’t hesitate to call me if he bothers you…see you next week.”

ALGIZ

Protection/spiritual guidance

Chapter 15a

Mae's Crossing *Preparing for Blessing*

What really defined Mae's Crossing were the people. The usual country occupations of farming, ranching, milling, logging, fishing, etc. were alive and well. Strong character built on old values reigned supreme, and keeping that spirit intact and inviolate was Samantha Sunshine's job. Every year for the last seven, she had strengthened the wards at the outermost reaches of the town. Time tested and true, the materials for the job awaited her final ministrations.

Kris Knudsen had built a large metal barrel, fitting it with a spigot and elevating it several feet off the ground. This housed the two hundred pounds of sand Sam needed for the operation. Daniel had collected the herbs which were now hanging in the sanctuary. She had bits and pieces from most of the population; lambs wool, goat hairs, cow hairs, honey comb, grain, wood chips, ash (from Kris's forge), flowers, vegetables, etc. Sam took inventory, making sure she had the widest representation of the population as was possible. Outback Jack was on the calendar for the day after tomorrow, when the actual warding would take place. Now she needed to cleanse, purify and empower. *Whew! Big job!*

Samantha stood on a ladder overlooking the open barrel of sand, incense placed and burning beneath it. Beside her was the stack of consecrated articles which she dropped into the barrel, stirring lightly with a long paddle to cover them. Her assistant, Olga, stood by the incense, occasionally tossing in the sacred herbs and flowers. As Sam swirled the mixture, she intoned, "Mighty Ones! Empower this charm! Bless and protect each ranch, home and farm!"

After a few minutes of stirring, she motioned to Olga who opened the spigot. Filling a bucket, Olga closed the spigot, fighting the pressure of the flowing sand. She hoisted the bucket up to Sam. Repeating the phrase, "Mighty Ones…" Samantha poured the sand into the barrel, covering the offerings. They continued in this manner until Sam had gone through the entire collection. All was in readiness for the upcoming flight.

Chapter 15a

Malachais ᛉ *Divine Guidance*

A week had passed since Malachais spotted Gerry on the street, and what came next was truly astounding. Laura came to work that Saturday morning, clearly excited about something. Asking if she could take a moment to talk with him before starting the cleaning, she related the following tale:

"Well, Mr. Merriwether, this is really important, and I thought you should know about it. Gerry and I had dinner together last night, and he told me what happened to him in BigCity. I still can't believe it, but listen to this. A couple of weeks ago, real late at night, he and his buddies were getting' real high and decided to go out and make some trouble. He says they were walkin' along and they saw two gay boys holdin' hands. Gerry says, "That's disgusting! Let's teach those little perverts a lesson they won't forget." He walks up to them, and just when he's getting ready to kick one kid in the nuts…sorry Mr. Merriwether, that's his words, not mine…just then Gerry gets this weird feeling like he's in a cage and his hands and feet are tied!" Malachais straightened up at that. "Try as he might, he can't move or kick the kids or nuthin'. His friend Duke starts yellin' at him, then it gets even weirder. Gerry says he feels like he's glowing, and the light freaks out his buddies and they run off. The two gay boys ran in the other direction, and there's Gerry, glowing and feeling stuck. The light got even brighter when the 'cage' melted, and he saw a symbol. I drew a picture of it for you." Mal looked at Laura's crude drawing of Dagaz, the very symbol he and Brianna had projected at him! "Gerry swears God talked to him, not really in words, but willing him to put his hands through the symbol. So he does it, and wham! The symbol wraps itself around him. He says it's like blinders were taken off his eyes, and he sees everything different. He knows his buddies aren't really his buddies, and that he's been bad, not being true to his spirit. Those were his words. So he packs up and gets out of BigCity as fast as he can to come back to Channing and apologize to me. Isn't that just the craziest story you ever heard? I'm still having trouble believing it, but Gerry, well, he's nicer than he's ever been and I think I'm still in love with him, and maybe I'll..."

"Hold up, Laura. This is amazing, just amazing! You have just given me the best news I've heard in a long, long time. Thank you for telling me. It sounds like Gerry's had what some people would call an epiphany, and if that's truly the case, you have nothing to worry about. I am so very happy to hear this. What a wonderful turn of events!" Mal patted her on the hand and was suddenly exuberant. *Wait 'til Brianna hears about this!* "I need to make a couple of private calls, so I'll be in my office. You go ahead and do the cleaning, Laura. Oh, and by the way, I'm giving you a raise. You deserve it."

Chapter 15b

Mae’s Crossing  *Earthing Spirit*

Moonface was out in the potter’s shed searching for the glue. Frustrated in her efforts, she decided to employ magick. *So much more efficient anyway.* On the worktable were two talisman fragments; one for Rosalind and one for Daniel. She carefully lined the two pieces up, held her finger to the seam and said “Mend!” The two pieces fused, creating a perfect clay talisman.

Later that evening, the three women went out to the faery circle at the edge of the woods. Dawn used a golden sickle to gouge a hole in the center of the ring while Sunny waited behind her, holding the talisman and Daniel’s yellow silk pouch. Moonface peered over their shoulders. “That’s good. Doesn’t need to be more that a few inches. Sunny, put the pouch in, then lay the talisman on top. Dawn, fold the pouch over the talisman.” Once it was placed to Moonface’s satisfaction, the three of them took turns piling earth over it, humming and chanting all the while.

Chapter 15b

Rosalind *Vulnerability*

Today was shop day for Rosalind, as she took her place behind the cases at Dot's Delights. She was really beginning to enjoy the interactions with the customers, and looked forward to the day's work. Much to her surprise, that gorgeous hunk, Kyle, walked in the door.

"Hi, Miss Rosalind. Am I glad you're here today, 'cause I have a special request for you."

"We here at Dot's are happy to oblige our customers if we can. What did you want?"

"Well, it's a personal request; not bakery goods. I was wondering if you'd be willing to drive my new jeep up from BigCity. That is, if you know how to drive a jeep. I need someone from here to go down with me and pick it up. Don't feel obligated. I can always ask Ed Janssen to recommend someone. It's just that I thought…if you were free…"

Rosalind was taken aback by the offer. *A three hour drive with Kyle Porter? What could be bad? Are the Fates smiling on me?* Trying to keep her cool, she replied; "Well, yes, I can drive a jeep. I do all the trade with the locals in our old stick shift pickup. I'm sure I could handle it. But why me?" *Is he blushing?*

Kyle stumbled a little over his words. It had been a long time since he had felt tongue-tied. *Thought that was 'kid stuff.'* "Because I like you, and was hoping to get to know you better."

Faced with such a straightforward reply, Rose felt her own cheeks heating up. "Okay, smooth talker. It's a deal. I'll drive your jeep back to town. It'll have to be on the weekend, though, 'cause I have a job that I can't walk away from."

"Great! It's a date, then. I mean, not really a date, but…dang…you know what I mean. Where do I pick you up and what time?"

Rosalind spent the rest of the day in the clouds. *A drive to BigCity with Kyle!* When she drove up to her house that evening, her mind was elsewhere when she saw the red silk pouch hanging from her doorknob! *Oh my Goddess!* Someone who knew her must have picked it up at the festival and brought it here. Relief flooded through her as she pulled it off of the knob and walked inside.

Several books were stacked on her night table; reading assignments from Brianna. Rose was eager to get started. Knowing that Bri would probably quiz her, she'd better read carefully. Not surprisingly, Rose had already read two of them, but thought it wouldn't hurt to re-read; kind of a refresher course. The new material, Rae Beth, Raven Grimassi, and Doreen Valiente teased at her mind as she cracked the cover of Spiral Dance for the second time and settled into her bed for some night-time reading.

Chapter 15c

Mae's Crossing ᛉ *Protection*

Samantha met Outback Jack in the middle of the pasture. She was a feisty little woman, but her 5'2" frame wasn't up to the task of heaving the sand bags. Stronger hands and backs than hers had moved the ten bags of sand out to the helicopter, and now Jack was putting them all in balance in the bay of the plane. Within moments they were airborne, heading out to the first of ten drop-offs. All had been marked with red flags to alert them as to their location. Hovering over the first spot, Samantha slowly tipped a bag, trailing a line of sand toward the next flag, chanting, "Mighty Ones! Empower this charm! Turn back the ones who mean us harm!" The rites were repeated nine times as they circled the perimeter of Mae's Crossing. Samantha could feel the energy emanating from the grains which encompassed the area, and swore she could see a pulsing electric blue line delineating the township.

Off in the woods, three women joined hands and echoed Samantha's chant.

At the southern edge of town, right before the sign identifying Mae's Crossing, a car filled with four young men was pulled to the edge of the road, hood up. "Damn! Don't know what's wrong with this car! It was running fine until now." Try as they might, they couldn't get the engine to turn over. The driver motioned his friends to put their shoulders into it, and they turned the car around, hoping to roll start the old stick shift on the downhill run. Success! But each time they reversed direction and tried to enter the township, the engine died. Defeated in their desire to stir up a little trouble, they resigned themselves to the downward slopes and drove off.

Chapter 15c

Brianna *Reaching for Guidance*

Brianna packed her little car with just the bare essentials, wondering where she was going to fit all the materials and supplies she'd be picking up in BigCity. . *Oh well, cross that bridge when I come to it.* She could have driven her old van and had room to spare, but the Ghia was the perfect touring car, and far easier on gas. She was in high spirits, which was evidenced by her actually singing 'Oh What a Beautiful Morning' instead of merely humming it. And not only would she be staying over at Malachais' tonight, but also next weekend for three nights! The world around her looked brighter, the birds were singing actual love songs, and the road ahead beckoned to her with open arms. Nothing could outshine the elixir of falling in love.

Before she closed up the house and got on the road, she kneeled at her altar. "Dear Goddess, bless and protect me on this journey. Let this love be true and grow deeper over time. May I always walk in the Light of the Old Ones and bring them honor."

Bri wafted the incense smoke over her then closed with "So mote it be!" She snuffed the candle and poured the burning incense into her fireplace, carefully closing the curtains.

Her trip was timed to arrive in the city, have lunch, do her shopping and end up at Malachais' in Channing for dinner. *Busy day!* On the long drive down, Brianna reflected on the news Mal had shared with her about Gerry's 'epiphany.'

SOWULO

Victory/Clear Vision

Chapter 16a

Mae's Crossing *Summer King accedes to Winter King*

September

The turnout at the temple for the Heathen Fallfest was larger than anticipated. Since it had been stipulated 'pot luck,' there was no shortage of food. Oliver, the Bee Man, brought two bottles of his home-made mead and Mikos Stauros brought his private vintage of pear and apple brandies. All in all, there was plenty for everyone. The ritual was rich and powerful; participants and spectators alike slaked their thirsty spirits. As Bors had predicted, the Wiccans had no trouble relating to the story, nor did the other faiths. This was clearly a thanksgiving and a celebration of the bounty in their lives. Strengthening the connection to spirit together like this created a bond between all present, and they basked in the glow of contentment. Mae's Crossing was truly blessed.

Chapter 16a

Brianna ᛊ *Victory / Bright Beginnings*

Fantasy Festival at the BigCity Fairgrounds opened to a record crowd that year. Brianna, dressed in filmy green and wearing a pair of faery wings, greeted the customers in her booth. She was well prepared, and had enough stock left on Sunday to keep customers speculating as to 'which one' was more suited to their needs, be it wings or masks. Big shows like this always took their toll. By Sunday evening breakdown, Bri was exhausted. Malachais had offered to help her pack, but was politely turned down. "If you could just show up at 8:00 pm and help carry stuff to my van, that would be great." The two of them made short work of it, and soon she was following Mal's car out of the fairgrounds and back to Channing. They'd agreed to lock her van in his garage. *No need to unpack the valuables!* Goods secured, they drove to his favorite Greek restaurant for a late night celebratory dinner. Seeing as how she was missing the Fallfest in Mae's Crossing, Bri made the customary blessings to the Gods over their meal.

Back at Malachais's home that night, the two sat out on his deck, smoking and having a cocktail. Bri had brought her pipe and stash, 'just in case.' It was pure heaven, sitting here together, enjoying the clear night sky and the easy comfort of their newly formed companionship.

Mal reached over and took her hand.

"Brianna, how can I say this? You've come into my life and changed it. I thought I was content…well, yes, I was content. But there's a big difference between contentment and joy. Not only are you beautiful and talented, you're also a powerful High Priestess. If I had written a 'wish list' I couldn't have anticipated such bounty! Now I'm afraid I've fallen in love with you. Knowing you're going back in the morning gives me an empty feeling, like I'm losing a part of myself."

"Oh Mal, me too…me too. This is all so unexpected and so welcome! It's all happening so fast. We've got the rest of our lives to figure it out, and if you couldn't tell, I love you too...there can be no other. Let's just grab the moment."

Malachais held out his arms to her and Brianna snuggled into his side. He could swear he heard her purring.

Chapter 16b

Mae's Crossing *Bright Future*

Between the fair and Blanton's gift, the town treasury was looking pretty healthy. The council convened, discussing possible uses for the money. Ed Janssen stood at the podium. "Well, folks, looks like we've had a good year. Now we can actually tackle some of those projects we've been kicking around. Let's hear some ideas, and then we'll put it to a vote. Show of hands for suggestions." Chester Burns' was the first hand up. Ed motioned for him to stand. "Hag's Wail tore out a couple of pilings on the bridge to my mill. I've been able to make it passable, but it's a real jury rig, an' I'd sure appreciate a bonafide repair." Kris Knudsen was called on next. "Right now, our town park is really bare bones. I suggest that we put in a pretty fountain, shallow enough for the little ones to play in." Bors Larsen waved his hand excitedly as Ed gave him the floor. "That's a great idea, Kris. But let's take it one step further. Water is the key. Since we need to pipe it in, we might as well have a drinking fountain, a few water spigots and an open air shower." Widow Thompson was next. "I'd love to see an open air gazebo large enough to hold several musicians, maybe even actors and performers, with plenty of seating. Then we could hold concerts and other stuff." Several more suggestions were made, then Ed called a fifteen minute recess. Upon reconvening, it was voted and approved to have the bridge repair as first priority. After that they would see how far their money would take them on their grandiose schemes for a town park proper. The focus of the park would be harmony and a reverence for nature. Each councilmember had their own ideas on how to portray that…plenty of room for personal touches.

Chapter 16b

Rosalind *Awakening Consciousness/Lightning Strike*

Kyle picked Rosalind up at 8:00 am Saturday morning. The clouds were gathering overhead, and rain was in the air. Rose slid into his silver Jaguar and tucked her bag into the narrow space behind the seat. Kyle flicked on his CD player. “Hope you like Miles Davis,” as the strains of ‘Take Five’ filled the car. For the next half hour, they debated the merits of Miles Davis versus John Coltrane. Conversation turned to personal history, and by the time they pulled up at the car dealer in BigCity, they were feeling like old friends off on an adventure. Kyle suggested lunch at Grison’s Steak House, as it was right around the corner and had a fine reputation as the best steak house in the city. Although Rose had lived in BigCity for several years, she’d never eaten at Grison’s. *What a treat!* Both sated, they walked to the dealership. Kyle finalized the paperwork with the salesman and handed her the keys to the Jeep.

“Let’s just drive around the block. I want to be sure you’ll be comfortable driving this beast.”

The new Jeep was a joy to drive, and Rosalind passed Kyle’s scrutiny with flying colors after a little Focus jumped in front of her and she had to do some quick maneuvering.

Driving up the winding mountain roads, Rose was relieved that the rain had stopped.

She could see a flash of green as Kyle stuck his elbow out the window. *Ah, another fresh air freak.* The road was still wet and treacherous as they approached Dead Man’s Curve. Ahead of her, Kyle suddenly swerved, tires screeching, and slid off the road. *No! No!* She headed for the narrow turnout, scraping the side of the Jeep as she jumped out and raced over to where he had disappeared. Just then, Farmer Johnson rounded the curve, and she frantically waved him down, screaming, "Help! Help! Kyle's gone off the road!" In an instant, Farmer Johnson had parked his truck and had run over to see Kyle, white fisted, gripping the steering wheel of his car which was teetering on the edge of a small outcropping. "Hang on there. Don't move! I'm gettin' a rope!" In record time he was trailing the rope down to Kyle, talking in a reassuring tone. "I want you to take that rope and very carefully tie it under your arms. Make sure it's a good knot." Kyle obliged, glad in that moment that he had studied knots in the Scouts. More help arrived as Tom Bradley pulled in behind Farmer Johnson's truck and hurried to his side. Together the two men held the rope as Kyle slowly edged his head and arms out the window. Not a minute too soon, as the car groaned and slid a few more inches. "That's good, that's good. Just grip that rope!" No sooner were the words out of Johnson's mouth than the car gave a final lurch and plummeted down the cliff side, bouncing a couple of times before it crashed to the bottom of the ravine, bursting into flames. Kyle dangled from the rope, hanging on for dear life as the two men hauled him up to safety.

The four of them stood at the side of the road and clasped each other in a tight hug. Rose fell to her knees. "Thank you Goddess!" Kyle had a deep gash in his forehead which Rose staunched with a kerchief from Farmer Johnson. They all looked down at the burning car, Tom breaking the silence with, "Quite a show, my man. Quite a show. Well, guess I'll be on my way." Farmer Johnson retrieved his rope, patting Kyle on the back, then drove away, leaving the two of them staring at each other in disbelief and shock. Kyle wrapped his arms around Rose. "When I was sitting there, I was thinking; 'Damn! I'm gonna die now that I've found the girl of my dreams!'" Rose hugged him back, speechless and shaken.

Chapter 16c

Kyle ᛊ *Success*

Outback Jack's Fishing Camp was doing a record business this year. Previous investments in a Land Rover and additional cabins had paid off nicely. Most clients drove up to Mae's Crossing where he would pick them up and drive them to his property. It was a fine spot, right on Diamond Lake, with a short trek to some good river fishing. Some fishermen preferred to be picked up by helicopter in BigCity; fine with him, as that was the 'premium package.' Kyle Porter had reserved a cabin for Sunday, and Jack was waiting for confirmation. Late Saturday night, Kyle called. "Hey Mr. Jack. Kyle Porter here. Sorry for calling so late. Had a little accident today, and I'm just glad to still be alive."

Outback Jack chuckled, "Don't take no accident fer me to be glad I'm alive. So will ya be comin' up tomorrow?"

"Yeah, well that's why I'm calling. I picked up my new Jeep today just so's I could drive up there tomorrow. Danged if I'm not going to do it. Still feelin' a little dizzy, but I'm sure I'll feel better in the morning. Your directions are pretty clear, and did you say you've got gear to rent? Can't seem to locate mine. Should be easy, but I've got stacks of boxes and stuff that I haven't unpacked yet. Anyhoo, just confirming with you 'bout coming up in the morning."

"I do thank ya fer checkin' in. Been some real good trout activity. Yer gonna love it. Just park anywhere ya like. Catch ya later." Jack still laughed every time he said that.

Chapter 16c

Malachais *Voice of Higher Self*

A flurry of activity couldn't quiet Malachais's thoughts about Brianna. His week was jammed with appointments, errands and visits to the point of ridiculousness. He really needed to slow down. By Friday, Mal's 'time off' was more than just a break in the routine; it was an imperative for his mental equilibrium. Being out on the deck in the moonlight brought forth visions of Brianna sitting across from him. There was no way around it---he needed her in his life. The way she 'got' his humor and returned it in like manner cheered him…to be able to share his thoughts with an equal intellect…and as if that weren't enough, Mal had forgotten how good it felt to receive loving approval. *What an elixir!*

Realizing and accepting his need for Brianna's constant presence, he went to bed and set adrift on the sea of dreams, searching for the solution.

Malachais awoke with a plan to rent a place in Mae's Crossing. It would entail a lot of packing and storing, but it was do-able and filled him with excitement as the idea fleshed out. He grabbed a pad, titled three pages Take, Leave and Store, and started an inventory of his home, room by room. *Yes, this just might work!* Given his penchant for order, the process could take up to three months. That would put the move sometime in December. Mal would have to run it past Brianna to see how she felt about it. One bad word, and the plan was nixed. Lost in thought, he was jarred out of his reverie by the doorbell. It was Laura. *Oh, cleaning time! Rats! I forgot.*

Tyr's
transformation · community

TEIWAZ

TEIWAZ, TEIWAZ

THE LOOSED ARROW
FINDS ITS MARK
THE MAN STANDS TALL
TYR, TYR, TYR!
JUSTICE LIGHTS THE DARK
AND COMES TO ALL!

Artwork by Katlyn at www.mermadearts.com

TEIWAZ

Justice/will power

Chapter 17a

Mae's Crossing → *Moving Towards Victory*

Work began on Chester's bridge within days of the council meeting. Congruent to that, water experts had been consulted to determine the best way to bring water into the park. It was a big hurdle, but not insurmountable. Three Feathers took his dowsing rods to the space, and located two possible wells; one fairly large. Once again, a council meeting voted to hire a well-drilling operation to put in a well. Pricey, but ultimately a boon to the community, especially considering the park would have its own water source. At the same meeting, it was voted on and approved to hold a naming contest for the park. A prize would be awarded to the winner at the official opening; i.e. when the fountain was turned on.

Chapter 17a

Malachais ↑ *Justice Served*

Saturday morning found a very excited Laura on Malachais's doorstep.

"Oh Mr. Merriwether! The best thing happened last night, well one of the two best things happened and wait 'til you hear!" Laura squeezed past him and put her bucket in the kitchen.

"Did you see it on the news? The big bust at Central Drug Store?" She reached over, shut the door and whispered. "Well, don't tell, but it was Gerry's anonymous tip that helped them to bust that creep who was selling crap to the kids. I am so proud of him. I wish I could shout it, but that would put Gerry in danger. And the other best thing is that Gerry proposed to me and I accepted! We're going to get married next summer after I graduate. My mom and dad…"

"Okay, okay. Slow down, Laura. No, I didn't watch the news last night, but Gerry turned the dealer in, really?" She nodded and fought to hold her tongue as Mal uttered, "Of course, it stands to reason the outcome would need an act of heroism." Totally perplexed, Laura was just about to speak when Malachais caught himself and said; "What I mean is, that was a heroic thing for him to do. I can see why you're proud.

I'd be proud too if it weren't for the unfinished business between Gerry and me. But I can be happy for you, Laura, and I am. Congratulations on your new future."

Chapter 17b

Mae's Crossing ᛏ *Honoring Spirit*

All Hallows Eve, Halloween, or if you will, Samhane, was a big celebration in Mae's Crossing. Something for everyone, you might say. The 31st fell on a Saturday this year, insuring a bigger than ever turnout. With three weeks to go, there was much to be done. The Temple billboard displayed the schedule: "Trick or treating, 6:00 pm to 9:00 pm; Young People's Costume Party (under 18 only) 8:00 pm to 10:00 pm; Masquerade Ball (18 and over) at the Temple, 9:00 pm to midnight; Samhane ritual in the inner Temple garden (dress warm) midnight to 2:00 am." Samantha had assigned much of the organizing of the young people's party to Jerrod. He was always around to help out any way he could. The boy really loved the Temple, not to mention having a schoolboy crush on Samantha. Sitters were lined up to care for the little ones while their parents were at the ball. There were decorations to be made (children at the grade school were making them for the young people's event), posters to be drawn up, and of course, costumes to create. The older children at the high school would be carving pumpkins during the week before Halloween (part of the Art Class assignment).

Chapter 17b

Rosalind → *Headlong into Future*

Saturday evening

As was previously arranged, Shelly showed up at Rosalind's Saturday night for a short overnight visit. She was greeted with so much enthusiasm when she got out of her car that she was immediately suspicious.

"Hey, Ro, what's up?" Shelly broke from their bear hug, holding Rose out at arm's length.

"Oh, Shelly, I'm so glad you're here. This has been such a crazy day, and I really need to talk with you. Come on in. Let's grab some wine and go sit out on the back porch."

Shelly pulled her overnight bag out of the car and followed Rosalind into the house. She was still in awe of the fact that Rose actually owned all this. *Good for her!* They detoured through the kitchen as Rosalind pulled a chardonnay out of the fridge and walked out the back door. Shelly snagged a couple of wine glasses, checking to be sure there was an ashtray outside.

Rose poured out some wine and the two clinked glasses. Shelly looked her in the eye. "Okay girl, cough it up. What's happening?"

And so Rosalind told her about Kyle; the drive, the accident, his words on the road…

"I thought I was going to die just as I met the girl of my dreams."

"Wow, Ro! I'm shakin' just hearing you talk about it! Damn! His car over the side; it's incredible that he didn't go down with it. Gotta meet this guy. See if he's good enough for you."

Rosalind spoke up: "That's not the half of it, Shel. There's Daniel, too."

"Daniel? Who's Daniel?"

Next in her 'true confessions,' Rose told her about her day with Daniel, and about the talisman and Dawn. Shelly shook her head. "Girl, you got me confused. You've never been that interested in getting involved, and now there's Daniel and Kyle. I don't get it."

Rosalind merely shrugged, then told her she'd lost the talisman at 'Glory Days Gala,' and how it mysteriously reappeared on her doorknob just the other day. She went in the house to get it, pulling it out of the pouch just as she stepped back onto the porch. "Oh my Goddess!"

Shelly grabbed her arm. "What?"

"This isn't the same talisman! It's a totally different symbol than the one that matched Daniel's. Oh, I didn't tell you, but I think the first one was a bindrune for fertility, and now I'm afraid I might be pregnant!"

Shelly downed her glass of wine and poured a hasty refill, lighting a cigarette and leaning back in her chair. *Omigod, Ro's way off the charts!.*

Rosalind continued, "I promised Daniel I wouldn't tell, but you're my best friend and you wouldn't breathe a word of this, would you?" Shelly nodded her head, waving her to continue. *How could this get any weirder?* "Well, I don't expect you'll believe this, but Daniel's an Elf!"

"That's it, girl! You've just outdone yourself on strange. How do you know he's an Elf?"

"Well, duh, when his cap fell off I saw his pointy ears! He was so scared. Dan'l said that nobody knows, and that his folks aren't happy with him hanging out with us humans."

"Damn! First Daniel, then Kyle, and now you might be pregnant? No wonder you're so wound up. Look, Ro, you're my best friend in the whole world, and I'll do anything I can to help you. Keep me posted about being pregnant. Wow! An Elf baby! You can count on me to keep my mouth shut, but if, well, if…you won't be able to hide it forever."

They hugged, Rose soaking up comfort and Shelly offering support. These two friends could handle anything together.

Come Sunday morning, over coffee and the inevitable pastry, Rose finished her 'catch-up.' She showed Shelly the painting she was working on. "Wow, Ro, that's awesome! I can almost feel her looking at me like she's saying, 'You're next, girl.' What a talent you've got!" Rose glowed with the compliments. Then she told Shelly about Miss Brianna, and how she was hoping to study with her for a year and a day.

"Do you think I could meet her? I mean maybe you could introduce us, 'cause you know I'm curious about Wicca. Wow! Wouldn't that be cool if we could both be her students?"

Rosalind considered the idea, and ushered Shelly out to the car. Rose thought of calling, but chose to cruise by Brianna's house first to see if her little yellow car was out front. *Oh good! She's home.* Rose stepped up to the porch and rang the doorbell.

Chapter 17c

Brianna ↓ *Feeling Absence of Male Force*

Brianna was torn between feelings of elation alternating with those of sorrowful separation. Somehow, there had to be a way that they could see each other more often. Right now, Bri was walking on clouds; visions of his smile and the warmth of his embrace teasing her mind. It was during this feeling of 'I've found my love and all is right with the world' that her front doorbell rang. "Coming."

Two young women were visible through the window. Bri opened the door to Rosalind and a wild looking woman. Rose's companion was a tall redhead whose hair looked like a large bird's nest. She was covered in tattoos, the most prominent being the writhing snakes on her arms. *The piercings are a mite distracting.* Her shirt and jeans were unquestionably top of the line in the 'casual but costly' genre; her leather jacket pure Harley.

"Sorry for just dropping in and not calling first, Miss Brianna. I really wanted to see you in person, and not talk on the phone. I was hoping you might have a little time for me and my best friend Shelly. Oh, Miss Brianna, Shelly LeFevre. Shelly, Miss Brianna McTavish."

LeFevre? Somehow that sounds familiar, but I can't quite place it. Sundays were Brianna's official 'kick back' days. No work, leastways not in the studio. She had no reason to turn them away. On the contrary, she was intrigued by Rosalind's girlfriend, and welcomed the distraction from her 'Mal obsession.' "Yes I do have time, please come in. Would you like some food or drink? Coffee, toast, fruit…"

"Oh no, Miss Brianna. We just had coffee and sweets, thanks all the same. No, we'd really just like to sit and talk if we could."

Shelly piped up with "Do you have a place we can sit outdoors so I can smoke while we talk?" and actually blushed.

Brianna walked them out to the back porch. It was a bit chilly but not unseasonable for October, so they all put their coats and jackets on. Bri grabbed a pile of afghans on her way out, tossing some to the girls.

Rosalind spoke. "I started on the book list you gave me. I was re-reading one, but then I told Shelly about 'us' and she wants to study too. So what do you think? Could we both study with you?"

"Give me a minute, please…I haven't even accepted you as a student yet, and you're asking me to take on a girl, I'm sorry, a young woman who I don't even know?"
Considering the opportunity and burden of taking on two new candidates, Brianna chewed it over. "Shelly, why did you choose snakes for your arms, and what do you know about Wicca?"

Shelly pulled the afghan in tighter. "Well, I know snakes are magical and that the Greeks considered them healers. I chose them because they're beautiful and I feel they protect me. And Wicca, well it's an earth religion. And they honor the Goddess. And you can do what you want as long as you don't hurt anyone."

"Hmm. I suppose that's how it might be seen. Do you know about the holidays?"

Shelly felt like she was under a magnifying glass. "Sure, I mean, kind of. There's Halloween and Mayday and a few others."

Brianna sighed. *Oh well, people have to start from somewhere, right?* "Okay, ladies. Here's the deal. First of all, Shelly, I want you to read the books on the list I gave Rosalind. I'll give you each a task; please write out the answers in your own hand; no computer print-outs. And don't discuss your assignments with each other. Come back in one month, give me your assignments, and I'll make my decision then. Will that work for you?"

Rosalind was surprised at the twinge of anger she felt for Shelly; now she'd have to wait another month before starting her training. Pushing that disturbing thought away, she smiled at Shelly, focusing on how glad she was that they were embarking on this trip together.

Chapter 17c

Kyle ↓ *Distraction/Self Absorbed*

Sunday

Kyle had a terrific time fishing, along with a terrific headache. He caught eleven trout, one of them just ounces under the record. Jack flash froze them for him, and Kyle looked forward to preparing several fine meals in his charming new kitchen. Outback Jack's Fishing Camp got star ratings from Kyle. Jack's partner, Arlo, was a trained chef. There was nothing common or down home about the food he prepared. Being the only guest that day, Kyle was invited to stay in the main house, a massive log cabin with prize fish trophies and crossed fishing poles on the walls. With rough hewn furniture and fur rugs, there was no question that this was truly a 'man cave.'

Fishing has a very meditative side to it. It was in this guise that Kyle immersed himself, unwinding from his life-changing experience through the auspices of nature at her best. The seasonal changes showed another face of the forest lining the lake, just as he felt about the changes within. He had tried several times to live with a woman, some mildly successful, none totally satisfying. There was always this nagging feeling that they were more interested in his money. Wealth, both liberating and burdensome, had come easily to him. Kyle was born into money, but was fearless in creating his own fortune when he entered the workforce. His fearlessness took the form of eccentric creativity. Unhindered by being under financed, he was free to experiment and was known in the industry for his sharp mind and innovative technologies. In a way, the creative process turned him on more than the women in his life.

Kyle took the time to examine his past life and motives, seeing himself clearly for the first time. *Where does Rosalind fit in all this?*

Love at first sight had always seemed like such a fairy tale to Kyle until he met Rosalind. He knew the moment their eyes met that here was a kindred spirit, someone he wanted to please, to hear laughing, to hold, to be with…*Uh oh, am I falling in love?*

While Kyle was lost in his reveries at the lake, Dawn crept up to his Jeep and tied a yellow silk pouch with 'Kyle' embroidered in gold onto the steering wheel.

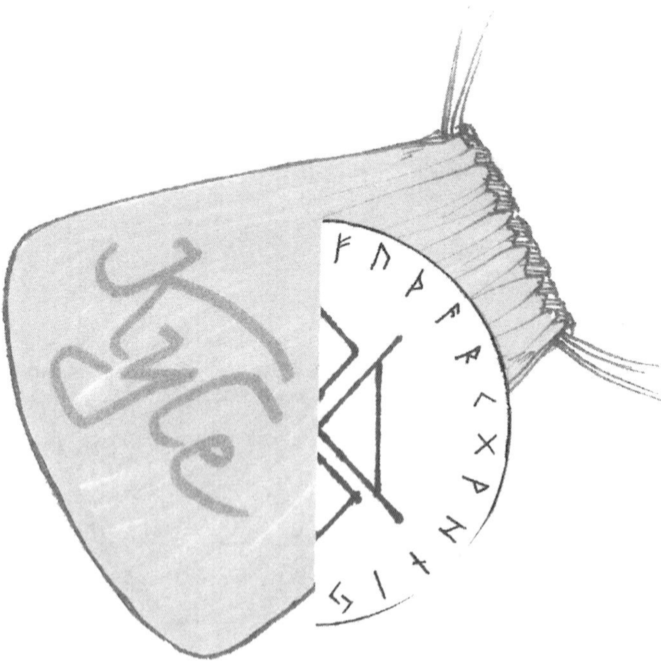

BERKANA

Divine feminine/growth

Chapter 18a

Mae's Crossing ᛒ *Goddess at Work*

Two weeks to Samhane

Once the well was dug and operational, work proceeded at a brisk pace as the town park got a facelift. Men with the know-how laid the foundation bricks for the fountain, factoring in openings for the ebb and flow of water. Teams of workers, mostly from the high school, built the wall enclosure. Tiles which had been hand made by local students were randomly placed in the wall. Other trinkets and souvenirs got imbedded as folk were inspired by the opportunity to personalize. The fountain became like a story book, telling the tales of the people of the place. The central figure was heatedly debated. Different themes were considered and discarded. Hoping the morning would bring a new perspective, the workers were dismissed for the day and went home.

Deep in the leafy woods, three women watched the vision in the cauldron. Moonface exclaimed, "I've got it! We can solve their problem and have some fun. Come on girls, we're going to the park!"

Late that night as the town lay sleeping, the Goddesses gathered in the unfinished fountain. Moonface directed the other two. "Dawn, step up to the pedestal and lean over as if you were pouring water out of a flagon. Sunny, stand next to her and do the same." The women followed her orders. "Yes, that's it. Now hold that pose." Moonface climbed up, completing the circle. "On the count of three; one, two, three. Bibbidy!" Sunny took the cue. "Bobbidy!" and then Dawn, "Boo!" They stepped down and looked back at the fountain, now portraying three women pouring water, forever captured in stone.

The next morning as word circulated, the crowds gathered around the fountain statuary grew, and grew, and grew. By noon over a hundred people were jostling each other to get an up front view of the miracle. Ed Janssen got out his bullhorn. "Listen up, folks." Conversations ceased as all eyes turned to him. "We've got a pretty amazing thing here to look at, and it's not about to get up and walk away. What I'm sayin' is you don't need to crowd and gawk. It was an anonymous donation, so if you know who did it, we'd like to thank 'em proper. Right now we're tryin' to get this fountain up and runnin', and when we do, there'll be a big celebration. And…" Someone in the crowd yelled 'Par-tee!' Ed smiling, continued "…and we're holding a naming contest for the park to be judged by the city council. We'll have a nice prize for the winner. So if you could please leave now, we can get on with our work. Plenty of chance for you to look at it at the grand opening celebration, 'cause you're all invited." The onlookers broke into little groups of twos and threes, slowly moving away from the wondrous fountain, chattering excitedly.

Chapter 18a

Brianna ᛒ *Goddess Revealed*

Brianna heard about the miraculous fountain, and went to the park to see for herself. Ed waved her through so she could get closer. There was no doubt about it; the Goddesses had created this sculpture. Brianna gazed upon them admiringly, and vowed to memorize their features. Moonface she'd already spent some time with, and the characterization was flawless. The other two must be the Mother and the Maiden. *Wonder what their names are?* Bri was struck once again by the sheer weight of magic that permeated Mae's Crossing. She was sure that was what made her settle here, along with visions of meeting up with her mysterious grandfather. Hoping to tap into some of that enchantment for her own benefit, Brianna returned home. She lit a candle on her altar and sat before it. After a few moments of quiet meditation she spoke:

"Mighty Goddesses, Power of Three
Bring my love closer to me!"

She sprinkled some rose petals on her briquette, then extinguished the candle with thanks.

Chapter 18b

Kyle *Woman of Mystery*

Kyle stopped by Dot's Delights in hopes of finding Rosalind behind the counter, but to his great disappointment she wasn't there. Daisy, the girl behind the cases, said it was Miss Rosalind's day to pick up the wheat from Farmer Johnson's. She was kind enough to tell him Rose would be in tomorrow. Buying a couple of their fabulous lemon bars, he thanked her, tipped generously, and left the shop munching.

Back in his little cottage, Kyle brewed up some coffee and got to work unpacking and arranging. By late evening he had made tremendous progress. Normally, he would have put it off and probably lived out of boxes for the next month. Now Kyle was motivated to have the place ship-shape by the weekend. His big plan was to prepare a trout dinner for Rosalind, employing some tips he got from Arlo.

The next day he caught her at work. "Hi Rosalind. How's it going? They keep you pretty busy around here, don't they?"

Rose still got nervous around him, but had a feeling that was going to change. "Yeah, well they do, that's for sure." She flashed him a smile as she studiously polished the glass in the cases. "So, how are you feeling? How's your head?"

"Oh, my head's still a little tender, but I'm okay. Just glad to be alive and talking to you. Say, I was wonderin'…if you're free this weekend…I'd like to cook up some of the trout I caught on Sunday. That is, if you'd like. I mean, would you like to come to my place for dinner this coming Saturday?"

“Why thank you, Kyle. I’d love to come to dinner. Would you like me to bring anything? What time should I be there?”

“How about 6:00 pm? And no, please don’t bother to bring anything. I’ve got it covered. See you then, okay?”

“Okay.” Kyle left the bakery, walking on air as Rosalind went back to her work, humming a jaunty tune.

Chapter 18b

Rosalind *Reluctant Mother*

That evening, Rosalind looked at the test again. Try as she might to deceive herself, there was no doubt that she was pregnant. If her calculations were right, that would put the birth somewhere around late April-early May. *Why, Goddess? Just when I was beginning to like Kyle!* She was totally overwhelmed by the prospect; it set her head to reeling. *Gotta call Shel.*

Shelly counseled Rosalind. "Hey girl, don't go off the deep end. This isn't the end of the world. Hell, who knows? It could be a good thing. You just gotta take one day at a time, and if you ask me, I think there's some 'Higher Power' at work here. I mean, check out that talisman, Ro. Don't look like no accident to me."

By the end of the conversation, Rose was feeling better and decided to talk with Daniel. Finding him was the problem; what a surprise when she saw him outside the bakery the next day!

Chapter 18c

Daniel ΔΔ *Parenthood Imminent*

Daniel drove into town on his shiny mountain bike. He'd just detailed it, and was bursting with pride. Peeking into Dot's Delights to see if Rosalind was in, he saw her walking into the back. *Now what?* Daniel didn't know what to do. He didn't want any pastries. No good excuse for going in. Dithering in the doorway, he didn't notice Rose coming up behind him. "Boo!" She laughed as he jumped and turned around. "Ooh! You scared me!" Rose smirked at him, "Yeah, right. Hey, Daniel, I need to talk with you in private. Could we go sit under those trees?"

When Rosalind told Daniel she was carrying his child, he was horrified. "Oh my gosh, oh my gosh! Oh, Miss Rose, I didn't mean for that to happen. Don't you worry, none, though. I'll talk to my parents. I'm sure they'll help. I bet you're really mad at me, aren't you?"

Rose studied Daniel, taking in the jaunty blue cap pulled tight over his ears. Any anger would have been pointless. It wasn't as if it wasn't mutual consent; a casual roll in the hay, mushroom induced. She took his hand. *Here I am, consoling him!* "Daniel, I can't be mad at you. I really like you, but I don't want to marry you. So what am I going to do about this child we've started?"

"Oh thank you, Miss Rose. Let me talk to my folks and I'll get back to you."

Just like Daniel to avoid the question. Or did he?

With that he hopped onto his bike and peddled off towards Dutchman's Creek.

Daniel slid into the back yard of his cabin, dust flying. He ran over to the horn hanging from the old oak and blew a clear, resounding note. The sound echoed through the canyon and hung on the air. In an instant, Lord Sylvan and Lady Alithea came riding out of the woods, bells a'jingling on their white horses. Lord Sylvan dismounted and held out a hand as Lady Alithea slipped down.

"All right son, what's more important than the feast we were just attending?"

Lady Alithea wrapped her arms around Daniel. "Oh, Dan'l my sweet. We've missed you so. Won't you please come back home?"

Daniel kissed his mother on the cheek. "No, mum, I'm not coming back. The folks here need me, and I'm doing something useful." Then he knelt before his father. "Da, I need your help. I got Rosalind with child."

The Lord and Lady looked at each other in shock, then hugged and danced in circles, merrily laughing. The Lady was exhuberant. "It worked! It worked!" Unbeknownst to Daniel, his parents had gone to the Goddesses with their problem. Moonface herself worked out the details to bring Rosalind and Daniel together, thus giving the rulers of Elfhame hope for the future. "We're going to have an Elf child! Oh, Dan'l, that's the best news you could have ever given us! Bless you. Bless Rosalind. We must meet her as soon as possible. Get her out here and call us." With that the two of them remounted their horses and rode off, singing and gesturing to the woodland creatures that accompanied them.

Chapter 18c

Malachais ▽▽ *Early Growth/Divine Feminine*

Things were falling into place for Malachais. How many of his students had he told "If you choose a direction where obstacles melt away and things just seem to fit, it's a clear indication of divine guidance and a confirmation of the rightness of your choices." Here he was, watching obstacles melt to reveal a clear path to his deepest desires. Mal was meeting with his broker on Thursday to discuss the ins and outs of making his townhome available for short term vacation/business rentals. He would keep the barest of furnishings in the home, but all drawers, cupboards and closets would be empty. A conversation with Brianna was imperative. Mal would be counting on her to keep her eye out for appropriate rentals in Mae's Crossing. Following up on that thought, he decided to give her a call.

"Hi, Mal. I'm so glad you called. I was just thinking about you, but then, that's nothing new. What's up?"

"Hi darlin'. Listen, I just had a brainstorm, and wanted to run it by you. I'm considering leaving Channing and renting a place in Mae's Crossing."

Brianna gasped. *Could it be true?* "Oh my Goddess, Mal! That's a wonderful idea! I've just been trying to figure out how we could spend more time together."

"Well, I've been giving it a lot of thought myself. I feel the same, and, well, you're pretty well established in Mae's Crossing, what with your home and business. I, on the other hand, am retired and really just want home and comfort…and you. It will take me a couple of months to get everything in order here. I really like Mae's Crossing, and you know I feel that the Gods have destined us to be together. What I'd like you to do is to scout around for a place for me. It has to be at least two bedrooms, even three or four would be okay, and I'd like a garage. Well, whatever. What do you think?"

"You know what I think. My prayers have been answered. Yes, yes! I'll start looking immediately. Oh, and would you like to come up for Samhane? Really big here in Mae's Crossing, and I'll be conducting the ritual on Saturday the 31st. If you come up a couple of days ahead of time, I could write you into the script if you like."

Malachais was grinning ear to ear. *What a glorious life! What a remarkable woman! Mal, old man, you've scored big time!* "I'd love to have a part in the ritual. I could be Hades, or maybe Cereberus. Just joking. Yes, that sounds great. It will be hard breaking from my group here; harder for them than for me. How far ahead do you want me to come up? Tuesday, Wednesday…"

"I want you here this very minute, but I'll settle for Tuesday the 27th. Oh, Mal, this is just too good to be true…I love you so much. I can't wait to be in your arms again."

"And me in yours. Please be patient with me. I've never done well with relationships, but they weren't you, and you...well you're all I've ever wanted without even knowing it. You light up my life, Brianna. Let's make this last forever, shall we?"

"Yes, Malachais, forever and ever."

E H W A Z

Change/teamwork

Chapter 19a

Mae's Crossing *Teamwork Growing*

Jerrod and Olga turned out to be indispensible helpers for Samantha. Not only were they tireless, they were imaginative. Ideas on how to decorate the young people's event had blossomed into a miniature 'haunted house' set up at the entrance. All participants would walk through spider webs with lit jack o'lanterns leering in the background. Jerrod and Olga had volunteered to be the creepy voices urging the partiers to continue 'at their peril.' All would emerge into a festive arena complete with musicians and dance floor (actually quite similar to the grown-ups' arrangement). A panel of five teen-agers would judge the costumes and award the prize of a gold ribbon and ten free passes to the movies. Samantha was impressed. She was also relieved that she was free to focus on the adult Masquerade Ball. Sam took the cue from the young folks, and planned an equally eerie entrance to the temple where the masquerade ball would be held. Planning the food and drink tables fell on her shoulders as well. Pastries for both parties were generously donated by Dot's Delights. Emmet Hudson's Hillside Market would provide sandwiches, snacks and non-alcoholic beverages. Ed's Hardware Store supplied paper plates, napkins, etc. He had also assured her that he would cover wine and beer.

A ‘Donations’ jar would be discreetly displayed *(to cover costs, thank you)*. Nicely decorated trash cans would be readily available. She enlisted the help of Jackie Flanagan, a lovely, quick-witted 17 year old. Jackie made over one of the temple rooms as a lounge/play area for children in need of supervision, and had several of her friends lined up to be in attendance for one hour each.

This was a small part of what went into a night of such delights. No wonder it was one of the town’s favorites.

Chapter 19a

Brianna Σ *Union Gathering Strength*

Brianna's recently straightened workshop was a disaster area after two major back to back shows. *At least it's orderly underneath.* She set about putting things away, happily filling out drawers and cupboards with her newly bought supplies. By lunchtime her task was completed. *Good, 'cause I'm starving.* After lunch Bri would look over her custom and wholesale orders, making sure to arrange them by priority. She had enough work coming in plus supplies on hand to hold her over until the next major Christmas shows. *Goddess, I love this life!*

Malachais was like frosting on the cake. He brought cohesion to her scattered ways, along with the bliss of being held in a loving embrace. She stopped in front of the hall mirror and examined herself. *How do I look to him?* Looking out at her from the mirror was a slightly wild-eyed middle-aged woman. Some curls had pulled out of her tie, and her face was framed in an auburn aura. Her eyes were definitely blue today, and were those crow's feet developing? *Oh, what the heck. I look fine.* Not one to dwell on personal image, Bri usually dressed casually with light make-up when she thought of it. Whatever she wore, she ended up looking like a butterfly; brightly colored gauzy materials clearly her favorites. With Mal arriving on Tuesday, she'd have to tidy up the house some. Nervous excitement ran through her at the thought of his constant presence. He'd stay for five days, and she was curious to see how he fit into her routines. *They could be altered.*

It happened right around dusk. Brianna was enjoying an after dinner wine on her back porch when a pair of riders on white horses came galloping wildly out of the woods.

Oh my Goddess! They're Elves! The elegantly clad gentleman jerked on his horse's reins, causing him to paw the air. The Lady *(she could be no less)* veered to miss him and came to a halt just inches from Bri's porch. Clearly disoriented and looking a bit disheveled, her violet eyes locked onto Bri's. "Oh dear, please excuse our intrusion! We were on our way to Moonface's when something frightened the horses and they wouldn't listen to us. Highly unusual for our fine steeds." The Lady looked to the Lord, her surprise echoed in his eyes. *She can see us!*

She reached down and patted the horse's quivering neck as it slowly calmed. The Lady gestured toward her husband. "We are the Lord and Lady of the Forest, actually Sylvan and I'm Alithea. And you would be…"

Brianna found her voice. "Brianna McTavish, your Lordships." She made a slight bow from her chair. "You say you're on your way to Moonface's? Would you be so kind as to give her a message from me? And maybe ask if I could drop in some time?"

Lord Sylvan cocked his head at her. "We aren't couriers, Miss Brianna. And asking if you can 'drop in' on the Goddesses is laughable."

"Now Sylvan, you musn't be so harsh with her. We just rudely intruded on her privacy." The Lady turned to Brianna. "What was your message dear? I'd be happy to give it to her. And I'll even ask her if you can visit." With that she turned towards Lord Sylvan, an impish smirk on her face.

“If you please, let her and the other two know that their fountain is a joy and a blessing to our community, and that we thank them very much.”

“Done and done, my dear. And now we really must be off. The horses have recovered from their fright, and we still have a long ways to ride. It’s been nice meeting you, Brianna. Our paths will cross again. Farewell.” The two smartly turned their horses back to the woods and cantered off.

Chapter 19b

Mae's Crossing  *Hidden Change/ Reluctant Cooperation*

Up until the day before the scheduled grand opening of the park, there was dissension in the city council. Naming the park, which seemed like such a good idea at the time, had taken on epic proportions as advocates of different names pressed for approval. The choices had been narrowed down to 'Blessing Park,' 'Central Park,' 'People's Park' and 'Blessed Ladies Park.' Finally, choosing between 'Blessing Park' and 'Blessed Ladies Park,' it was unanimously agreed that 'Ladies' Park' sounded too exclusive of males and children, and the name of 'Blessing Park' was chosen. A certain amount of grumbling came from the 'Ladies' contingent as they grudgingly gave in to peer pressure.

Crowds gathered at the fountain, eager to see it operational. Ed Janssen signaled to Kris, who manned the spigots, and the water shot into the air with oohs and aahs from the onlookers. It was a fine spectacle, and quite easily the most beautiful fountain any of them had ever seen. Face wreathed in a very satisfied smile, Ed called for the group's attention. "I know you're all wondering what this park will be called. After much debate, the council has chosen the name 'Blessing Park.' Olga screamed with delight, as that was her entry, and ran up to Ed's side. "Congratulations on your excellent name, Olga. As a thank you for your contribution, the council would like to award you with a check for one hundred dollars." Beaming, Olga accepted the check and curtseyed first to Ed and then to the audience amidst cheers and accolades. Blessing Park had become a central feature of a very proud town.

Chapter 19b

Rosalind *Warming up to a Union*

Saturday snuck up on Rosalind and caught her by surprise. *Dinner tonight at Kyle's!* She had been so preoccupied with the seemingly endless ripples of effect emanating from her pregnancy that all else got scant attention from her. Mabel had even snapped at her a bit. Rose tried to put it out of her mind and focus on the moment. She left the house and her trepidations behind, anticipating the wonder of having an intimate meal with Kyle Porter. *And he even cooks!*

Rosalind pulled up alongside a shiny new jeep with a big scrape in the side. *Ouch!* Although Rose had seen this cottage when she was younger, she was seeing it through different eyes today. *It's so charming, and the foliage must be wonderful in the summer.* Even now, with winter breathing her frosty breath in the dark of night, the days still held enough warmth to nurture the lush growth. Kyle was standing on the porch, arms crossed over his chest and a big grin on his face. "Pretty enchanting, isn't it? Least I thought so when I first saw it. Come on in, Rose. Welcome to my home."

Once inside, Kyle took her on a tour, discreetly indicating the nicely appointed bathroom. Still smiling, he took her arm, directing her to the cozy living room with a small fire going in the fireplace. "Just barely cold enough for a fire. Couldn't wait to try it out. It's the first time I've used it." He pointed to a large trophy on the mantle. "This is a trophy I won in high school for long distance running, my major childhood accomplishment. So, what do you think?"

"You've done a great job of decorating. Did you take interior design in college? Oh, and what college did you go to?"

"I graduated from Stanford. And no, I didn't take interior design, but thanks for the compliment. I've always been interested in home décor, but my folks felt it was 'inappropriate' as a major discipline for me. So I focused on computer graphics, which is just as well. Great field for innovation, and I was able to come up with some practical advances. It actually financed my way into an early retirement. So here I am, retired and ready to enjoy my life while I'm still young enough." The tour ended in the kitchen, which had a sweet little breakfast nook that he had staged for the meal. There was a vase of flowers "From the Widow's garden; last of the season" and some scented candles flickering on the backside. There were small paned windows all around the nook, looking out onto a beautifully tended garden.

"I can see why you took this place. It's just adorable. Thanks so much for having me over. Can't wait to see what you've cooked up."

The meal continued with pleasant conversation, and ended with two very satisfied diners. The trout was unbelievable; some subtle seasoning had brought out the sweetness of the flesh. Rosalind was impressed.

Kyle suggested a stroll through the garden after dinner. Rose had had no idea what pains the Widow had gone to with her property. Paved paths wound their way through carefully tended rose bushes and topiary converging on a small fountain with colorful fish swimming about.

"I feel like I'm in some kind of fairyland," she said as she chose a bench with a good view of the fountain.

"Me too," responded Kyle while seating himself next to her. Before long, he had his arm about her shoulders. Rose nestled into the crook of his arm, and the two silently basked in the feeling of contentment and budding love.

Chapter 19c

Kyle M *Proposal*

As dusk was falling, Kyle and Rosalind walked hand in hand back to the cottage. Kyle steered her into the living room, and asked her to sit on the sofa. He left the room momentarily, then returned with both hands behind his back.

Holding out a dainty bunch of forget-me-nots *(where on earth did he get them in late October?),* he knelt before her and brought his other hand forward. There was a little red velvet box nestled in the palm of his hand. “Miss Rosalind Duncan, I am hopelessly in love with you, and need you by my side for the rest of my days. Would you please be my wife?” Kyle opened the box to reveal a stunning diamond engagement ring. Rose had never seen such a large diamond. She sat there, speechless, groping for the right words to say.

“Oh my Goddess, Kyle! This is the most gorgeous stone I’ve ever seen! But…but you hardly know me, and I you. This is so sudden. I don’t know. I mean, I think I love you too, but…”

“Then just say yes, please. When I was hanging on the edge of that cliff, I saw in a flash how we were meant to be together. I vowed that if I survived, I would make you my wife. I’ve never been more sure of anything in my life.”

“Kyle, Kyle…I can’t. I just can’t. You don’t know what’s happening with me. You wouldn’t want to marry me if you knew.” Tears appeared in the corners of her eyes.

Kyle got up from his knees and sat next to her, pulling her in close to him. "Nothing you can say can change how I feel about you. What are you worried about? Whatever it is, I'm here for you, and will help in any way I can."

Rose struggled with the need to tell him, fearing that this precious bubble would burst once he knew. Somehow, she gathered her strength and the words came tumbling out. "Oh Kyle, I hate to tell you this, I'm so sorry…but I'm pregnant."

Kyle stiffened at the news. He certainly wasn't prepared for this. The silence extended as Rose sniffled and wiped at her eyes. "Oh…I thought you weren't involved with anyone else. Silly me, I should have asked. He's a very lucky man." He shifted his weight and put a little distance between them.

Now Rose began to cry in earnest. "No, no Kyle. It's not what you think. I'm not in love with him. It was just a crazy moment. We'd taken magic mushrooms, and, well, I guess my inhibitions vanished. This is such a shock… I really don't know what I'm going to do. And now, and now," her sniffling was reaching epic proportions, "now you're proposing. It's like a dream come true turning into a nightmare. I'm so sorry, I'm so sorry…"

Kyle scooped her into his arms, comforting her as best he could. "Didn't I say I'm here for you? You had me going for a minute there, thinking you had a secret love. It's a bit more than I bargained for, but to have you in my life, you could have a litter and I wouldn't care. Let me take care of you. Marry me and I'll see you through this. Who knows? Maybe I'll be a good father."

With the fire burning low, Kyle and Rose lie curled in each other's arms, contemplating their future. Just as her lids began to droop, Rose's eyes were drawn to the diamond on her finger, mesmerizing in the firelight.

Chapter 19c

Malachais M *Horsepower*

Tuesday before Samhane

The road stretched out before him. Malachais felt like a magick genie was beckoning him to Mae's Crossing. *Well, Brianna is certainly that.* He thought back to yesterday, pleased that the meeting he'd arranged between Jarnath and Willem had reaped the hoped for results. The two had hit it off immediately, and he could see a friendship beginning.

Mal was about an hour past BigCity when the red Camaro came up on him from behind, hugging his bumper. The driver held a cell to his ear, and through the rear view Mal could see he must be shouting. He pulled as far to the right as was safe, hoping to give the enraged driver room to pass. It was only a two lane road now, all the way into the mountains, and there really weren't enough pull-outs along the route. The Camaro shot past him, just as an SUV topped the hill, coming towards them. The red car swerved in front of Malachais as he braked, barely missing him by inches. The SUV wasn't as fortunate. Seeing a car coming straight at him, the driver chose badly, careening off the shoulder. Suddenly it flipped and landed upside down, wheels spinning and dust flying as the red Camaro raced over the rise. Badly shaken, Mal pulled over to the side of the road, and ran over to the wrecked car, simultaneously grabbing his cell and punching 911. "There's a bad accident. Route 71 north, about one hour out of BigCity. You'll need an ambulance." His heart fell when he got to the car. It looked like there were three people, and from their positions and the blood everywhere, he held little hope for their survival.

Sirens sounded in the distance, getting louder as the ambulance approached. Mal's knees buckled, and he sat on the ground, head in hands. "Dear Goddess, wrap your loving arms around these folks and give them peace."

It was better than an hour before Malachais got back on the road again. First there was the ambulance with trained folk springing into action. One of the passengers was still barely hanging on to life; the other two were gone. Then the police showed up, and Mal spent most of that time explaining what had happened as the officer stood writing in his pad. Car description, a fleeting glimpse of numbers and letters on the license plate, rough description of the driver…Mal was wrung out by the time he slid into the driver's seat. He called ahead to Brianna to let her know why the delay, then slowly pulled back onto the road. Mal shook his head, trying to dislodge the gruesome scene from his mind. It didn't work.

When he finally pulled up in front of Brianna's, she ran out to him and the two just stood there for the longest time, arms wrapped around each other. Malachais sobbed fitfully, not caring how it looked, only how it felt. Later that night, their lovemaking took on a new intensity as they learned to cherish the moment.

MANNAZ

Community/mental prowess

Chapter 20a

Mae's Crossing ᛞ *Community*

It was 7:30 pm, All Hallow's Eve, and all was in readiness at the Temple. Jerrod was nervously watching the older kids line up at the spooky entrance. Olga couldn't pass up trick or treating, so she would be showing up later. Samantha soothed him, promising to be a creepy voice in the haunted house if Olga didn't appear in time. Sure enough, 8:00 pm rolled around, and the youngster still hadn't arrived. As the excited crowd started moving through the tangle of webs, Sam and Jerrod stationed themselves on either side of the path, moaning and beckoning the kids along. "Proceed at your peril," Jerrod said in a scary voice. Samantha chimed in, "Come into my parlor, you of stout hearts," followed by an eerie laugh. Soon enough all had navigated the scary straits, and emerged into a well-lit area surrounded by glowing jack-o-lanterns. Food tables were at the back and musicians off to the side. The evening was a resounding success. Even the older kids were enjoying it as they showed off their costumes on the dance floor. At 9:30, Jerrod picked up the bullhorn and announced the winner. Screaming with joy, Bjorn ran up and accepted his gold ribbon and movie passes, wowing the crowd in his guise as Justin Bieber, complete with tattoos. Bjorn did a quick impersonation to jeers and cheers from an appreciative audience.

Samantha had slipped away near 9:00 pm, making sure that Jerrod, Olga and Jackie had things under control. As she was ushering the first arrivals through to the Masquerade Ball, she saw Jackie leading a group of younger children into another part of the Temple. *Good!* The little ones were safe for the night. A young girl stood close by Samantha, ready to take more children back to the nursery. Sam had draped the entrance with Spanish moss, spiderwebs and huge black plastic tarantulas. The inner passage was lit by wavering blue lights. She ushered in pirates and princesses, elves and fairies, fantastic animals (one very creative unicorn), gods and goddesses. Sam didn't envy the judge's job. One by one the masquers shuddered their way through the eerie tunnel into the softly lit, gaily decorated 'ballroom.'

Daniel wouldn't miss it for the world. *One of my most favorite parties!* He just put a lot of paste on his ears and painted them; folks thought he could have done a better job, but they complimented him politely. Even the true Goddesses attended, vying with the likes of Aphrodite and Freya. What a night of fantasy! Many wore Brianna's inspired creations. At 11:30 pm, the judges called all to attention. "I swear you folk have outdone yourselves this year. We had one heck of a time just choosing three. In my mind you're all winners. That bein' said, I'd like to give the third place award of a fine dinner for two at The Grand Hotel to….Violet Burns, or should I say "Cat Woman" for her masterful rendition." Applause. Pregnant pause. "Second place, a weekend for two at Bea's Bed and Breakfast to….Mikos Stauros for The Lord of the Forest…I swear those horns are real." Applause. Breathless pause. "And first place, a week's stay at Cancun, goes to the young lady we don't know but will never forget…Miss Thistledown Head!"

Moonface whispered forcefully, " Now you've gone and done it, Dawn. You better make this good, or you're in deep kimchee."

Dawn darted through the crowd as admirers reached out to touch her star spangled dress and hair. She smiled and curtseyed, twirling her way to the podium. Holding out her hand for the prize, Dawn stepped up to the microphone.

"Thank you, everyone, for your kindness. My name is Dawn, and I'm sorry but I can't accept this prize, 'cause I'm deathly afraid of airplanes and boats and cars. Please allow me to award this lovely gift to the fantastic Unicorn, who certainly deserves it more than I."

Gasps of surprise followed the unicorn as he bounded up to the platform and accepted the prize. Dawn slipped out the back door and rejoined the other two women. "Nicely done, Dawn, nicely done." Granny patted her on the back and they vanished into the mist.

Chapter 20a

Brianna ᛗ *Community*

At precisely midnight on Samhane Eve, red lights were turned on to illuminate the black curtains pulled across the doorway leading to the inner garden. Coven members and guests waited quietly as the Summoner entered through the curtains. She carried an elegantly decorated scroll and read from it in a Town Crier's voice. Directly on the other side of the curtains, Caroline Spivack stood with abalone shell and smoldering sage, ready to smudge each one as they came through. The Summoner held the curtains open, and one by one admitted each to the sacred space.

There were stations to visit on the way to the ritual circle. The first stop was at the Ancestor's Altar. A family size tent provided the structure for some carefully placed straw and pieces of wood, giving it the semblance of a little cottage. Inside, large cushions surrounded a round table filled with tea lights. Each participant had brought a memento to be placed within the hut. Photos of loved ones and favorite pets, a token, a statue; whatever helped them to connect. Here they sat in silent meditation as they communed with the spirits, lighting a candle and perhaps writing some words (paper and pencils at hand) which would be slipped under the tea light. When ready to go on, the participant raised a hand, and the Summoner took them to the next station.

A witches' hut, covered in green cloth with golden symbols on it, was the next stop. The Summoner rang a bell. From inside came the quavering voice, "Who goes there?" Summoner replies, "It is a supplicant asking for your guidance." "State your name." Supplicant responds. "Then enter." Various types of divination were displayed as the guest chose one. After the reading, the bell inside the hut was wrung, and the Summoner came for the guest, taking him/her to the main ritual area.

At the final destination, benches and a few cushions circled the altar area. A refreshment table was at the back with hot mulled cider, both spirited and non-alcoholic.
Various instruments were scattered about, and folks were encouraged to have whispered conversations or to play an instrument. Singing, if very low, was acceptable. The last of the supplicants entered the circle area, followed by the Summoner. The Summoner turned and called the High Priestess, who came swooping in like a bird flying low, broom close by her side. Dressed in a hooded black cloak with a simple black eye mask, the mystery woman shook the broom at the edges of the circle and recited the besom chant. More than this can't be told outside of the sacred circle.

After the rites were completed, Brianna and Malachais stood in the center of a group of well-wishers. Malachais was introduced to the community. Some even suggested he might be eligible for a special dedication ritual to welcome him into the coven (provided, of course, that all coveners were in accord). He certainly had the credentials, and since Mal would soon be moving to Mae's Crossing, it seemed inevitable. Brianna was beside herself with pride and joy. *They like him!* Life was opening up in new and dynamic ways for both of them.

Chapter 20b

Daniel *Anticipating Family*

Daniel struggled with the concept of fatherhood, preferring his simpler relationships with the woodland creatures. *Parenting is scary; all that responsibility!* Not knowing what his parents had in mind was troublesome. Finally in desperation, Daniel dismissed the whole problem; *Que sera, sera.* It was far easier to just follow orders. And the orders were to bring Rosalind to his parents.

Tuesday morning found Daniel camped outside of Dot's Delights. (Daisy had finally told him Tuesdays were Rosalind's days in the bakery.) Sure enough, she just drove in and parked in back. "Hi Dan'l. What's up?" Rosalind looked at him through expectant mother's eyes, seeing a handsome child in the offing. *So hard to feel angry.*

"Hi Miss Rose. Am I glad to see you. My parents really want to meet you, and I was hopin' you could come out to my place soon. Like tonight maybe?" He quirked his head at her, looking more Elfin than usual. *Are my eyes just playing tricks with me?*

Intrigued by the chance of meeting Elf Elders, Rose felt herself being drawn in by the prospect. *Why not now? Gotta meet them eventually.* "I get out of here around 6. I could be there no later than 7. Sure, Dan'l, I'd like to meet them, too."

Funny how Rose had lost much of her uncertainty and distrust since Kyle's proposal. It was like Kyle was her safety net, and she knew that she would never again fall alone. The fears built up around the impending birth evaporated, freeing her to go with the flow. It was also part of her training to learn to merge with her life's direction rather than resist it. Rosalind was an excellent student.

Daniel jumped on his bike. "That's great Miss Rose! See ya later."

Chapter 20b

Rosalind ⵣ *Yearning for Family*

Last minute details kept Rosalind at Dot's Delights until after 6:00 pm. Hurriedly tidying up and locking the door behind her, Rose was on the road and arrived at Daniel's with minutes to spare. Not as if he would know; there wasn't a clock to be found in his domain. Daniel popped out the door, Mr. Crafty squeezing past him and high-tailing it into the woods. "Hey Miss Rose. Really glad you could come by tonight. Let's go out back and I'll call my folks."

Call his folks? Rose's curiosity was soon quenched as Daniel raised the horn to his lips and blew a long, mournful note into the deepening dusk. Within moments, two riders on white horses emerged from the trees, magnificently clad in bright colors with flashing jewels adorning their fingers and necks. Lord Sylvan and Lady Alithea dismounted and walked towards Rosalind, hands extended in greeting. Just as Rose was going to grasp the Lady's hand, Alithea withdrew hers and knelt before her, placing her hands on Rose's stomach. "Welcome, blessed child." Lord Sylvan placed his hands over hers and repeated, "Welcome, blessed child." Stunned, Rosalind gazed upon their ecstatic faces, drinking in the warmth and acceptance pouring off of them like sweetened water.

Lady Alithea rose, then bowed to her. "Thank you, Rosalind, for your most generous gift. We are in awe of your willingness to bear this child. Long and long have we waited for a moment such as this. Elfdom has been dwindling, and we are in great need of offspring, lest we vanish completely. You are exalted among our people for your sacrifice."

Before Rosalind could respond to this outlandish statement, three women appeared in a puff of smoke. *Dawn!* Rose recognized her immediately and puzzled over her companions. One looked ancient, were it not for her glossy black hair reaching down her back. The other was younger with bright red hair, braided and wound about her head.

Granny spoke up. "Oh Alithea, you can be so oblique at times! The poor girl has no idea what you're talking about." Moonface turned to Rose. "Rosalind, my love, you have been chosen to bring great joy to Elfdom through the birth of your Elven daughter, Blossom Dearie. In April, you will travel to Elfhame where you will be looked after until the birth. They will raise the child to her 18th summer, at which time she may or may not choose to visit you in your realm. Until then, we will allow you one visit per year. Daniel will bring you to her. Is this clear?"

Rose plunked down on the porch step, overwhelmed by the impact of their remarks. *It's a girl! And they want me to give it up! No, no!* On the verge of tears, she blubbered, "I can't give up my baby. How can you ask that of me?" She stood up, defiant in her decision, nervously twisting the ring on her finger.

The five of them joined hands and encircled her. Sunny spoke. "The Mother commands it. It shall be done." Dawn spoke. "The Maiden commands it. It shall be done." Moonface spoke "The Crone commands it. It shall be done." Lord Sylvan and Lady Alithea spoke together. "Elfhame commands it. It shall be done."

When they dropped hands and stepped back, Rosalind bowed her head in glamoured acceptance.

"As your time draws near, come to Daniel. He will bring you to us, where you will be well cared for until the birth. You will always be welcome in Elfhame, and honored for your gift." Lady Alithea bowed to her, took the Lord's hand, and walked back to the horses. The three women bowed to her and disappeared in a puff of smoke, leaving her staring at Daniel, who stood wringing his cap in his hands.

Chapter 20c

Mae's Crossing ᛞ *Isolation/pessimism*

November 1

Al took the news of Brianna's affair badly. Feelings of loss coupled with anxiety for her well-being fueled his fire. Early on, he had established himself as the local recluse, and never managed a close friendship with anyone other than Willem and Brianna. She was his touchstone with reality; his glimpse of the magical. *Would that change now?* He moped about for a few days after she told him. The days lengthened into months. By the time he was celebrating New Year's, Al was at the bottom of his pity-pot.

His phone rang; it was Willem. *Probably calling to wish me Happy New Year.* "Yo, Will. How goes it, laddie?"

"Hey Al. Just another New Year's call. An' ya know, well, I had an idee. Wondered how it might grab ya."

"I'll letcha know if'n it hurts. Wha's up?"

"Well, I bin feelin' a little old an' feeble of late, an' it'd sure be good if'n us two could share a house. I mean, I was thinkin' of retirin', and why not to Mae's Crossing. So whaddya think?"

Grabbing the lifeline which was just tossed to him, Al pulled himself back to a purposeful reality. *Thanks, Will.* "Ya think I could stand to look at yer sour puss every day? Well, ya got me ta rights. I'll start lookin' fer a place. That suit ya? Happy New Year."

Chapter 20c

Malachais ᛞ *Victims*

Sunday found Malachais itching to get back on the road and home again, in spite of the draw Brianna exerted. There was much to do in the way of inventorying; culling out the storables, choosing the necessities, etc. Truth be told, he wanted some time to himself to sort things out in his mind. The accident lay like a heavy rock in the pit of his stomach, and try as he might, he couldn't seem to budge it. Brianna, bless her heart, had brought out an old Three Stooges movie. The two of them had laughed until tears rolled down their cheeks. After sweet hugs and loving words, Mal slid into the driver's seat and drove away.

Malachais chose a Beethoven CD, Pastorale, and for a while felt the weight lifting off of him as he motored down the mountainside.

Back in Channing and settled into his lounge with drink and smoke, Mal gave Jarnath a ring.

"Hey Mal, old man, so you're back?"

"Yes, I'm back…Sort of…You know, I'm feeling in strong need of the services of a sweat lodge. Do you have the time to join me? "

Jarnath detected an underlying tension in his friend's voice. "Hey now, that's a great idea. I've sure got the time. I could use a little cleaning out myself. I'll check with Luke Stronghand and get back to you. Any particular day?"

"As soon as possible, Jarny. The sooner the better." They talked of inconsequentials for a bit, then said their good-byes.

A calmness settled over Malachais as he sank into the cushions and studied the starry sky.

Sure enough, two days later saw them emerging from the sweat lodge, lighter than when they had entered. During the drive back, they both spoke of the burdens each carried, and how symbolically tossing them onto the steaming stones helped. Jarnath admitted to excessive grief and was ready to relegate it to a special corner of his heart. Now he could re-enter the world with an eagerness that Nellie would have approved of. Malachais let go of his obsession with 'victims,' knowing that joy was his if only he accepted it. There would always be victims; folks who felt out of control and manipulated or senselessly abused. Mal promised himself to make a contribution to the new women's shelter. Jarnath vowed to tend the garden, which had been woefully neglected. All in all, both men benefitted from the experience, feeling renewed and invigorated.

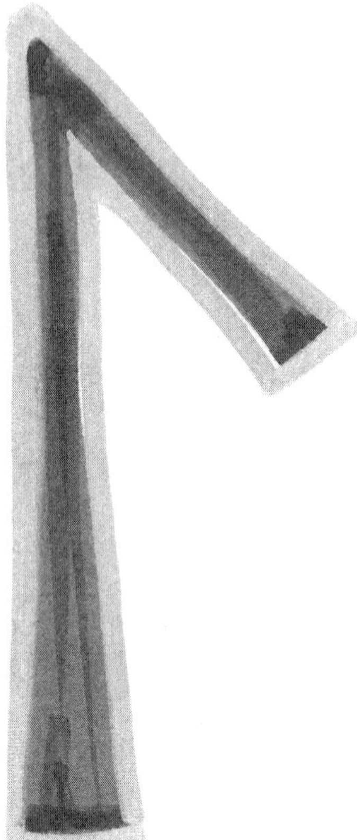

LAGUZ

Emotions/flow

Chapter 21a

Mae's Crossing ✓ *Buried Yearnings*

The little house was tucked away in the neighborhood directly behind Al's Antiques, a short walk of two blocks between them. Seeking a better solution to his woes as a landlord, Ed Janssen wanted a lease/buy commitment. He had bought it years ago, thinking to supplement his income with rental fees. Ed was sorely disappointed. The 'investment' cost him more than it was worth for the constant repairs and upkeep inherent in an older home. Al knew all this, and felt that he was in the driver's seat. If all worked out and the living arrangement suited the men, he knew he could pretty much name his own price.

Al stood at the gated entrance to the yard, door key in his pocket. He savored the moment. The cottage spilled out onto a yard that had great potential. Scruffy lilac bushes formed a frame around the verandah, shading the porch swing off to the right. It was recently painted a cheery yellow with white trim. 'Spill' aptly described the obvious additions to the original building which seemed to be attached in a haphazard way. Large trees dotted the yard; elm, poplar, beech and walnut. Smaller lemon trees hugged the house. The garage was a separate building with a workshop/apartment bulging out behind it. Unknowingly, Al had stumbled upon his dream. Hard to believe, but he'd been around Brianna long enough to know magic was real. And this had to be magic in its most potent form: actual physical manifestation. The house before him was the same as the one in his dreams. He couldn't wait to show it to Willem.

Chapter 21a

Brianna *Leaving Disappointment Behind*

Finding a place for Mal turned out to be less than the snap Brianna thought it would be. She hadn't had this trouble twenty years ago. There was certainly no glut in the market of desirable 2 bedroom homes. Bri had checked out a half dozen possibilities and was getting discouraged. Time to go inward; talk to the Gods. Always, when she felt this kind of franticness building in her, she turned to the Goddess. She never asked the Goddess to solve her problems; only to point her in the right direction.

Sure enough, after a brief ritual and a bowl on the back porch, it came to her. Caroline Spivack had been talking about moving out of her large house into something more manageable. She had been alone in this home since her husband's passing twelve years ago, and was ready for something more suited to her single personality.

Bri checked her contacts and pressed Caroline. "Hi Bri. What's up?"

"Hi Caroline. Say, I was wondering about your house, and if you had anyone lined up for it yet."

"Well, no, Bri, I don't. I did find a place I'd like to move into, but I need to get my own house settled before I can make the move. Why? Did you have someone in mind?"

"You bet. Remember Malachais? You met him at Samhane."

"Sure I remember. Who could forget such a beautiful man? And by the way, congratulations!"

"Thanks Caroline. I'm still getting used to the idea of an 'us.' Now Malachais wants to move to Mae's Crossing, and I was hoping that he might be the perfect tenant for you."

"Wow, Bri! That's a terrific idea! It would clear the way for me to make my move. And to have Mr. Merriwether as my tenant…I can't think of a better arrangement."

And so it was settled. All that was needed now was final approval by Malachais. Brianna couldn't wait to let him know.

Chapter 21b

Mae's Crossing ᛚ *Going with the Flow*

Willem got off the bus in front of Nelson's Department Store and walked the short distance to Al's Antiques. As he entered the shop and saw that Al was involved with a customer, Will wandered about, struck by his friend's expertise in sniffing out exceptional pieces. The door bells tinkled as the customer left, and Al appeared at his elbow.

"Yer not gonna believe this house I found. Let's lock up and walk over." Al motioned Willem outside as he turned the open sign over and closed the door behind him.

The two friends strolled down Chestnut Street until Al stopped in front of #33. "This be it, Will. Whatcha think?"

Willem did a double-take. He'd seen this house before. Where was it? *Could it really be the house that's bin popping up in my dreams?* "Danged if'n it aint the very place keeps poppin' up in my dreams!"

Al looked at him incredulously. "Ya don't say! Well I'll be damned. Willum, I do believe there's some mighty strong magic goin' on here, 'cause ya know what? I bin dreamin' of it too. Oh hell, no need to go no futher. I'll give Ed a call, an' ya better get ta packin'. We've done found ourselves a home." Old habits melted as the two men broke form to give each other a hug that held years of friendship in one gesture.

Chapter 21b

Rosalind ᛚ *Love*

Trying to digest the enormity of her situation, Rosalind fairly gagged with the effort. Just when she was getting used to the idea of motherhood *an Elfin child!,* she felt compelled to help the Elves of Elfhame by letting them raise her child *(Blossom Dearie*!). In her heart of hearts, she knew it was the right thing. Still, there was a sense of loss nagging at her mind.

Kyle picked her up from her home that evening to treat her to another fabulous trout dinner. When he had closed his front door behind them, he turned to Rose with outstretched arms. “Rose, Rose…” She entered his embrace, soaking up the peace and security she felt with him. Kyle nuzzled her hair, whispering in her ear: “I am the luckiest man in the world.” Rosalind lifted a tear-stained face to his. “Can we share the prize, ‘cause I’m the luckiest girl in the world.” Their kiss became a flame, kindling their desire. In a throaty voice, Kyle said, “Come into my bedroom.” Rose replied “So you can show me your etchings?”

When Kyle opened the door to his room, Rosalind gasped. Puzzled, Kyle asked her, “What, Rose? What do you see?” She pointed at the yellow silk pouch embroidered with his name, dangling off of a bedpost. Feeling the moment slip away, Kyle retrieved the pouch. “This just mysteriously appeared in my jeep when I was at Outback Jack’s,” and led Rose to the sofa. He opened it up and handed her the talisman.

Rose sat staring silently at it, her mind in a whirl. “Could you give me paper and pencil, Kyle? I want to figure this out.”
“What’s to figure? Can you read this? What are these markings?”

He gave her a tablet and pencil, and she drew out his half of the bindrune, filling it out with her half. “These are runes, Kyle, and this is a magical talisman created by the Great Goddesses themselves.”

“It’s a what by who? You’ve got to be kidding me. The Great Goddesses? Just who are they, and why would they be giving this to me?”

“Because they want to bind us together.” She sat hunched over the coffee table and completed the drawing, making out the sign for partnerships/gift intersected by new beginnings/breakthrough. After some more scrutinizing, she deciphered the two loose inguz runes. “They say we’re going to be very passionate, and that we will have two children!”

Rose got up from the couch and motioned to the kitchen. “Come on Kyle, I’m starving. Let me help you with the meal, and I’ll tell you the whole story.”

And so it all came out, between chopping vegetables and cooking pasta. Rosalind shared everything; the talisman, her mushroom madness, Daniel's talisman, his true origins, meeting his folks and then the most recent meeting with the Goddesses. Several times during her tale, Kyle either dropped a knife or a cloth. Once he dropped the broiler pan (when she told him of her last meeting with 'magickal folk') *who only live in fairytales*!

Deep down inside, it thrilled Kyle that Rosalind was in actual touch with Elves and Goddesses. Never doubting her for a minute *deception's not her style,* he hoped he might be able to meet them. He'd certainly meet Daniel sometime or other. *How will I handle that?*

"Oh my God, Rosalind! I had no idea you were so, so…connected. Don't you fret, though, 'cause it just makes me feel luckier and luckier that I found you. Or that 'the Goddesses' brought us together. However it happened, whatever comes around, I want us to see it all together. You are incredible!" He grabbed her in his arms and whirled around, gave her a big, wet kiss, then shooed her out of the kitchen. "Can't watch this part. Top secret doings on the trout. Go sit and pour us some wine. This'll only take 5 minutes or so."

Before long they were happily diving into the sumptuous meal, big smiles all around.

Later, as they were sleepily entwined in each other's arms, Kyle whispered, "What do you think about a June wedding?"

Chapter 21c

Mae's Crossing *Moving On*

Caroline Spivack viewed the future with mixed feelings. It was way past time to 'get on with her life' since her husband died twelve years ago. *Easier said than done*. Theirs was an exceptional relationship, navigating the ups and downs with a strong and steady love.

The house held too much of Doug's energy; so much so that his absence was even more difficult to handle. She had to move on; to create a new life without the constant reminders of what they had shared. Much of her personal growth was credited to the coven, which had not only been a support in her time of need, but had also provided her with the courage to explore new directions. Living in a four bedroom house with large grounds was too demanding, and no longer suited her. Caroline yearned for a little cottage, maybe with a garden. Something that would be all her own.

With vision and purpose, Caroline set out to find her new home. After a couple of weeks of checking out leads and suggestions, she came upon the perfect solution. Situated within walking distance of the market, it was a one bedroom cottage with a carport. She would have preferred a garage, but that was the only deterrent. *It could use a little paint.* All else was as she had pictured it, complete with the white picket fence and rose bushes. The owner was willing to give her a little time before signing the lease, as Caroline needed to rent her own house to give her the necessary financial balance. Already, she had rented storage space and had begun to move things she wouldn't need but wasn't ready to let go of quite yet. The big house was emptying out. She was contemplating doing a yard sale when Brianna called. *Amazing how the Goddess just seemed to appear in one's life at the right time!* If Malachais liked the place, her move was assured.

Chapter 21c

Malachais *Growing in Love*

News of the perfect house on the horizon filled Malachais with joyful anticipation. Just another sign of the rightness of his choices. He'd completed the inventorying of his entire holdings, then figured out what size storage unit he'd need. Who knows? Mal might eventually move everything into the new home if all worked out. Before contracting with the movers, he'd best take a look at Caroline's house.

Once again, Malachais was on the long road to Mae's Crossing. *What a relief it will be to do away with this commute!* His heart was light, thinking of his love waiting for him.
In an unusual display of emotion, Mal began singing. First it was, "Oh, What a Beautiful Morning" followed by "Somewhere Over the Rainbow." The sounds filled the air around him, deep and sonorous. Mal actually had a fine singing voice; good pitch with lots of feeling.

Just past the township sign for Mae's Crossing, a woman appeared by the side of the road, frantically waving him down. Malachais pulled over and got out of his car. Breathless, Sunny flashed him a seductive smile. "Oh thank you, kind sir, for stopping. I'm stranded. My car died and I've been walking in these boots which aren't really meant for walking, if you know what I mean." She leaned on his arm and lifted a gracefully turned ankle to display dangerously spikey high heels. "If you could give me a lift, I would certainly appreciate it." Again, a smile flickered at the corners of her mouth, giving her a bit of a pixieish look. Mal made a slight bow. "It would be my pleasure. Where would you like me to drop you?" "Oh, anywhere on 1st Street will do, thanks."

As they drove the short distance into town, her hand moved to rest on his leg…the heat practically burned through the cloth. Mal gently picked up her hand and moved it away, and could swear he saw a shimmering wash of color rolling off of her as she turned and gestured in the air. “That’s the tree that I was looking for! Can you pull over here?” Seeing that she couldn’t arouse the hunger and desire she was aiming at, Sunny decided on another approach.

Mal pulled over, leaving the engine running as she gingerly stepped out of the car. “Are you sure this is where you want to go?”

“Oh yes, this is it. I’ve been wanting to see this tree close up, and…”

Leaning over in the seat, Malachais said, “Okay,” shut the passenger door and drove off, leaving Sunny staring unbelievingly at the retreating vehicle.

What was that about? He felt like he was moving through molasses. *Was it Glamour?* The redheaded woman had been spilling over with lust, enough to make most men’s blood boil. Mal shivered, throwing off the veil she had thrown over him. *Wait ‘til I tell Brianna about this!*

Malachais continued his drive out to the eastern fringe of Mae's Crossing, following Brianna's directions. He just wanted to look at the Spivack home from the outside before showing up at 'Bri-Gris.' True to Bri's description, the house was quietly elegant, painted in soft hues of blue grey and solid grey. The yard would need a gardener---not one of Mal's talents. He loved the half circle driveway up to and away from the house. Mal feasted his eyes on the property, knowing without looking inside that it was the right place for him. What would also be right for him would be to hear Brianna say 'Yes' to his suggestion of a hand-fasting. *Yule, maybe?*

INGUZ

Potential/seed

Chapter 22a

Shelly *Potential*

Shelly had completed Brianna's assignment, and was looking forward to their meeting tomorrow. Everything she'd read seemed to confirm her choice; Wicca was definitely calling her. Memorizing 'The Charge' was a big challenge. Standing before the mirror, Shelly recited the piece perfectly. *Will I do as well in front of Miss Brianna?* It was such a beautiful bit of prose *but sooo long!* Doreen Valiente was one awesome witch. *I wish I could have met her.* Gathering up her paperwork, she stuffed it in her purse and grabbed her overnight bag.

The drive went smoothly. *I'll have to ask Miss Brianna if there is a special warding I could do for all the travelling ahead of me.* Pulling up to Rosalind's home, she felt a certain pride in Rose's accomplishments, and maybe just a bit of envy.

Rose stood on the porch, a big grin on her face.

"Okay girl, cough it up. What's got you so cheery?"

Rosalind waved her left hand before Shelly. Hard to miss a diamond of that size!

"Oh my God, Ro! That's a boulder you're wearing! How can you stand the weight?" Shelly examined the rock, oohing and aahing to Rosalind's delight.

"So when am I going to meet Mr. Wonderful?" They linked arms and walked inside.

Chapter 22a

Brianna ◇ *Hearth Fire*

Hearing Malachais' tale of the mysterious redheaded woman, Brianna felt a twinge of jealousy. Even though he had resisted the woman's pull, Bri resented the woman's attempts. *Hands off!* They were both bundled up for the cold as they sat on the back porch, basking in the moon's glow. "You know, hon," Brianna said "I'm pretty sure I know who that was. But why she would do that puzzles me. Do you remember seeing her at the Masquerade Ball? Did she wear her hair in braids twisted around her head?"

"Well I'll be…yes! She was at the ball. I thought I'd seen her before."

"Come on. I want to show you something." Brianna motioned to the door, grabbing her keys and going out to her car. "Hop in. It's just a short drive. Check behind the seat to see if there's a flashlight."

Brianna drove to Blessing Park, and led Malachais to the fountain. "Did you bring the flashlight? Shine it on the sculpture. Now move the light to the right. That's it! Do you recognize her?"

"Oh my Goddess, Bri! You're right. It *is* her! That's the woman who stopped me on the road. So who is she?"

"She's one of the Triple Godesses; obviously the Hot Mama. I met her mother," Bri directed the light to Moonface, then moved it over to the last figure. "And this is the Maiden."

Shivering with the cold, Malachais draped his arm around Bri's shoulders and took her back to the car. "Let's go warm up," he felt himself blushing *glad it's dark out* "and talk this over at home." *Did I just say home?*

After getting a nice fire blazing, the two kicked back on the soft, cushy divan. "I was wondering…just what are the Goddesses up to?" Bri stretched out like a cat, gently pawing at his shoulder. "I mean, why would they be messing with us like this?"

Malachais ran his finger down her arm, lingering on her hand. Lifting it to his lips, he kissed it tenderly. "Maybe they're testing us. Well, just go ahead, I say. Test away. My love is as solid as the oak in your yard. You live in my heart, darlin', and none can turn me." Brianna purred and snuggled into his shoulder. "You know, Bri, I'd like to shout it from the rooftops just how grand it is to be with you. How would you feel about us being handfasted…maybe at Yule with all our friends as witnesses?"

"Oh yes, Mal, yes! I'd been thinking the same thing! And Yule, yes, that's perfect. I could proclaim my love as the Sun God rises," she smirked, he chuckled.

Chapter 22b

Kyle *Reaching for Fulfillment*

November

Hard to believe that at 34, Kyle had never been married. He had lived with Emily for almost 3 years; that was the longest relationship he'd ever been involved in. Kyle found the thought of being Rosalind's husband very appealing, even more so now that it had an undertone of fantasy. All this stuff with make believe characters that turned out to be real, well...he'd always secretly felt an attraction to the magickal realms. Kyle had even read up a bit on Wicca, and envied Rosalind her training. He felt that sharing a life and planning a future together was his destiny, and he embraced it wholeheartedly. *Isn't there some kind of marriage ceremony they practice? Handfeasting?*

Over the course of time, Kyle had learned that Rose owned the bakery and the big old house she lived in. She was an independent woman with a secure income; that was a big plus. He happily buried fears of 'gold-digging.' Knowing the truth about her pregnancy actually gave him a secret sense of relief. The next pregnancy would be their child, and this one would give him some practical experience without the responsibility of raising the child. Kyle wanted his parents to meet her, but it would have to be soon before she started showing too much. It would raise too many questions that he didn't want to be fielding. *Maybe a Christmas visit?* Kyle promised himself to ask her about it the next time they got together.

Chapter 22b

Rosalind ◇ *Walking the Path of Spirit*

Rosalind and Shelly showed up at Brianna's right on schedule. "Wow! Look at that cool old Mustang!" Shelly walked around the car, admiring all the fine detailing. "Somebody must really love this car. It even has sheepskin seat covers and a sheepskin steering wheel cover. Totally bitchin'!"

Just at that moment, Malachais walked out of the house and up to his car, smiling at the two young women. "You must be Shelly. I'm Malachais Merriwether," he held out his hand to her. "And of course, Miss Rosalind." He made a slight bow. "I'm off to the market. Brianna's expecting you. Nice meeting you, Shelly."

Shelly looked after him longingly. *Ooh, what a gorgeous man!* The two girls went up to the porch and to the open door Brianna was holding. "Come in, girls. You're right on time. Excellent. Let's go out to the back porch." The table was arranged nicely with a sweating decanter of juice in the center, flanked by three glasses and an ashtray.

Once settled, Brianna took their two assignments and spent a few minutes looking over them. Nervously lighting up, Shelly tried to relax and take in her surroundings. Brianna had an incredible garden with a large circular space in the center. *Must be for rituals.*

"Rosalind, in answering the first question, I see that you just sort of stumbled on Wicca as peripheral to your study of runes. Runes can be a very effective tool in ritual work, but we'll get to that later. Your interest, Shelly, is a direct result of Rosalind's focus. There are many ways to be introduced to the Goddess, but there's no mistaking the calling." Brianna leaned over and poured herself a glass of juice. "Help yourself," as she waved at the glasses. "I'll go over the rest of your answers later. There were places I'd like to write comments on, so give me some time on that. For now, I'd like to hear Shelly recite the first part of the Charge of the Goddess."

To her own amazement, Shelly breezed through the charge, only faltering twice.

"Very good, Shelly." Brianna turned to Rosalind. "Rose, please recite the charge relating to esbats."

Rosalind pondered for a bit before remembering that esbats were moon rituals. *Oh, right that's what she means.*

"Whenever ye have need of any thing, once a month, and better it be when the moon is full, then shall ye assemble in…." Not a stumble, not a pause. The words rolled off her tongue like she wrote them herself. Both Brianna and Shelly were impressed. Rose shook herself, feeling like she had just returned from a long trip, and smiled shyly.

"Thank you, ladies, for your exceptional performances. You have shown me that you have the determination to learn and the ability to apply that learning. I would be pleased to train you both."

Rosa and Shelly looked at each other, barely holding in their excitement.

"First off, since you're starting out together, we'll approach this as a team. There will be exercises that will work nicely with you as a pair. Please keep in mind that this is not a competition. From now on, you will have identical assignments, but responses are individual and not to be 'bettered' or 'lessened.' Can you apply yourselves without making comparisons?"

Both women nodded in affirmation.

And so the afternoon wore on while Brianna quizzed the girls. They were encouraged to ask questions, which turned out to be a long listing. Dusk found them still deep in discussion when Brianna glanced up at the sky. "Look girls. The moon's rising. Salute Her."

Rosalind cocked her head. *Salute Her? How in the heck am I supposed to do that?* "Uh, Miss Brianna, that wasn't covered in the lessons."

"Use your imagination. Or copy me." Brianna genuflected at the moon, throwing Her a kiss.

Calling an end to the meeting, Brianna handed them the next month's assignment. The two picked up their things and headed for the door. Just as she was letting them out, Brianna announced, "Oh, by the way. Malachais and I are being handfasted in the Temple at Yule. We'd love for you to attend."

"How wonderful! Congratulations, Miss Brianna. Yes, we'll come." She turned to Shelly. "Right?" Shelly nodded enthusiastically, excited about seeing a real handfasting. "Kyle and I just got engaged…" Rose indicated the ring on her finger, "and we're planning a June wedding."

"Yah, that's really great, Miss Brianna. Sure your eyes'll never get tired of lookin' at the likes of him." Shelly laughed and hugged Bri.

Chapter 22c

Kyle ◇ *Possessive*

Kyle met up with Rosalind as she was closing the bakery. He leaned over and lightly kissed her cheek. "Say, how do you feel about walking over to the park? Get you out into some fresh air." "Great idea. Let's walk." They held hands as they walked down to Blessing Park.

There were three benches set back from the fountain, each one facing a different Goddess. Rosalind picked the bench facing the Maiden, patting the seat next to her. Winter had stolen the leaves off the trees. Seeing the naked trees as a backdrop to the sculpture gave the observer a sense of the dance of life and death. Different Goddesses, different views. It was truly a magical fountain for those who watched and listened.

Kyle rubbed at a branch he'd picked up along the way. "Do you think this is an oak branch?" Rosalind examined it. "It's the right color. Yeah, I think it's oak." He started nervously stripping the bark, clearing his throat as he turned to her. "It's about Daniel, Rose. I just can't stop thinking about punching him in the nose, or something."

"As if that would make things better!" Rosalind's back stiffened as she tried to focus on the Maiden, blithely pouring water into the fountain. She realized suddenly that she held no animosity towards Daniel, and actually wanted to defend him from Kyle's anger. Although their coupling had been obscured by a mushroom haze, what she could remember was sweet and sensual. Were it not for Kyle coming into her life, Rose might have sought out a repeat performance. Putting those musings aside, she reached out to Kyle. "Kyle, honey, please try to understand about Daniel. In some ways, he's like a little kid. Doesn't have a mean bone in his body. He's no threat to you, and you must know I love you more than life itself." She inhaled deeply, letting it out slowly before continuing. "I was afraid this might come between us." Rose stroked his hand then held it to her cheek. "And I really don't blame you for your feelings. I'm going to have a baby, and damn it, it's not ours. If only I could have met you sooner…" She looked to the Maiden for strength, willing herself not to cry.

"Oh, Rose, I'm so sorry. Thinking about you with another man, well, it just makes me crazy. I'll have to work it out somehow. How can I be so selfish when your road is going to be so much tougher? I want to be there for you, always and always." Kyle draped his arm around her shoulders, pulling her in tight to him. "Listen, I know a little about Wicca, and I was thinking it would be really good if we could get handfeasted this winter. We could jump over this oak branch, right? I mean, June is a long ways off, and with you growing all the while, it might be easier for you if folks thought, well, if they thought it was mine, you know?"

Rosalind smothered a laugh. "It's called handfasting, hon. And you're right, it might be just the thing, what with me being a shopkeeper and all, that folks might think like you say…Oh wow! I just had the greatest idea!"

"Handfeasting, handfasting, whatever...so what's your great idea?"

"Miss Brianna and Malachais Merriwether are being handfasted at Yule. Maybe we could make it a double handfasting! Wouldn't that be terrific?"

Chapter 22c

Malachais ◇ *Completion*

Malachais had pretty much emptied out his town house, leaving just the bare essentials for future short term rentals. He'd decided to throw himself a party; a farewell to Channing. All was in readiness as the first guests arrived. Jarnath stood at the door with Willem at his elbow.

"Come on in, guys. Help yourselves to the food and drink. I'll be right with you." Mal closed the door behind them and grabbed the special bottle of champagne he'd been saving for this very moment. Jarnath and Will took seats at the dining table and filled their plates while Mal popped the cork. Jarnath cocked his head at Willem. "Hey, Mal, did you know Willem here is moving to Mae's Crossing, too?"

"No, really? What about Channing Exchange?"

Willem replied, "I put it up fer sale. Ready to retire, I am, an' Al 'n me found us a little house on Chestnut Street. Looks like we'll be neighbors, eh? Mr. Jarnath tells me yer marryin' Miss Brianna. Congratulations, Mr. Mal. She be one fine lady."

"Well, it's not really a wedding, it's a Wiccan handfasting. It has to be renewed annually. But, yes, it's basically the same thing. Thanks, Will. I'm so fortunate to have found Brianna. She's an exceptional woman." With that, he filled their glasses and they all toasted to the rosy future.

The next arrivals were John and Marcia Dillingham, Malachais' property managers. Soon, the house was filled to capacity as one by one, all toasted and congratulated Malachais on his new life. Mal rose to answer the doorbell to find Shelly, Laura and Gerry standing on his doorstep. Unsure as to how to deal with Gerry, he stepped back. Shelly took the lead. “Mr. Merriwether, Gerry has something to say to you.” She pushed her brother into the room, as he looked sheepishly down at his feet.

“Uh, Mr. Merriwether, uh…I just wanted to say how very sorry I am for taking your vase. I know I can’t replace it, but I thought maybe I could offer my services as groundskeeper and handyman, say for maybe a year…for free?”

Mal considered his proposal. He was fairly certain the boy had turned a corner in his life, and that his offer was sincere. “Gerry, do you have any idea how much mental pain and suffering you caused me by stealing my chalice? It was irreplaceable, you know. Theft is a great violation of personal space.”

“Yah, Mr. Merriwether, I know, I know. I was so crazy back then, but I’ve changed, honest I’ve changed. Please let me make it up to you.”

Malachais turned to Laura, melting at the pleading look in her eyes. “Okay, Gerry.” He extended his hand to the young man. “I’ll introduce you to John Dillingham. He’ll be handling my property, and if you work out, he might even use you on some of his other holdings.”

“Oh, thank you, thank you, Mr. Merriwether! You won’t be sorry. And, and…I need to settle up with Mr. Douglas. Is he here?” Mal pointed Will out to him, and Gerry hurried over to where he was sitting.

Willem stiffened as he recognized the young man approaching him, feeling a twinge in his ribs.

Gerry actually got down on his knees before the old man, extending his hand holding two hundred dollar bills. "Mr. Douglas, I know money can't mend the hurt I caused you, but please take this with my apologies."

Surprised at the young man's gesture, Will looked him square in the eye. "Ya done hurt me bad, boy. Real bad. An' you be right…money don't mend it…but it helps." With that he smiled, took the bills and said, "Apology accepted."

"Thank you so much, Mr. Douglas. And if you can stand havin' me around, I'd like to help you with your move…free of charge, of course."

Out on the deck, Laura gave Shelly a big hug, fairly bursting with pride.

Off in the corner, Jarnath nursed his champagne, fighting the urge to wallow in self-pity. *Oh poor me, everyone I love goes away!*

DAGAZ

Breakthrough/balance/meeting of opposites

Chapter 23a

Mae's Crossing ᛞ *the Sun is Born/a New Day Dawns*

Christmas season was one of Mae's Crossing's all time favorites. The town glittered with ornaments and lights. There was a big Christmas tree inside the park entrance, sparkling in bright colors at night, shimmering with tinsel during the day. Good will and excitement filled the air as folk bustled about doing last minute shopping. Samantha was finishing up the final touches inside the Temple, preparing for three ceremonies. A double handfasting was scheduled for the afternoon, followed by the Yule celebration in the evening. A traditional Christian observance would be celebrated on the 25th, truly a busy time for the Temple Chaplain.

Chapter 23a

Brianna ᛞ *New Beginnings/ Magical Moment*

Yule dawned crisp and clear in the mountain valley town. Brianna and Malachais slept apart in their own homes the previous night at Mal's insistence. *He's such a traditionalist.* She looked out upon the first magical snowfall of the season; a fleeting pleasure which would soon be supplanted by the hard work of shoveling. The ceremony was scheduled for 2 in the afternoon, freeing up the Temple for the annual Yule circle at 7:00 pm. Brianna breathed a sigh of relief; this wasn't the first time she'd felt gratitude for being second in command rather than the official High Priestess of her coven. She didn't envy Lady Fawn her position. *Such a huge responsibility.*

When Rosalind suggested a double handfasting, Brianna's first reaction was one of non-acceptance. *This is Our Big Day*! Knowing it for the selfish thought it was, Bri hugged Rose and graciously welcomed the idea.

The two 'brides' met in the Temple lounge at one o'clock. Both were nervous as kittens. "Oh, Miss Brianna, I'm really afraid we'll forget our lines. We've only had a few days to look them over, and oh my Goddess, it's all so scary and so wonderful!"

Brianna was agitated as well, but knew hers was the calming hand needed. "Let's go over the lines together, Rosalind. Someone will be there to cue you if you should stumble. Don't you worry. This will be one of your most cherished memories. Give it your best." And so the two women repeated the ceremony, word for word. First Rose took Malachais' part, prompting Bri's responses. With the first run-through fresh in her mind, Rosalind responded to Brianna as she spoke Kyle's part. By the third time through, both of them were more at ease, and started fussing with their clothing. Rosalind was radiant. She had fashioned garlands of mistletoe fastened with festive red and green ribbons, draping them over her white robe and down her back. On her brow was a wreath echoing the garlands. Brianna was stunning in a black robe offset by twining red and white silk scarves. A simple silver headpiece with the sign of the High Priestess encircled her head, while her Tree of Life pendant rested on her chest.

When they were summoned into the chapel, the two couples saw each other in their ritual garb for the first time. Smiles and looks of admiration confirmed the desired effects. Kyle wore a simple brown robe with a golden undershirt whose sleeves and high neck extended out from the covering. Hanging from his neck was a large gold sun pendant. A soft brown cap, wrapped around with lines of holly leaves and berries, was pulled tightly over his bright red curls. Rosalind did a double-take as she took in the full implications of the cap. But by far the most commanding in appearance was Malachais with his Cernunnos headdress; the 7-tined silver antlers reaching above his head. He, too, wore a black robe. His medallion was a simple gold pentagram. A black satin paten flowed over his shoulders, patterned with golden suns.

Samantha was in awe of the magnificence of the gathering *This is truly a magical moment.* She delivered her lines, welcomed the responses, and blessed the couples as Kyle and Rosalind jumped over an oak branch and Malachais and Brianna leaped over a broom.

All retired to the reception area, aglow with the wonder of their new standing. Friends mingled. Shelly spotted Daniel and walked up to him. "Hi Daniel." He turned and jumped at first sight of her, *Wow, look at those tattoos and that ring in her nose!* then grinned and tugged at his blue cap. "Uh, hello it's Miss Shelly right?" She grinned back. While they were idiotically grinning at each other, a woman with wild white hair tugged at his sleeve. She leaned over and whispered in Daniel's ear. "Yes, ma'm. Gotta go, Shelly. Nice meeting you."

Daniel left for the dance floor where he found Rosalind. He slipped up next to her, trying to dodge Kyle's vision. "Hi Dan'l. What's up?" He fidgeted, feeling Kyle's displeasure. "Miss Rosalind, the newlyweds are wanted outside right now! Could you please bring them out to the courtyard?" Kyle bristled. It was the first time he had seen Daniel, and the moment's enchantment lost some of its luster as he glowered at him. Daniel averted his gaze and crept backwards.

Rosalind whispered in Kyle's ear, who reluctantly passed it on to Malachais as she then turned to Brianna. Smiling and waving, Brianna spoke. "Please excuse us for a moment. We won't be long. Help yourself to the food and drinks." The four of them followed Daniel out to the courtyard.

Chapter 23b

Mae's Crossing ᛞ *the Balancing Point*

Moonface waved her hand in a circle encompassing those she had gathered. A shimmering dome now covered them, making them invisible to folks on the outside. "Sorry to crash your party, or should I say handfeasting?" Granny leaned over and tweaked one of Kyle's curls. "This will only take a moment of their time." she motioned toward the Temple and the merry crowd. "On a more serious note, I have a special announcement to make." Moonface cleared her throat and looked at the couples before her. "All of you will have a key role to play in the coming Dark Days, days of chaos and violence." The couples huddled together. Brianna took shelter in Malachais' arms. "You will each be called upon to complete a task. You two, Brianna and Malachais, will be teachers and ritualists. Brianna is a chosen one, as she carries Elfin blood." Mal stared at Bri in shocked amazement, who stiffened at being 'outed.' *Of course, I should have guessed it! The eyes that never seem to settle into one color; the ears that have a definite Elfin shape…*"Malachais has shown himself to be of stout heart and strong in magic, and will be instrumental in instilling inspiration and courage." Sunny winked at Mal. He felt his cheeks redden as he leaned into Bri. "Teach the children well. Endow them with the wisdom of the Ancient Ones and there is no doubt that the Light will prevail, although it will be a mighty struggle. Bringing forth the young Spiritual Warriors who will face the coming Darkness is a task that has already been started. You, Rosalind and Daniel, are preserving the Elfin lineage." Brianna raised her eyebrows. "Lord Sylvan and Lady Alithea will be here shortly, and they'll tell you more about that. The coming children of Rosalind and Kyle will be strong leaders in the hard times ahead."

"It is not in my nature to apologize, but know that I meant you no harm and hope that I haven't caused too much discomfort. The lurking danger is all too real, and you are all needed. Nay, you are all compelled to help, if the truth be known. In exchange, I have given each of you the greatest love of your life…one who will stand by your side through the trying times."

A booming sound filled the dome. It was The Lord and Lady knocking to be let in. Granny pointed her finger like an athame, cutting a door for them to enter and effectively closing it behind them as they rode in on their white chargers. The Lord swung down from his horse and held out a hand to the Lady. They each bowed to the three Goddesses. Facing Rose, the Lord fell to one knee: "We pay honor to Rosalind Duncan, who carries the precious seed of Elfhame within her. Her daughter will strengthen our numbers, and bring great joy to all of us." Mal and Bri both expressed surprise at the news. Bri leaned over and hugged Rose. The Lord rose and he and the Lady bowed to Rosalind. The Lady spoke; "I am here to sadly announce the near extinction of the Elfin race. A melancholy has fallen over our kind as the mortal world turns away from us, relegating us to mere figments of their imagination. In order to preserve our race, we have come to understand that our "purity" is strangling us, and we need to strengthen our physical bodies by union with humans. As it is, there are few of our Elves who are able to bear children. I bore one child with great difficulty. Our existence is necessary to keep the balance between nature and humanity, and to keep the magic alive. If you know of any woman who would be willing to bear children for us, we would like to interview them. We will reward them quite handsomely. Daniel can call us at any time." With that they remounted, glancing back at Moonface as she cut a door for their exit, again sealing it after their departure.

Granny continued, "Our work here is done, and we must be going. There is a Druidic couple who has attracted our attention, but we will return once a year to help strengthen your wards. If at anytime you find your path murky or obstructed, I give you three symbols to call us." Moonface pointed at the shell of dome over them and a deep, velvety black Hagalaz dominated the shimmering backdrop. "That is my symbol. If you want help from Sunny, visualize this:" She seemingly threw the rune at the side of the dome…a fiery red Nauthiz. "And if Dawn's help is needed, imagine this rune"…a scintillating white Isa filled the air. "It's been a pleasure playing with you. Be well." Poof! All returned to 'normal' as the Goddesses vanished, along with the dome. Suddenly, the two couples were surrounded by friends filled with good wishes, as Daniel slipped away.

HAGALAZ
Moonface
Past, Ancestors

NAUTHIZ
Sunny
Present, Active

ISA
Dawn
Future, Unformed

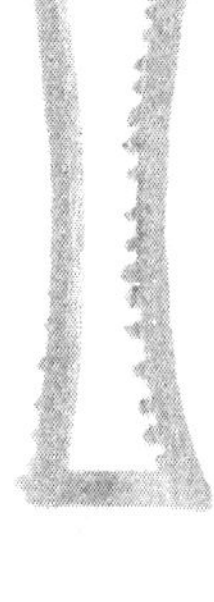

Chapter 23b

Rosalind ᛞ *New Beginnings*

Rosalind and Kyle walked into his house, still high from the afternoon's proceedings. They both changed out of their ceremonial garb and met in the kitchen.

"I've booked our flight to New York for tomorrow morning. My folks are really excited about meeting you. I know you'll like them; they're good people." Kyle stood behind Rose as she sat at the table, massaging her shoulders and kissing the top of her head. "Dad can be a little gruff at times. Don't let that fool you. He's soft as a marshmallow. And Mom, well, she's just a doll. Everybody loves her." He walked around and sat opposite her, taking her hands in his. "This is all so fantastic, Rose. I just can't find the words to say how happy and proud I am to be your man. And you're right about Daniel; I'll just have to find a way to deal with my feelings. I almost lost it when I met him. I mean, damn! You're carrying an Elfin child! I know it's an honor. I'm in awe of you and your part in all of this." He looked her steadily in the eye. "I swear, Rose, I'm going to do my level best for you."

Rose silently soaked up the love and acceptance Kyle offered her. She gently pulled her hand away and caressed his curls. *A lasting love! Could this really be happening?* Putting all her years of loss and abandonment behind her, Rose bravely stepped into her new life as Kyle's chosen companion.

"You know, Kyle, we shouldn't be living apart. I'd like you to move into my house. Then it will be 'our' house."

"Yes! I'd love to! But I've made a deal with Widow Thompson for a year. I'll just keep the place, and take my time moving out. We can always use it as our secret hideaway."

The two of them moved to the couch and curled up together. Outside, as the evening sky deepened into purple, the full moon shone through the diamond paned windows, bathing them in gossamer enchantment.

Chapter 23c

Daniel *Reluctant Change*

Daniel attacked the chaos in his cabin, trying to toss similar things together. Behind him, the broom was silently sweeping. His thoughts kept straying back to that enchanted afternoon with Rosalind, a dream come true. Now that she was handfasted to Kyle, she was no longer a free woman. Future fantasies came crashing down around his Elfin ears. Even though he could no longer hope to hold her, there was an unbelievable future opening up for him. He was going to have a daughter! Blossom Dearie would be his true child; one he could love and play with and watch grow. Through this babe, he and Rosalind would be bound for life. Daniel started humming a new tune; one composed especially for Blossom.

Chapter 23c

Malachais *Waking up to Change*

As the morning sun streamed in Brianna's bedroom window, Malachais stretched and turned over. Seeing her in peaceful slumber lying next to him filled him with joy. *What a beautiful woman!* And to think she chose him to be her lover, well, it was more than he had ever hoped for. He lifted a curl off her forehead and she stirred, reaching her arms out to him. "Good morning, love."

Later they sat bundled up on the back porch, coffee and cigarette sending streams of steam and smoke into the cold December air. Malachais drank in the beauty of the moment, sighed, then reached out for Brianna's hand. "So, Bri, darlin', when were you going to tell me about your Elfin blood?"

"I'm sorry I kept it from you. Really I am. Now the Goddesses have announced it, and four of you know. Certainly Daniel sensed it. I've never discussed it with anyone other than my mother, and I've fallen into the habit of conveniently forgetting it. Truthfully, I wish I knew more myself. I know my grandfather, Govannan, was a full Elf. I never met him, and my mom rarely spoke of him. There were little things she taught me; places to seek out in the woods, plants that had special properties, animals that had certain kinships to us. But of grandfather himself, nothing. I keep hoping that someday we'll meet. I'm sorry I can't tell you more. Were it not for the Goddess' speech, I may not have told you. Leastways, not for a while yet."

Mal sat in silent contemplation. "You know you can trust me, don't you? I would never betray a confidence." He blew a few smoke rings in the air, then continued. "So…what do you think about us living together?"

"I want to, but I'm not sure how. I mean, we're both pretty settled in our ways. I've been trying to work out a plan myself. Should you move in here? I just don't know. Somehow, it doesn't feel right." Brianna looked to Mal for confirmation.

"I certainly agree, darlin'. I don't think I should move into your space, nor you into mine. At least, not yet." Mal leaned over and kissed the tip of her ear. "We could continue like this for the term of my lease, then re-open the case at that time." He smiled one of his more endearing smiles. "Actually, I did have a thought. If I really take to Caroline's property, I might make an offer on the house. If I owned the house, you could move in and the downstairs front bedroom could be your studio/workshop. It's not as roomy as your studio here, but…we could always put up a separate building. The lot's big enough."

"Wow, what an offer!...I'll have to think on it some… I really love my space here." Leaving what she had so carefully built on Hummingbird Lane was daunting. "Let's just spend the year bouncing in and out of each other's lives. Then if we renew our vows *silly girl, if?* next Yule, we'll look at it from there. I have promised to be your companion, to love and support you in all you do. That should be enough for now."

Wrapped up together in the chill morning air, they reveled in the sparkle and brilliance of the snow dusted scenery...and the sparkle and brilliance of their new-found love.

OTHALA

Ancestors/homestead/completion

Chapter 24a

Rosalind ᛟ *Home/Family*

The day before Christmas Eve

Kyle's parents arrived at the airport in a chauffeured limousine to pick them up. Rosalind immediately fell in love with them. She could see the physical traits he inherited from each of them, but the most striking feature of all was the open acceptance they extended to her. They drove off into the cold afternoon, chatting gaily as they moved through the city and into the reaches of a snowy upstate New York. When the gates clicked open, they proceeded down the tree-lined lane. Rose was truly overwhelmed by the opulence spread out before her. The grounds were artistically landscaped, and as they approached the entrance to the mansion, a group of servants stood shivering on the broad steps leading up to the double doors. As soon as they parked, a few of them peeled off the porch and began tending to them. Luggage was retrieved, and Kyle held out his arm to Rosalind. She was escorted to a private bedroom to change and freshen up, promising to meet up with the family in the solarium in half an hour. *Wherever that was!* Rose gazed in wonder out the bedroom window at a dramatic garden complete with a maze, an enormous swimming pool taking up the center. There was a light tapping at the door. "Yes, who is it?"

"It's Dulce, the maid. May I come in?"

"Sure, okay." Curiosity aroused, Rose opened the door to an imposing woman in uniform who did a slight curtsey then flowed past her into the room. Dulce's graying hair was tightly confined by her maid's cap, and her white apron was starched and spotless. *Wow, she looks like business. Reminds me of Mabel.*

"I've come to assist you in preparing for the little soiree. Is that what you'll be wearing? Can I help you with your hair?"

As Rose was into her fourth month, there was a definite baby bump emerging which needed disguising. The layered skirt and blouse were loose fitting and flowing; a gift from Shelly and certainly in high fashion. Much to her surprise, Dulce cluck-clucked about her dress then moved her attention to Rose's hair. She pulled the barrettes out and started fussing. Within moments, Dulce had transformed Rosalind's do into an elegant layering of her blond locks. When she looked in the mirror, Rose was stupefied. *That's me?* "Wow, Dulce, you're a magician! What a beautiful job you did! Thank you so much." She turned towards the door. "Is it time to go down? Do I look okay?" Dulce made an awkward attempt at a smile, as Rose followed her downstairs to the solarium. Kyle rose and came to her side while his folks turned and smiled, motioning her to take a seat. Mr. Porter made a cursory lift and dip as they moved toward the divan.

"Rosalind, you look lovely. What pretty hair you have." Mrs. Porter leaned forward in her chair, extending her hand.

Rose grasped it, hesitated, then planted a light kiss on the matron's cheek. "Thank you, ma'am. You'll have to give Dulce the credit. This is her handiwork, not mine." She joined Kyle on the couch, smiling sweetly *I hope it looks sweet.* Rosalind struggled to feel comfortable in the midst of all this opulence.

Mr. Porter bent towards her, an inquisitive look on his face. "Kyle tells me that you inherited your Grandmother's bakery when she passed away. You're so young, 23 is it, to be saddled with such a burden. Why should it go to you, and not your parents?" Kyle groaned. *Damn it for putting Rose on the spot!* His dad probably thought her parents were unreliable, or at the least, unstable.

Rosalind straightened her posture, dreading the coming conversation. *Why hasn't Kyle told them?* She threw an accusing look at Kyle, then cleared her throat. "Uh, Mr. Porter, they're gone. Remember Flight 93 in 2001? The one that crashed in Pennsylvania?" He nodded. "Well, my folks were on that plane, on their way to a National Executives Conference."

Mrs. Porter expressed shock. "Oh, my dear. How dreadful! I am so sorry to hear that." She turned to Kyle. "Kyle, why didn't you tell us?"

Kyle squirmed in his chair. "Sorry, Mom. I just didn't get around to it yet. I was going to tell you, but Rosalind walked in right at that moment." He looked sheepishly at Rose, his eyes begging forgiveness for putting her in an awkward position.

Just then, dinner was announced, and they all filed into the dining room. Time passed easily, the discomfort of the previous conversation forgotten. Rosalind entertained them by recounting stories of the various suppliers she had met through the route with Mabel. Both parents seemed impressed with her level-headedness and willingness to learn the business. Mrs. Porter was especially touched about Rose's story of Mr. Crafty.

As the meal concluded and the servants started to clear the table, Mrs. Porter stood and turned to face Rosalind. "Kyle tells me you're planning on a June wedding. Would you please allow us to host it here?"

Realizing that she had been avoiding planning for the wedding, Rose readily accepted, happily shifting the responsibility to Kyle's parents.

Later, as Kyle was escorting her to her room, she whispered in his ear. "She's moving! Here, feel this. I think she's kicking." Rosalind laid Kyle's hand on the exact spot. Sure enough, "Wow! I felt it!" He wrapped his arms around her in a very proprietary way. Rose felt like she was in the safest harbor in the world as she gratefully leaned into his loving presence.

Chapter 24a

Mae's Crossing *Home/Community*

Christmas Eve

Thanks to a very generous anonymous donation to the Temple, Samantha got to play Santa Claus in a big way for her beloved town. The directions accompanying the donation were explicit: "Prepare a large Christmas feast to be served to those without family to share with. Buy gifts for man, woman, boy and girl. Wrap and mark them, distributing at your discretion." Sam posted a sign-up sheet for the dinner, and was surprised at how many responses she got. She decided to have a tree in the cafeteria, and would give out the presents after dinner as a surprise.

At 5:00 pm on Christmas Eve, folks lined up outside the Temple cafeteria. Woodsman Otter was first in line, clearly pleased to be sharing a holiday dinner. Tom Bradley and John Simpson were actually standing together, chatting amiably. Right behind them, Al and Willem stamped in place to warm up, while Mikos Stauros breathed wreathes in the cold air. Samantha opened the doors and started letting people in, checking them off her list. By the time Widow Thompson squeezed inside, the list was complete. Sam saw a group of unfamiliar faces under the covered porch. They looked like a family on holiday, probably drawn by the milling crowd and excessive ornamentation. She mentally tallied the numbers, then waved them over, confident that there was plenty for everyone. Samantha took a quick walk around the temple grounds, gathering up strays and sending them into the warm and cheery dining hall.

Al and Willem cleaned up their plates, put them in the bins, and hurried back to a table that was just bustin' with good talk. The Fates were kind in seating Woodsman Otter and

Widow Thompson at the same table, who turned out to be great story tellers and conversationalists. There were a few more unfamiliar faces, but they were all glowing with good will and good eats. Samantha called their table number, and the group rose and went to the Christmas tree, choosing gifts with the right colored ribbon (red for women, green for men, pink for girls and blue for boys) and taking them back to the table to open. There's a certain magic in the air when a group gathers and opens gifts together. Some took their time, carefully lifting the tape off the paper and saving the ribbons, while others simply tore the wrappings off. Will held up a brightly colored knit neck scarf. "Well, thankee, thankee. Durned if'n this aint just the thing. I bin needin' one o' these. It's a mite colder up here in the winter than it twas in Channing. I be happy to get this, and happier to be wearin' it." With that he wrapped it around his neck and sat down, all smiles.

After the meal, a group started making the rounds, singing all the familiar Christmas carols. Widow Thompson had a fine soprano voice. Many at the tables sang along, some even getting up and joining the strollers. Non-Christians alike were drawn into the revelry as they sat back and enjoyed the melodies and harmonies.

Willem nudged Al. "I sure be glad I moved to this fine town, Al. 'Specially 'cause I bin havin' a weird feelin' lately 'bout sumthin' really dark brewin'."

Chapter 24b

Brianna ᛟ *Delay in Establishing Home*

New Year's Eve

Brianna struggled with the overpowering presence Malachais presented in her life. *Do I really want to live with him! Yes! Do I want to change my life to make room for him? I don't know.* Given some time to herself after he went home, Bri formulated a workable solution. Now that the holidays were over (almost; New Year's Eve tonight), she wanted to establish 'work time' with Mal lest her business suffer. The coming year would prove out the viability of the plan. *Plenty of breathing space. Now just go with the flow.*

Mal picked her up at 8:00 pm. At Brianna's suggestion, reservations had been made at the Grand Hotel for the annual New Year's bash. It was a good turnout, and Mal and Bri made the rounds, wishing all a good new year. He was truly gratified to be so heartily welcomed into the community, and Brianna was bursting with pride. *That's my man!*

They danced…oh, how they danced! Each knew this for the precious moment it was as they put their all into it. Malachais glided on the floor, dipping and twirling Brianna. The crowd parted and circled 'round them, clapping to the beat. He lowered her to the floor, then swooped her up above him as the song ended. The clapping continued, along with a couple of cheers and huzzahs!

Totally exhilarated, they returned to their table, flushed and breathless. Such a love had grown between them that all was said with a look. Malachais lifted his glass to Brianna. "To the future, my love." Brianna clinked glasses with him. "To the future, my love."

Chapter 24b

Mae's Crossing *Reaching for Ancestral Connections*

Mid-January

Mabel Collins lived in a modest two bedroom home situated on the edge of the forest.
What the home lacked in size was made up for by the land surrounding it. The nearest neighbor was two miles down the road, and the seclusion was ideal for the High Priestess of Forest Grove Coven. As Lady Fawn, she conducted most of their rituals in her back yard, weather permitting. On occasions of inclement weather, they would go indoors or to the Temple. The doorbell rang, and Mabel emerged from her kitchen to answer the door.

"Welcome, Malachais. Glad ya could make it. Please come in."

Mal wiped his feet on the doormat and entered into her private domain, marveling at the powerful energies emanating from the little home. He glimpsed bundles of herbs hanging in the kitchen. The living area was filled with figurines of Gods and Goddesses, antlers and animal skulls interspersed amongst them.

Mabel directed him to a seat in the living room, then brought in a tea set from the kitchen, complete with *wouldn't you know it* fresh cannoli. Pouring out the cups, she came to the point. "I wanted to talk with ya bout joinin' our coven. Bin thinkin' of it since Yule. I'd like to know a bit more of yer background, if'n ya don' mind tellin' me. Coven memberships, status, years in the Craft…" she trailed off as Malachais set his cup down and wiped his sugary fingers.

"I self-dedicated to Wicca when I was 18. That makes 42 years in the Craft. I am a member of five covens, and hold position of High Priest in two. Thirty years ago, I was trained in the Gardnerian tradition. I currently practice Modern Celtic Wicca, but will conduct ritual to Deities of other traditions. I can give you my High Priestess' number in Channing who can verify my membership in Coven of the Quaking Aspen. Quite honestly, I was hoping you might invite me. I need folks I can observe the holidays with."

Mabel hummphed a couple of times while he was speaking, then responded, "Well, I guess ya be qualified, all right. Hope your Gardnerian training was in a warm climate." She chuckled. Mal relaxed a bit, allowing himself a little laugh as well. "Miami would certainly qualify as warm."

"Good nuff. I'd like to schedule the dedication for Imbolc. Truth be known, we really be needin' a High Priest. None o' our men want to go that high. The Gods seem to be favorin' us to bring you here." She smiled as she lifted her cup to him.

"I would be honored to be a part of Forest Grove, and Imbolc is perfect. Thank you, Lady Fawn. You won't be disappointed."

Chapter 24c

Malachais ᛟ *Seeking Ancestral Connection/ Homestead*

Imbolc

The box of Ogham was still perched on top of the bookcase where he had stuck it as he was arranging his books. Caroline's house suited Malachais to a tee, and he was thoroughly enjoying the new views and layout. When his eye caught the box sticking out, he instinctively reached for it. Checking the contents once again, Mal brought it to the dining table. He laid out the silk cloth, placing the bag of Ogham sticks next to it. A quick trip upstairs to the Temple Room, and Mal came back with incense, lighting the briquette. He walked around the room, holding the incense burner, and wafted the smoke over the windows and doors. Satisfied that he had secured the area, Mal kneeled before the makeshift altar, asking for Oghma's guidance. Standing, he pulled three sticks from the bag and dropped them on the cloth. Beith, Luis, Fearn…the first three signs of the 'alphabet.'

Malachais began his interpretations. The first impression he received was the unlikely possibility of these three showing up, laid out in order. Beith held the position of the lowest layer with Luis crossing, then Fearn just barely touching the tip of Luis as it pointed in an easterly direction. The next level of meaning delved into their placement on the calendar. Mal had never taken to all the information in "The White Goddess," finding other authors who better suited him as he chose a side in the 'controversy.' Beith, Luis, Fearn: November, December, January.

The Ogham had accompanied him on his journey quite literally as he was now looking forward to Imbolc. How fitting that initiations and dedications are scheduled for the month of the Willow. Having January branch off in a new direction from the events of November and December underlined Mal's determination to establish a meaningful life of his own, independent of Brianna's. Not that he yearned for separation. On the contrary, he was fighting the urge to merge. She was way too precious to scare away with too much confinement, like the butterfly she was. Malachais wondered if, the next time he threw them, it would be the next three in the series…So…Beith could be Bri, Luis him, and Fearn his new direction. Mal opened his Ogham journal and drew the reading, carefully noting the date and time, then packed up the fews.

Out on the back porch, drink and cigarette to hand, Mal resolved to set aside a 'smoking room' indoors. *Way too cold out here!* He puzzled over the cryptic message the Goddesses had delivered at the handfasting. "Days of chaos and violence" certainly had an ominous ring to it.

He pulled himself back into the moment, and went inside to prepare for the ritual that night. Mal had fasted all day, *Did a drink and cigarette count?* wanting to approach the occasion empty, ready to be filled. Taking a purifying shower, he watched his distractions swirl in the salty water and disappear down the drain.

Chapter 24c

Mae's Crossing *Laying Down/Home/Ancestral Land*

Groundhog Day

Hester Janssen turned over in bed, responding to Ed's light touch on her shoulder.

On the northern edge of town, Kris and Inge wrestled beneath their duna.

Out at Blanton's Dairy, James and Tanya tangled on the spotted cowhide rug before the fire.

Louise and Chester Burns flowed together like the waters outside their bedroom window.

Muffled sounds of ecstasy came from the private bedroom of Allan and Betty Nelson.

Caroline Spivack and Emmet Hudson watched a racy movie from his bed.

With Jason staying with his best friend, Mr. and Mrs. Miller chased each other, naked, around the house.

Meanwhile, Jason and his 'best friend' rolled in the hay at Blanton's.

Candlelight threw two shadows, intertwined, on the shades of an upstairs room in Dot's old house.

Malachais and Brianna worked their way through his new home, making love in each room. Mal called it a 'handfasting blessing' for the house. Brianna called it pure lust.

Deep in the woods, at the edge of an enchanted glade, the faery circle quivered with excitement. The earth trembled in the very center, cracking and sending fissures out in all directions. Slowly, slowly a blazing red and yellow tendril emerged, testing the air with its newborn shoot.

BE THESE THE CHARACTERS:

In order of appearance:

RESIDENTS OF MAE'S CROSSING :

Mae Duncan: Born 1809 died 1902, established settlement of Mae's Crossing.

Brenda (Brianna) Jeanne McTavish: 52 years old, moved to Mae's Crossing from Big City in her early 30's, artist; Wiccan High Priestess.

Al Cooper: 70 years old, born and raised in Mae's Crossing, proprietor of Al's Antiques; Native American heritage.

Tom Bradley: 32 years old, moved to Mae's Crossing from Oregon in 2004, raises goats; Agnostic.

Widow Thompson: 65 years old, born and raised in Channing. Moved to Mae's Crossing at 25 after marrying Stuart Thompson. owner of the Sewing Basket; Lutheran

Joyce Duncan: Deceased, former city council head, born and raised in Mae's Crossing.

Rosalind Mae Duncan: 22 years old, born in BigCity. Parents died 2001; Rosalind and older sister Jennifer Anne (ages at that time 10 and 15 respectively) moved to Mae's Crossing to live with grandmother Dot; Seeker.

Dorothy (Dot) Florinda Duncan: Born and raised in Mae's Crossing, died at the age of 73, owner of Dot's Delights; Pagan.

Mabel Collins: Age 60, moved to Mae's crossing when a toddler, manager of Dot's Delights; Pagan.

Caroline Spivack: Age 55, widow, bookkeeper/accountant for Dot's Delights; Pagan

Woodsman Otter: Age 47, hermit, lives in cabin in the woods; Zen Buddhist.

Jennifer Anne Duncan: Born in BigCity in 1986-died 2009. Sister to Rosalind. Lived in Mae's Crossing ages 15 thru 18 then moved back to Big City to attend college. Died in BigCity at age 23 of injuries sustained in domestic violence.

Jedediah Germaine: Born 1900, died 1978; ceremonial magician

Alan Nelson Junior: Age 62; born and raised in Mae's Crossing; owner of Nelson's Department Store; homeowner; CUUP

Ed Janssen: Age 45; Head of town council; Owner of Mae's Crossing Hardware and Lumber; homeowner, Married to Hester; 5 children; Asatru

Chester Burns: Age 49; Moved from Ohio in 1997; Owns Burns Mill; married to Louise; 3 children: Violet age 20, Willow age 18 and Spruce age 15; Native American

Dawn, Sunny and Moonface: The Norns; Maiden, Mother and Crone; The Fates

Billy Higgins: 41 years old; Foreman of Blanton's Dairy. Native American shaman.

Daniel: About 26 years old. Cow whisperer.

Kris Knudsen: Age 36; Village smith; homeowner; married to Inge; 3 children; Bjorn 14 yrs old, Olga 10 and Heidi 8. Asatru godhi.

Betty Nelson: Age 61; Married to Alan Nelson Jr., CUUP

Jerrod Janssen: 14 years old, son of Ed Janssen, Asatru.

Samantha Sunrise: 32 years old, Temple Chaplain.

Bors Larsen: 30 years old, Asatru.

Tanya Blanton: 44 yrs old, Married to James, CUUP.

Butcher Gordon: 37 yrs old; Pagan

James Blanton: 46 yrs old, Co-owner of Blanton's Dairy, CUUP.

Old Man Blanton: 81 yrs old, Founder of Blanton's Dairy, CUUP.

Farmer Johnson: 37 years old; owns wheat and tobacco farm in lower Mae's Crossing; Agnostic

John Simpson: 38 years old; owns sheep ranch; Buddhist

Mr. & Mrs. Miller: son Jason 17 yrs old

Mikos Stauros: 40 years old; raises grapes, apples, pears, etc. and creates wines and liqueurs. Strega witch.

Samuel Germaine; 65 years old; son of Jedediah Germaine

Outback Jack: 50 years old; owner of fishing camp, 2 helicopters, one small plane and two four wheel drive jeeps. Partner Arlo; Native American

Emmet Hudson: 53 years old, owner of Hillside Market; CUUP

Jackie Flanagan: 17 years old; Senior at Mae's Crossing High School

Lord Sylvan and Lady Alithea; Lord & Lady of Elfhame

OUTSIDERS:

Malachais Merriwether: Age 60, worked in CA for 30 years, retired to Channing in 2008; Wiccan High Priest

Jarnath: Age 54,Master Glassworker; married to Nellie; Gardnerian High Priest

Laura Black: Age 17; born and raised in Channing. Senior in high school. Cleaning girl for Malachais

Gerry Le Fevre: Age 18; born and raised in Channing. Laura's boyfriend

Willem Douglas: 73 years old; Owner of Channing Exchange; Pagan

Shelly Le Fevre: 22 years old; born and raised in Channing; moved to BigCity 2009. Sister to Gerry Le Fevre; Seeker

Dr. Victoria Cellini: 32 years old; Bone specialist at BigCity Memorial Hospital

Kyle Porter: 34 years old, retired billionaire, born in New York; Seeker

Luke Stronghand; 62 yrs old; Native American Shaman, Channing area

John and Marcia Dillingham: Property managers in Channing

Mr. And Mrs. Victor H. Porter: Kyle's parents; Mr. 62 years old, Mrs. 58; retired in upstate New York; Methodist

Dulce: Mrs. Porter's private maid; Episcopalian

Some words from the author:

I am convinced that all life proceeds from God/Goddess/All That Is, and that a divine spark dwells within all consciousness. Many are separated from this knowledge, thus horrors result. My dilemma is how to awaken humanity to its own divinity, and in turn to the divinity within all life itself. Would that I could truly summon Elves and Goddesses to aid me in my quest, and have refuge in Mae's Crossing! So I write a book and plant a seed. May you all grow in balance.

To the Heathens who read this: I traverse the path to Spirit under the wide, encompassing umbrella of modern Wicca. As such, it would be presumptuous of me to narrate from an Asatru viewpoint. Know that a part of my spirit is kindred to yours, and that you may see me walking beside you.

Blessings, wren

30 years ago, wren became intrigued by the Runes. Over the years, she put her talents to engraving and eventually teaching the intricacies of this ancient symbol system. Examples of her work can be seen on the Myth & Magic site appended to her jewelry site, Wild Nature Theme Jewelry at **www.wildnaturethemejewelry.com**. This book, The Runic Trilogy, is a complex unfolding of the system, using the various meanings of the runes to dictate the story's form.

Wren has dedicated her life to a number of artistic endeavors, and was first recognized for her pen and ink drawings in the 60's. From there she progressed to calligraphy. As The Village Scribe, she helped found the Sea Scribes, a Monterey calligraphy guild. With the onset of computerized calligraphy, she re-directed her efforts to engraving in 1990, and continues to create her original works to this day. Wren presently lives in Austin, Texas, where a booming explosion of artists and musicians are being nurtured by its progressive outlooks.

Following this will be at least three more volumes, all based on various alphabets. The series is called "Alphabet Soup," and the next book will be entitled "Treespeak or the Druid's Curse," based on the Celtic Ogham.

17067032R00183

Printed in Great Britain
by Amazon